There seems
nightclub.

Everyone is talking about the hot spot's sexy new bartender who has the female clientele lining up and vying for his attention. However, these ladies better act quickly. Seems that the sought-after bachelor has been seen "rendezvousing" with the nightclub's lovely blond manager.

Was anyone but the *Savannah Spectator* wondering why a certain redheaded cocktail waitress at the aforementioned nightspot dumped a tray of drinks in a handsome navy SEAL's lap? Well, it turns out the hunky guy is her former fiancé. Although the beauty claims she is immune to the navy SEAL'S charms, sources say that the sizzle between these two is steaming up the nightclub. However, the navy SEAL has some serious romancing to do if he's going to get this feisty woman down the aisle.

Another enticing tidbit: Which Savannah socialite, whose engagement was recently called off, has been spied in very close company with a certain dashing club owner? Those in the know reveal that these opposites have nothing in common—except a passionate attraction that neither is strong enough to deny.

The *Savannah Spectator* plans to keep close tabs on these three couples and keep you updated with further romantic details....

BARBARA McCAULEY

who has written more than twenty novels for Silhouette Books, lives in Southern California with her own handsome hero husband, Frank, who makes it easy to believe in and write about the magic of romance. Barbara's stories have won—and been nominated for—numerous awards, including the prestigious RITA® Award from the Romance Writers of America, Best Desire of the Year from *Romantic Times* and Best Short Contemporary from the National Reader's Choice Awards.

MAUREEN CHILD

is a California native who loves to travel. Every chance they get, she and her husband are taking off on another research trip. The author of more than sixty books, Maureen loves a happy ending and still swears that she has the best job in the world. She lives in Southern California with her husband, two children and a golden retriever with delusions of grandeur.

Visit her Web site at www.maureenchild.com.

SHERI WHITEFEATHER

lives in Southern California and enjoys ethnic dining, attending powwows and visiting art galleries and vintage clothing stores near the beach. When she isn't writing, she often reads until the wee hours of the morning.

Sheri's husband, a member of the Muscogee Creek Nation, inspires many of her stories. They have a son, a daughter and a trio of cats—domestic and wild. She loves to hear from her readers. You may write to her at: P.O. Box 17146, Anaheim, California 92817. Visit her Web site at www.SheriWhiteFeather.com.

DYNASTIES:
Summer in Savannah

Barbara McCauley
Maureen Child
Sheri WhiteFeather

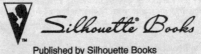
Silhouette® Books

Published by Silhouette Books
America's Publisher of Contemporary Romance

Special thanks and acknowledgment are given to Barbara McCauley,
Maureen Child and Sheri WhiteFeather for their contributions
to the DYNASTIES: SUMMER IN SAVANNAH collection.

 SILHOUETTE BOOKS

CONTENTS

UNDER THE COVER OF NIGHT

Barbara McCauley

To Kathy Bennett—
romance writer and policewoman.
You are the ultimate heroine!
Thanks for sharing your expertise with me.

Chapter 1

He felt naked without a gun.

Normally, Nick could hide a piece somewhere, the small of his back or the boot holster he often wore when he was undercover. But security at Steam had been tight as a tick and he hadn't dared draw any attention to himself. An informant had tipped the DEA that one of the bartenders who worked at the newest, trendiest nightclub and restaurant in Savannah was smuggling drugs. The information, though sketchy, had been reliable enough for the department to set up an operation.

Nick, lucky dog that he was, had drawn the duty.

Because it was a Saturday night, the club was at maximum capacity. Though Steam wasn't the kind of place Nick would have ever stepped foot into usually, he supposed he could understand the draw. The live blues bands were top-notch, the food five-star and the ambience in the club oozed sex. Deep verandas, black iron lacework, red velvet draperies, dark mahogany floors. Beautiful people.

Lots of beautiful people.

Glancing around the room while he filled an order for one of the cocktail waitresses, Nick took in the tempting, not to mention abundant, display of female skin surrounding him. The women who frequented the club were too chi-chi for his taste, but he'd have to be dead not to appreciate their assets. He had a glove box full of phone numbers slipped to him over the past two weeks, and while he wouldn't mind a night of uncomplicated sex, he wasn't interested in being some spoiled princess's pet.

While the band in the adjacent room slipped into a ballad as soulful as it was sultry, Nick slid a finger under the collar of the dark-red bartender's shirt he wore and stretched his neck. All night he'd had a feeling. Nothing he could put a name to. Just a feeling. But so far the evening had been as routine, as *boring,* as it had been for the past two weeks.

"Raferty," the head bartender, Grady, called to Nick from the cash register, "you close with Joyce tonight. Marcos, you're off in ten."

"Sure thing." Nick smiled amiably and Marcos, who'd already started cleaning his station, waved a hand of acknowledgment.

The bartenders at Steam were an odd mix. Grady, a burly Boston Irishman who ran the bar with the stern arm of a militia man. Bronx, aptly named since his transplant from a popular New York club. Marcos, a Savannah native and son of an affluent plastic surgeon. Grady was the only one of the group who'd ever been arrested, once for assault and once for destruction of private property, but both charges had been dropped.

On the surface, none of the men fit the profile of a drug smuggler, but Nick knew better than to trust what was on the surface. If in fact one of these men were in the drug business, sooner or later they'd give themselves away. Nick just hoped it would be sooner.

Knowing that Grady would be busy with Bronx while they balanced the night's till, Nick considered ducking out for a few minutes to search the head bartender's private office. He'd tried once before, but the club's manager, Sophia Alexander, had nearly caught him. Though the blonde rarely spoke to him, Nick had felt the icy chill of her green gaze more than once. He knew that she was watching him, that she was suspicious. One wrong move on his part and she could blow his cover and the operation. She frustrated the hell out of him.

In more ways than one.

Nick had seen beautiful women before, but Sophia had the kind of looks that turned men into drooling fools. Skin as smooth as cream, exotic, jade-green eyes fringed with dark lashes, golden blond hair that always looked as if she'd just tumbled out of bed. She had a body that matched her face, with legs that never seemed to end. He'd allowed himself a fantasy or two. He was human, after all.

But Nick was no fool, and he never drooled over any woman.

Because it was his job to know everything going on around him, Nick had listened to the rumors about Sophia. Heard that she was hands-off to employees and customers alike. The owner's personal property, one cocktail waitress had said with a wink. He'd heard another waitress say that the blonde was just an ornament for Clay Crawford, that she was shallow and conceited and self-centered. Though Nick had never seen any evidence that the gossip was true, it didn't matter to him one way or the other. Whatever Sophia Alexander was, and whoever, had no impact on Nick's world at all. He simply wanted her out of his way.

"Hey, pal, how 'bout a Bud?"

Nick looked up at the familiar voice. His partner, Kurt Matthews, who'd been assigned to mingle with the club regulars and the staff, grinned at him from the other side of the bar.

"Lite?" Nick asked casually.

"Regular."

Nick nodded. Kurt's response was the code they'd set up between them. Regular meant nothing was going down, but lite meant something was suspicious.

While Nick filled a mug, Kurt turned to flirt with a pretty redhead standing behind him. The ladies were drawn to Kurt's Tom Cruise smile and clever pickup lines, Nick had learned in the two weeks they'd been working together, and though it was against policy, Nick knew that Kurt had gone home with more than one of the women from the club, including a couple of the waitresses.

Not that Nick gave a damn about policy or who Kurt went home with. He just wanted this job over.

He worked better alone. Blending in with the homeless near the riverfront was more his style or stakeouts at cash motels that rented rooms by the hour. Fancy nightclubs and wealthy jet-setters simply weren't his glass of whiskey.

At the sound of roaring applause following the band's final song, Nick grabbed a towel and wiped down the now-closed bar. The club was starting to empty, yet still, Nick couldn't shake the niggling feeling that something wasn't right. He scanned the stream of people leaving the bar area, noticed that Kurt and the redhead were already gone.

Apparently, Kurt had managed to score again, Nick thought with a sigh. But tonight the only score Nick really cared about was the Braves game that he'd missed. He had ten bucks on the Atlanta team and hadn't heard the outcome yet.

He was dreaming about watching that game, a cold beer in one hand, a sandwich in the other, when he caught a flash of red shirt disappearing behind a set of velvet drapes in the far corner of the bar. The exit sign was clearly lit over the drapes, but it was an emergency exit that led to an alley used only for deliveries.

There were no deliveries at two in the morning.

Nick quickly glanced around. Grady and Bronx were at the cash register going over receipts, but

Marcos was nowhere to be seen. It was probably nothing, Nick thought, but what the hell, it wouldn't hurt to check it out.

Tossing his rag under the bar, Nick made his way through the lingering crowd, then quietly slipped out the back exit into the darkness.

The record-breaking heat of the day had stretched into the night. Water dripped from an overhead air conditioner, and the stench of ripe garbage filled the air. At the sound of muffled voices, Nick ducked behind a trio of metal trash cans. Two men stood no more than fifteen feet away; their figures outlined by moonlight. Nick recognized Marcos, but the second man had his back turned to him.

Nick froze at a sudden movement in the shadows two feet away, but he realized it was an alley cat that had been sniffing around the trash. Slowly Nick released his breath, then turned his attention back to the two men.

Dammit, he wished he had a gun.

"I tell you I can't do this anymore," Nick heard Marcos say. "I want out."

"I don't give a damn what you want," the second man snarled. "Everything's set to go. One more drop and you can disappear with your share."

"I can't take the pressure," Marcos whined.

"Two million dollars won't do me any good if I'm in jail. He was looking at me today like he knows something."

Turn around, Nick silently begged the second man. *Let me see your face.*

As if the man heard Nick's thoughts, he did turn.

Nick's eyes widened, then narrowed in anger. His hand clenched into a fist.

Kurt.

Sonofabitch.

Sophia Alexander didn't care that outside her office walls the city of Savannah was sweltering in the worst June heat wave they'd seen in twenty years. She didn't even care that the humidity nearly equaled the soaring temperatures, though her thick mass of hair would certainly complain quite loudly the minute she stepped outside into the muggy night air. But on the happiest night of her life, what did a few unruly curls matter? Tonight was a night for champagne. A night for toasts and celebration.

A night for making love.

She ran her fingertips over the ruffled front of her black silk blouse and sighed. She'd been too busy for the past six months to even date, let alone have a boyfriend. Men required more attention than she'd had time for lately, and while she hadn't especially missed being in a relationship—even if she was twenty-eight and practically a spinster, so her mother thought—there were times like now that Sophia wished she had that special person she could share a moment like this with. Times when she craved the strong arms of a man and the comfort of knowing that someone was waiting at home for her.

But she had her parents and her sisters, and though they all drove her crazy at times, Sophia loved them desperately. Tomorrow night everyone—her mother and father, her sisters and their new husbands—would all be gathered for the mandatory Sunday dinner at the Alexander house. It was killing her, but she'd wait until then to break her good news to the people who mattered most in the world to her.

She couldn't wait.

Forcing her attention back to the computer screen in front of her, Sophia entered the last figure for the accounts receivables she'd been working on. Even without the champagne, she felt lightheaded and giddy and couldn't stop smiling.

"For God's sake, Sophia, it's almost two in the morning. Didn't I tell you to go home an hour ago?"

Clay Crawford closed the office door behind

him, but not before the soulful sound of the music playing in the nightclub below drifted up the stairs. The band Sophia had hired for the month had been extremely popular with the clientele at Steam and reservations were booked solid for the next month.

Sophia leaned back in her chair, refusing to let the scowl on Clay's handsome face darken her mood. She thought about telling him her good news, then decided against it. He'd been a great friend and mentor these past few months, but it was important to her that her family be the first ones to know.

"Two in the morning is just getting started around here, Clay," she said, stretching her arms. "Since you own the place, you ought to know that."

"And since I own the place—" Clay took hold of Sophia's shoulders, lifted her out of her chair, then handed her the pair of black high heels from under her desk "—I'm telling you to go home. You've worked until three every night for the past four weeks straight, and I happen to know you're working extra hours at your parents' bakery, as well."

"We have a lot of weddings and parties this month." Sophia slipped her heels on, then smoothed her skirt into place. "Don't tell me my mother called you."

"She's worried about you."

Sophia sighed. "She's worried that her oldest daughter is never going to get married. You know she's got her eye on you to fill the position."

"Me?" Clay lifted a brow. "Why me?"

"You're handsome, charming and rich." Sophia cocked her head and smiled. "Maybe I *should* marry you."

"Yeah, well, maybe you should." He grinned back at her. "You busy Tuesday at three?"

"I'll check my schedule and get back to you," she said, but they both knew they were just kidding around. Despite all the rumors constantly circulating among the employees and clientele that she and Clay were an item, the "spark" had simply never been there between them. They were both single and liked it that way.

"You do that." Clay turned her around and pushed her toward the door. "Now, get the hell out of here. And I better not see you tomorrow or the day after that, either. You got that?"

"I have to go over the bar order with Grady for the private party on Wednesday," she argued.

"I can handle it." He grabbed her purse and

shoved it at her. "Believe it or not, I really can run this place without you."

Sophia yanked the strap of her purse over her shoulder and sniffed. "You'll be calling me by four tomorrow and begging me to come down here."

Clay opened the door. "I never beg."

Sophia arched a brow and lifted one corner of her mouth. "That's what they all say—at first."

He smiled back. "I'll bet they do."

When he closed the door in her face, she stuck her tongue out, then sighed and took the elevator down to the first level. Maybe she could use a couple of days off, she thought. Not because she was tired—if anything, she was pumped. But she had a thousand things to do in the upcoming weeks and there was no time like the present to get started.

That thought had her smiling again. It wouldn't take a moment to talk to Grady, she decided as she stepped off the elevator. She made her way through the still-crowded entry into the bar area. Joyce, one of the cocktail waitresses, was bussing the empty tables by herself.

"Grady around?" Sophia asked Joyce.

The perky, twenty-four-year-old design student, smiled at Sophia. "In the storeroom with Bronx, taking inventory."

Frowning, Sophia glanced around the room. It

was policy that at least one bartender and one waitress stayed until the room was cleared. "Who's
supposed to close with you tonight?"

"It's okay." Joyce quickly wiped down a table.
"I'm almost done, anyway."

Sophia folded her arms. "Who?"

"Nick." Joyce dropped her gaze, then added,
"But he didn't leave, I think he just stepped out
the back exit to get some air. Really, it's okay."

Sophia set her teeth. Raferty. She wasn't sure
why, she just had a bad feeling about the guy. With
his rugged face and bad-boy attitude, the female
clientele flocked to his station. In the two long
weeks since Clay had hired the new bartender, the
man had assembled himself quite a fan club. Even
Joyce was trying to cover for him.

Sophia supposed she could understand the attraction. There was a certain...*edge* to Nick. An
intensity that appealed to most women. Not that he
appealed to *her,* of course. The man wasn't at all
her type. She wasn't exactly sure what her type
was, she just knew it wasn't Nick Raferty.

She should be pleased as party punch over the
guy. His sales were up twenty percent over any one
else's, he showed up for work on time and there'd
been no complaints. So far he'd been the perfect
employee.

But something kept niggling at her, especially since she'd found him in Grady's private office, supposedly looking for a stapler, or so he'd said. She wasn't even sure why she hadn't believed him. Something in those dark eyes of his. Nothing she could put a finger on, just *something*. She'd tried to talk to Clay about the man, but he'd simply told her not to worry, that there was no problem.

But there *was* a problem. She was certain of it.

Maybe the problem was simply the fact that he distracted her. Kept her just a little off balance. Sophia didn't like to be distracted and she definitely didn't like to be off balance. That alone was reason to dislike the man.

And leaving Joyce by herself to clean up while he sneaked off to have a smoke or meet one of his groupies was inexcusable. She'd have a few words with Mr. Raferty herself, Sophia decided.

"I'll finish up here," Sophia told Joyce.

"But—"

"No arguing." Sophia took the rag out of Joyce's hand and tossed it on the table. "I know you've got a final next week and you need sleep. Now get out of here."

Her teeth set and her back up, Sophia headed for the exit door, then stepped out into the hot night air, ready for a confrontation. When the alley appeared to be empty, she nearly stepped back inside, but then she spotted him kneeling in front of a row of trash cans.

Was he sick? Forgetting that she was angry, she stepped closer. "Nick? What's wrong?"

The sound of his name echoed in the darkness. On a raw curse, he whirled. *"Get back inside!"*

What in the world…? Confused, Sophia stepped back, but it was too late. A shot rang out, and Nick crumpled to the ground.

Chapter 2

White-hot pain surged through Nick's shoulder; the damp asphalt pressed against his cheek. His mind told him to move, but his body refused to cooperate.

"Nick, I swear, I didn't mean to shoot. You just surprised me. Come on out and let's talk."

Nick blinked, let the words take shape in his brain. It took a moment for their meaning to register. At the touch of a hand on his back, adrenaline kicked in. Jerking upward, he grabbed the body attached to that hand and pinned it underneath his own.

"Get off me!"

Even in his dazed state, Nick recognized the body and the breathless voice as female. He blinked again, remembered that Sophia had stepped into the alley and given him away.

"What the hell is—"

He covered her mouth with his hand. "I'm undercover with DEA. Now keep quiet or we both die. Understand?"

That seemed to stop her struggling. Though he couldn't see her face in the dark, he felt her nod.

"Nick, you okay?" Kurt called out, and Nick could tell the man was moving closer. "Let's talk about this, face to face. You know how it is, buddy. I'm just building a retirement fund beyond the department pension. Four million dollars with just this one drop, pal. Look the other way and you've got yourself five hundred big ones. Take care of the woman and I'll make it an even seven-fifty."

Nick heard Sophia's sharp intake of breath at Kurt's offer. Slowly he released his hand and whispered in her ear, "If you want to live, do as I say."

She nodded again, then he rolled off her and crouched behind the trash cans. "Take off your heels."

"My heels?"

"Don't argue with me, dammit," he growled quietly.

Sophia slipped off her shoes and knelt beside him. He could feel her shaking, but he hadn't the time or the inclination to lie to the woman and tell her if she stayed calm that she would be fine. It would take a miracle or one hell of a stroke of luck to survive this. Nick didn't believe in either.

"Dammit, Kurt, let's just get out of here." Marcos's voice had risen to a near whine. "I'm not going to be part of any murder. You never said anything about—"

Another shot rang out, then a strangled cry.

Then silence.

Sophia's fingers clawed into Nick's arm. He had to bite back the searing pain that tore through his shoulder.

"Seeing's how my own profit just went up significantly, my offer to you is now a million," Kurt said calmly. "Come on, Nick, it's like winning the lottery. We pin the smuggling on Marcos, a spoiled rich kid with gambling debts, then we take the drop and who's the wiser?"

Dammit. Nick knew he and Sophia were trapped. If they made a run for the door leading back into the bar, Kurt was close enough to easily pick them both off. At the moment the only thing saving their butts was the darkness and the wall of metal trash cans.

A movement to Nick's left nearly had him lashing out, but he caught himself as the alley cat strolled out from the shadows, his back arched and tail swishing. Nick frowned at the feline, then turned his attention back to Kurt.

"We could use a good man like you, Nick." Kurt's voice was no more than six feet away. "A million, and that's my final offer. But that's just for starters. There's another shipment in a few days that could set you up for life."

Kurt stepped around the trash cans and pointed his gun directly at Nick. "Stand up, nice and slow."

Nick stayed on his knees. "I'm hit."

Kurt swung his gun toward Sophia. "You, up."

Struggling to breathe and to keep her knees from collapsing underneath her, Sophia slowly rose. She *hated* guns. Had never even been close to one before, let alone have one pointed at her.

How was this happening? she thought wildly. One second life was perfect, then in the blink of an eye, it was over.

Not yet, she told herself. She'd never been a quitter, and dammit, she wasn't about to start now. She glanced down at Nick, and even in the darkness, could see the dark stain spreading across his shoulder. He swayed on his knees, and she worried that he was going to pass out. *Stay with me, Nick,* she urged mentally. If they were going to get out of this alive, she knew they needed each other.

Kurt slid a longing gaze up to Sophia. "Damn, but you are one fine woman."

"And you're scum," Sophia spat, then cursed her own loose tongue. In spite of the fear consuming her, she was angry. Angry that Marcos, a man she'd trusted and considered a friend, had been using Steam to smuggle drugs right under her nose. Angry that her life was about to end because of bad timing and a dirty cop.

"At least I'll be rich scum," Kurt said with a grin. "And you'll just be dead."

"You'll never get away with this." She prayed she could reason with him. "My sister is married to Reid Danforth. They'll find out the truth, no matter how long it takes."

"Reid Danforth?" Kurt hesitated. "As in son of Abraham Danforth, who's running for Senate?"

Hope flickered in Sophia. Everyone in Savannah had heard of the Danforths. They were old money and well connected. "You can walk away now, just disappear, and if you get lucky you won't spend the rest of your useless life rotting in prison."

"After I plant the evidence incriminating you and Marcos, the only thing rotting will be you." Kurt reached into his pocket and pulled out a small ziplock bag filled with white powder. He tossed it at Sophia. "Pick it up."

When she hesitated, he cocked his gun and his grin flattened. "Now."

Sophia looked at Nick, prayed that he had some kind of an ace to play here. But the man was slumped forward, his head down, and she knew she was on her own. With no other option, she picked up the bag.

"So what do you say, Nick?" Kurt turned his attention back to Nick. "Are we partners or not?"

Sophia watched as Nick slowly lifted his head. His eyes were narrowed in pain, his mouth set in a hard line. "How about...*not!*"

When Nick's arm swung forward, Sophia hadn't time to breathe, let alone scream. An unearthly howl rent the air at the same time Kurt's gun exploded. Then it was Kurt who was howling, grabbing at the snarling, spitting cat attached to his head.

"Let's go," Nick yelled, grabbing Sophia's arm.

With their escape back into the club blocked by Kurt's thrashing body, they had no where to go but down the alley. Sophia stepped on a rock and stumbled, but with Nick dragging her, she had no choice but to keep going.

A bullet struck the wall just above their heads; brick and mortar exploded like shrapnel.

"This way." Sophia pulled Nick to the left when they made it out of the alley into the side street. She could see that he was already slowing down and he'd never make it around the building to the front of Steam where people might still be hanging out. She took the lead now, dragging Nick behind her into an underground parking structure.

"That's my car," she managed between breaths, pulling him toward the black BMW as she dug frantically through her purse for her keys.

"I'll drive," Nick said when Sophia yanked her keychain out.

Her hands shook as she unlocked the door and jumped in the front seat. "Like hell you will."

With no time to argue, Nick slid in the front seat beside her. Five seconds later, with a screech of tires and the smell of rubber behind them, the car flew through the exit at the same time Kurt came running out of the alley.

"Get down!" Nick yelled when Kurt pointed his gun at them.

A bullet grazed the driver side mirror, shattering plastic and glass. Screaming, Sophia jerked the car toward Kurt and he leaped out of the way, falling backward as the BMW tore down the street.

"We've got to get you to Memorial." Sophia swerved around a corner and headed toward the hospital.

"No." Nick laid his head back against the leather seat. "He'll expect that. He'll find us."

Her heart pounded so hard she could barely hear over the roar in her ears. "So what if he finds us? We'll be safe there, at least."

"We aren't safe anywhere."

"I don't understand." Shaking her head, she white-knuckled the steering wheel. "What the hell just happened?"

"I'm on a DEA task force with the Savannah Police Department. We had information that a major drug deal was going down at Steam, but we didn't know who the contact was. Kurt and I were working undercover."

"*You* were working undercover, you mean," Sophia said sarcastically. "It looks to me like Kurt was working you."

Nick's mouth pressed into a scowl. "Kurt must have found out that Marcos was the middleman and decided he wanted in on the deal himself."

"So he would have just let the drugs come

through?'' she asked. ''Turned his head, then collected two million dollars?''

''If I hadn't walked out there tonight, no one would have ever known,'' Nick said. ''When nothing panned out at the club, the task force would just move on to the next operation.''

''Did Clay know about this?'' She turned down a dark, residential street, nearly sideswiping a van parked at the curb.

''Slow down, would you?'' Nick snapped. ''We won't get far if you crash the car. And yes, Clay was cooperating with us, but he was instructed not to discuss it with anyone.''

''I'm his manager.'' She was yelling, but she didn't care. ''Are you saying I was a suspect?''

''You weren't high on the list, but we hadn't ruled anyone out, either.'' He gestured to a church at the end of the street. ''Pull into the parking lot behind that church and cut the lights.''

''I'm not pulling over anywhere.'' She didn't even look at him. ''You're bleeding, for God's sake. We've got to—hey!''

Nick grabbed the wheel and yanked it sharply to the left, then jammed his foot over Sophia's. The car swerved sideways, jumped the curb and swerved into the dark parking lot, out of view from the street.

"Are you crazy?" she yelled at him. "Do you want to get us both killed?"

He snatched the keys out of the ignition. "We'll both be good as dead if you take me to a hospital. He'll be waiting for us."

"So what if he's waiting?" It was all she could do not to grab Nick's collar and shake him, but even in the darkness she could see how ashen his face was. "What can he possibly do in a public place?"

"With millions of dollars at stake, not to mention we're witnesses to Marcos's murder, Kurt will do whatever he has to do. There's no way he's letting us get away. Either he kills us, or sets us up to take the fall. Probably both."

"Then call your department." Sophia looked back over her shoulder. Even though the dark streets were empty, her nerves were running too high to relax. "Tell them you're coming in."

Nick shook his head. "Kurt was too confident, too sure of himself. And even after he killed Marcos, he said 'we.' He's working with someone on the inside. I can feel it. There's no telling who or how high up. I make the wrong phone call and we're dead."

"How is that possible?" Sophia pressed a shaking hand to her temple. It felt as if a hammer were pounding inside her skull. "We didn't do anything wrong."

There was no humor in his laugh, only sarcasm. "Kurt's spin on what happened will be that you and I were on the take together."

"No one will believe that," she argued. "Clay will back me up, and my family."

"God, you are naive." He sank back against the seat. "Kurt's got your fingerprints on a bag of cocaine, and he'll plant that and more evidence against you and me. It's his word against ours, plus anyone else he buys off. And it won't matter, anyway, because once he finds us, we won't be around to talk. Our only chance is to lay low for a few days, figure out who he's working with and flush them out."

"A few days!" This wasn't happening. It *couldn't* be happening. In spite of the heat, Sophia felt chilled to the bone. "I can't possibly do that."

"You will if you want to keep breathing. I need to think," he said, closing his eyes. "Just...give me a minute..."

"No!" Sophia grabbed Nick's head when it rolled to the side. "You are *not* doing this to me. Wake up, dammit!"

But he couldn't hear her. She was on her own, and she didn't have a clue what to do.

Chapter 3

The woman's shrill scream jerked Nick awake. He sat up quickly, sucked in a breath at the lightning bolt of pain that exploded in his shoulder. When the second scream came, he realized it wasn't a woman in distress. It was a bird.

A seagull.

A wave of nausea rolled through him, forcing him to close his eyes and lie back on the bed. He had no idea where he was or how he'd gotten here. The only thing he felt fairly certain about was the fact that he was alive, and he figured even that wasn't a sure bet.

When the nausea and pain passed, he opened his eyes again, blinked at the sunlight streaming through the double set of four-paned windows. It felt as if the room was moving, a room that was barely big enough for the bed and a side table, he noted. The vintage rose wallpaper had darkened with age, the hardwood floors were well-worn. A musty scent permeated the white sheet covering his naked body. And was that whiskey he smelled?

He spotted the bottle of Jack Daniels on the nightstand beside the bed, wondered briefly if he'd tied one on, but then the night before came rushing back. Kurt shooting him. The close escape with Sophia, parking behind the church. His memories ended there. He glanced at the tight, neat bandage wrapped around his shoulder, then slowly moved his arm to test the damage done.

His single swear word was as crude as the pain was sharp.

"Feeling better, I see."

Through the stars dancing in front of his eyes, Nick glanced up at Sophia. She stood in the doorway, holding a coffee mug in her hand.

"I will be if that's coffee you've got there," he said, though the words came out rough and sluggish.

The black skirt and ruffled blouse she'd been

wearing the night before were gone. She now wore gray workout sweats and a white tank top. Wisps of blond hair escaped from her ponytail; her face was free of makeup. And still she looked as if she'd stepped out of the pages of a fashion magazine.

"It's coffee." She moved toward him and held out the cup. "Sort of."

"Sort of?" He took the mug and sniffed.

"There's no coffeepot. I had to boil the grounds in water and strain them through paper towels. It might be a little strong."

He took a sip and choked. Damn. If he didn't already have hair on his chest, he would now. "A little?"

"Maybe more than a little. How's the shoulder?"

"Fine."

"Liar. It hurts like hell."

"After this coffee, what's a little pain?" Because he needed the caffeine, he took another sip. And grimaced.

"Just like a man." Sophia shook her head. "Quit your complaining and thank your lucky stars you're alive, buster."

"I wasn't complaining." He frowned at her. "I was merely stating a fact. You want to fill me in on what happened?"

"You passed out. I brought you here."

"And where exactly is 'here'?"

"A riverboat." She walked to the window and glanced outside. "The *Savannah Sweetheart.*"

A riverboat. That explained why the room was rocking. "Are we safe here?"

"For the moment. There's no one else onboard, and we're the last boat docked on the wharf."

"Where did you get a change of clothes?"

"I didn't go home, if that's what you're asking," she said. "I had a gym bag in the trunk of the car. Working the hours I do, I always keep my workout clothes and spare toiletries with me."

He sat, then swore at the pain that ricocheted through his shoulder. Sophia hurried back to the bed, took the coffee mug from his hand and set it on the bedside table.

"So you're fine, are you?" The mattress dipped when she sat on the edge of the bed. Frowning, she eased him back onto the pillows. "You start bleeding again and I swear I'll shoot you myself."

Her words were tough, but her hands were gentle. Carefully she untied the knot at his shoulder, then loosened the bandage and looked at the wound. Her fingertips against his skin were soft and cool. Comforting. It had been a long time since a woman had touched him with such tenderness.

He wanted to prolong the feeling as badly as he wanted to stop it.

"How did you get me here?" Questions would distract him, keep his mind focused on the situation and off the feel of Sophia's hands. "I must have sixty pounds on you."

"Sixty-four to be exact, according to your driver's license."

He arched a brow. "Snooping, were we?"

"I earned the right," she said without apology. "Nicholas Raferty, 552 W. 64th, six-two, 185 pounds, blue eyes. Thirty-three. You have good vision and you're an organ donor. Last night you came close to being one."

"We both did, darlin'. And it's Sloane, not Raferty." When she glanced up at him, he stilled her fingers with his hand. "You did good last night."

Eyes the color of cut jade held his, then she shrugged. "I did what I had to."

"Most women—and men—would have panicked. You kept a head on your shoulders."

"Keeping my head was my motivator," she said. "But if I'd have stopped to think about it, I would have been paralyzed with fear."

"Sometimes it's best not to think. Especially when you're afraid." He felt her pulse quicken under his fingers. Her skin was soft and warm, and she smelled as if she'd just stepped out of a shower. "You didn't tell me how you got me here."

"I swore at you a lot." She slipped her fingers from his and handed him the coffee mug, then turned her attention to retying the knot at his shoulder. "Getting you out of my car, on your feet, then in here was the toughest part. You also didn't like it when I cleaned the wound with whiskey."

"What a waste of JD," he said, shaking his head. "I don't remember anything after I passed out in your—" He sat suddenly, took hold of her arm. "Where's your car? Kurt will be looking for it."

"It's parked in the dock lot. But don't worry. It's not actually mine. Mine's in the shop, so I've been driving my sister's for the past week. There're no license plates yet."

He relaxed a little, then laid back against the pillows. "Your sister actually let you drive her brand-new BMW?"

"I had to beg a little," Sophia said with a shrug. "But she is married to Reid Danforth, remember? She's driving his Porsche, so it's not as if she's walking."

"And my clothes?"

"I washed the blood out of them. The pants are

all right, but there's a hole in your shirt where the bullet grazed your shoulder.''

"I meant," he said evenly, "did you undress me?"

"Oh." She grinned at him. "Are you shy, Nick?"

"Just unlucky. A woman gets me naked, and I can't even remember it."

"You're not *naked* naked." Her gaze slid across his bare chest, then down lower to where the sheet covered his midsection. "You cost me two bucks, by the way."

"Yeah?" He took a sip of coffee and chewed. "How's that?"

"The girls at the club had a pool going on you. Boxers or briefs, white, black or other."

Coffee nearly spewed forth. "What!"

She smiled. "Who'd have thought you were the black brief type?"

He glared at her. "You girls have too much time on your hands."

"Are you telling me you didn't throw in five bucks for the wager on Melanie?" She arched a brow and leaned in. "Every guy in the place wants to know if they're real."

"My job requires me to interact with the staff."

Sophia laughed softly. "So you're telling me you weren't interested?"

"Not in Melanie."

Her gaze met his, and the smile on her lips faded. He slid a hand behind her neck, heard her breath catch and felt her body tighten. But she didn't move away.

"Bad timing, Sloane," she said, still holding his gaze.

"Story of my life, darlin'."

She resisted when he tugged her to him. He held firm, waiting for her. He might push the issue, but he wouldn't force it.

I must be insane, she thought. What else would explain the heat racing across her skin and the pounding of her heart? She barely knew this man, and besides that, the circumstances that had brought them here, the danger, the threat, still closed around them like a noose. How could she possibly be sitting here, wondering what Nick's mouth would feel like on hers?

Wanting his mouth on hers.

Maybe it was the realization of how close she'd come to death, and at some primitive level she felt a need to experience, to celebrate life. Maybe it was what she and Nick had shared in that alley— that somehow, together, they had managed to escape. Or maybe it was the knowledge that she could be an hour, a minute, away from death again.

Whatever it was, it didn't seem to matter at the moment. The only thing that mattered was the desire swimming in her veins, the absolute need to be physically closer to this man.

Sanity be damned, she thought, and brought her mouth to his.

The zap of electricity startled her, nearly had her jumping back. But the current was too strong to let go, the pressure of his hand dragging her closer, irresistible. She felt the tingle all the way down to her toes, then back up again. His lips were firm under her own, insistent but not demanding. When his tongue traced the seam of her lips, she shuddered at the thrill racing up her spine.

Her mind went blank, and all she could do was feel.

The taste of coffee, the masculine scent of his skin, the raspy stubble of his beard rubbing against her chin and cheek, everything heightened her senses. She let herself sink into the kiss, into Nick. Luxuriated in the feel of his muscled chest under her hands and the press of his firm mouth against her own.

Surely this was a mistake, she thought, but it was too late for regrets. Together they'd stepped over an edge and it seemed that all she could do was hold on. He deepened the kiss and she followed, met his tongue, thrust for thrust. It was as if she'd known this man, his taste, his smell, his touch, for a lifetime.

She'd never experienced anything like this, but then, she'd never been shot at and on the run with a man she barely knew, either. The thought sobered her just enough to let a trickle of reason back into her muddled brain. Despite the fact that she wanted to crawl under the sheets with Nick and finish what they'd started, she found the strength to pull away.

They stared at each other for a long moment, then he said, "We'll get out of this."

Will we? she wondered, not completely certain what he meant by "this." But she nodded, anyway, then rose and stepped away from the bed. "There are a few canned goods in the galley. I'll see what I can put together for us."

It surprised her how weak her knees were when she walked to the door.

"Hey, Soph," he called, then grinned at her when she turned. "How come no one ever just asked me?"

"Asked you what?"

"Briefs or boxers."

She grinned back. "That would be cheating. Winning the bet required a personal inspection."

His brow lifted, then he shook his head and sighed. "I swear I'll never understand women."

"That's the way we like it," Sophia said lightly. "Now get some rest, Nick. I need you strong and healthy and out of that bed as soon as possible."

She walked out of the room, but not before she heard him say, "What a waste."

In spite of herself, she chuckled.

On the deck outside, the early-morning sun was already promising another hot day. Sophia leaned against the wall and gulped in a deep breath of damp river air. She'd always been in control of her life and her emotions, had always known what she wanted and how to get it. In a moment all that had changed. It infuriated her, yet made her more determined than ever.

She knew that she and Nick needed to work together, that they needed each other to get through this. She touched her fingers to her still-tingling lips and glanced back at the doorway.

This thing between them, whatever it was, was a dangerous distraction that neither one of them could afford. Once she had some food and rest she'd be fine, she told herself. She'd be able to think clearly and reasonably.

Reassured by that thought, she headed for the galley, eager to have a task to keep her mind and hands busy.

Chapter 4

It was dark when Nick woke. He pressed the button on his wristwatch display and the dial glowed pale green. Nine o'clock. *Damn*. After Sophia had brought him a can of peaches and a protein bar earlier in the day, he'd fallen back into a deep sleep. It annoyed him he'd lost precious time, but there was nothing he could do about that now.

Slivers of moonlight poured through the cabin's windows. When his vision adjusted to the dim light, Nick sat on the edge of the bed, relieved that the room stayed put under his feet this time, even though the boat itself rocked slightly. He felt stronger now than he had this morning, the pain in his shoulder wasn't as intense, and his head was clearer, too. He might not have wanted the sleep, but he knew he'd needed it.

Testing his legs, he found they were steady, then made his way to the bathroom. When he came out again, he tugged his pants on, then realized how quiet it was. The kind of quiet that made him stop and listen.

He heard something on the deck outside, a slight shuffling sound. He moved behind the door, pressed his back to the wall and waited. The doorknob turned, then the door slowly opened and someone—a man?—crept into the room. He couldn't see the guy's face, but he had a heavy build, short dark hair and was wearing glasses. Nick waited a moment, until the man was completely in the room, then tackled him. They both went down on the floor in a cacophony of grunts and groans.

"Get off me, you idiot!"

What the hell? At the sound of Sophia shrieking at him, Nick stilled, then rolled away from her. Muttering curses under her breath, Sophia stood, then stomped to the bedside table and turned on the light. Nick blinked to clear his vision.

It was Sophia, though it sure as hell didn't look

like her. She wore a wig, wire-framed eyeglasses, a padded, oversize gray sweatshirt and sweatpants. She snatched off the glasses, then the wig and tossed them on the bed. When she shook her head, her long, blond hair tumbled around her shoulders.

"For god's sake, Nick." She set her fists on her well-padded hips and scowled down at him. "What the hell are you doing?"

"What the hell was *I* doing?" He stood, forced himself not to wince at the fresh pain shooting through his shoulder. "What are *you* doing, sneaking in here like that?"

"I wasn't sneaking. I just didn't want to wake you. Good Lord, I'm dying in this."

Nick's heart jumped when she dragged the thick sweatshirt over her head. Underneath she wore the same white tank top she'd had on earlier. He watched when she pulled down the sweatpants, and even though she had clothes on underneath, he still felt a strong jolt of lust at her simple act of disrobing.

Focus, Sloane, he warned himself. He gestured to the disguise she'd tossed on the bed. "What is all this?"

"The *Savannah Sweetheart* used to be a floating theater." She tossed the sweatsuit beside the wig and glasses. "There's an entire room of costumes downstairs."

"And you're wearing this stuff because...?"

"I went out."

"You what?" His voice rose. "Are you insane?"

"It's insane not to eat. There's no more food onboard." She raked her fingers through her hair. "I walked to a small neighborhood store and bought a few groceries, plus toiletries for you and a first-aid kit. If your shoulder gets infected, you'll have to go to the hospital."

She was right, but that didn't mean he had to like it. "How do you know you weren't followed?"

"Actually, I was followed. By a cute little black terrier who liked the way I smelled. *Eau de* hamburger." She walked across the room and picked up the fast-food bag she'd dropped when he'd tackled her, then dug inside. "I was careful, Nick, and I used cash, from your wallet by the way. In spite of all the blonde jokes you've heard, I'm not stupid. Now sit down and eat."

Nick caught the wrapped hamburger she tossed at him. It did smell good, and he realized he was starving. "Kurt isn't stupid, either, Sophia. It's only a matter of time before he tracks us down here.''

"There's nothing to tie me to the *Savannah Sweetheart.* Not yet, anyway." She brought the bag and sat on the bed next to Nick. "Escrow just closed yesterday."

"Escrow?" He rooted through the bag and found French fries, then popped a salty handful in his mouth. A beer would have been great, but he doubted she'd included that item in her shopping. "Are you telling me you actually own this boat?"

"As of five o'clock yesterday. I was never sure the deal would go through, so I didn't tell anyone."

"You must have told someone," he said in disbelief. "Best friend, family. Boyfriend?"

She shook her head. "No one knows. I was going to surprise my parents and sisters with the news tonight."

Before she glanced away, Nick saw the pain in her eyes. She should be sitting around a table celebrating with her family, not hiding out from a killer. He felt a pang of guilt, then shrugged it off. Life wasn't perfect and it sure as hell wasn't fair. It simply was. He'd seen countless victims of countless crimes. Some survived, some didn't.

Before last night, Nick would never have thought Sophia would have lasted five minutes without melting down. Few things surprised him, but she did. And so did the unexpected need he felt to comfort and take her mind off her pain.

"So tell me." He intentionally changed the subject. "What's a gal like you doing with a boat like this?"

Smiling, she lifted her gaze to his. The spark was back, Nick noted. And the determination. Good.

"I'm going to open up a riverboat nightclub. That's why I've been working at Steam. Clay's been teaching me the business."

Lifting a brow, he took another bite of his burger. "So that's what he's doing, is it?"

She rolled her eyes. "I can see you listen to rumors."

"What rumors?"

"In spite of what everyone says, Clay and I are just friends," she said, shaking her head. "Neither one of us has time for a relationship, and even if we did, the chemistry simply isn't there."

He looked at her in amazement. "Is he gay?"

It was the first time Nick had truly heard Sophia laugh. He liked the sound, and the way her eyes lit up.

"You have no idea how absurd that question is." She was still chuckling when she bit a French fry in two. "But if that's your smooth way of giving me a compliment, thank you."

"You don't need smooth, Sophia." He watched her lick the salt from her lips, felt his blood drop below his waist. "And you sure as hell don't need compliments. You know exactly what you do to a man."

Their eyes met, and the smile slowly faded from her lips. "Why don't you tell me?"

"Why don't I show you?"

He set his food down and reached for her. She came to him willingly, slid her hands up his bare chest and moved into the kiss. Her lips were salty but sweet at the same time. He wanted more.

He wanted her.

His tongue traced her lips, then slipped inside. They were familiar to each other now and there was no hesitation. She met him, came alive in his arms and pressed closer, murmuring his name. When his hands slid down her arms and bracketed the sides of her breasts, she shuddered.

He nearly lost it.

There'd been women before, but none that made him forget who he was. None that made him feel weak yet powerful. None that evoked such a blinding tempest of emotion. He struggled to contain the feelings, knew he didn't dare unleash the need clawing at his insides.

He lifted his head, watched her thick eyelashes flutter open, saw the smoky green glaze of desire. Her lips were swollen and moist from his kiss, softly parted.

"What's happening?" she murmured.

It took a will of iron to release her, but somehow he managed. "Hell if I know."

She eased back, her eyes wide now as she watched him. "I've never asked a man for this before," she said, her voice shaky. "It never mattered before. But it matters now. I need you to tell me what's happening here. Because if it's just sex, I—"

"It's not." His hands snaked out and grabbed her. "It's not."

Her eyes met his and she nodded. Then she said with a smile, "Well, maybe a little it is."

"Oh, there's that, all right," he said with a grin. "But there's more."

"Yes," she said softly. "I think there is."

"Look." On a sigh, he slid his hands down her arms. "This, whatever this is, has never happened to me before. Taking a bullet was easier."

"Gosh, thanks." She laid a hand on her chest. "Your compliments make my heart all atwitter."

"Yeah?" His grin faded. "Well, here's another one for you. I want you, Sophia."

His declaration made her breath catch, then she reached out and touched his cheek. "I don't believe this is happening. But you're real. All of this is real. All we have to do is stay alive."

"We will. I won't let that bastard near you."

"I can take care of myself, Sloane," she said firmly. "You're the one who played dodge ball with the bullet and missed, remember?"

"I'll be fine by tomorrow." He pressed his mouth into the palm of her hand, felt the need rise in his blood again and forced it back down. "Completely fine."

"That's rather optimistic, don't you think?" Her voice had a breathless quality to it.

"It's not optimistic, sweetheart. It's a promise."

"Well then, I suggest you eat." She picked up the hamburger he'd set down and handed it to him. "You're going to need your strength."

He picked up her hamburger and handed it to her, as well. "So will you, sweetheart."

"Nick." She stared at the burger for a moment, then said, "I called my sister, Tina."

He swore softly. "Kurt will be expecting you to contact your family, Sophia. He'll have the ability to trace any calls you make."

"I called from a pay phone several blocks from here," she said defensively. "You don't know my parents and Sunday-night dinner. If I hadn't shown up, especially without calling them, they'd have the police out looking for me. And if I'm not at the bakery for my afternoon shift tomorrow, they'll have the fire department and coast guard called out, too. I needed Tina to run interference for me."

He closed his eyes on a heavy sigh. "What did you tell her?"

"I told her I had a problem that I couldn't explain right now and asked her to cover for me with the family for a few days. Nick, if anyone can help us, my sister's husband can. I don't have to tell you the kind of influence Reid Danforth and his family have in this city."

Nick couldn't argue that. Abraham Danforth, the patriarch of the wealthy family, was a decorated war hero running for state senator. Nevertheless, it was risky. "Did you tell her where you were?"

Sophia shook her head. "I just told her I'd be fine, and not to do anything or tell anyone she'd spoken to me. I promised I'd call her tomorrow."

"All right." It was risky to go out in public right now, but at the same time, he realized they couldn't stay on this boat and do nothing, either. "I need to make a call, too. If Kurt is working with someone in the department, I need to find out who.''

''How are you going to do that?''

''I don't know yet.'' He glanced at the wig and glasses on the bed, then smiled slowly. ''But I think I've got an idea.''

Chapter 5

Early the next morning Sophia stepped out of her room into a light cover of fog. It would burn off within the hour, but for the moment, the soft blanket of gray gave her a sense of security. It was probably foolish thinking, but she figured if she couldn't see out, then no one else could see in. Right now she needed every little kernel of calm she could find.

Her pulse jumped at the sight of the man standing at the railing several feet away. She relaxed when she realized it was Nick, but when he turned, her pulse jumped for an entirely different reason.

His shirt was open to the waist, as was the top button on his pants. With his hair rumpled and his face shadowed with a two-day-old beard, all he needed was a patch over one eye and a saber in his hand to make him the perfect pirate.

She couldn't imagine how she'd ever thought this man wasn't her type. He was every woman's type.

"Mornin'." He leaned back against the railing and nodded at her.

Lord, even his voice had the rough, husky sound of a pirate. She closed the door behind her and stepped out onto the deck. "You're up early."

"So are you."

How could she sleep, knowing that all she had to do was walk the few feet from her cabin to Nick's and she wouldn't have to be alone? She wouldn't have to be afraid. Not in Nick's arms.

When she caught the scent of bacon on the air, she glanced toward the galley. "You're cooking?"

"Don't look so surprised." He pushed away from the railing. "Eggs are one of my specialties."

"Is that so?" She held her ground when he moved toward her. "What are your other specialties?"

"Coffee." He slid his hands up her arms and

pulled her closer. "Potatoes. I'm a pro with potatoes."

"Potatoes?" Her breath caught when he lowered his head. "Heavens, you do know how to impress a girl."

"Good," he murmured, lightly brushing his mouth over hers. "Let's eat."

When he turned and walked away, Sophia wished she had a potato. She'd throw it at him. How could he leave her like this? With her body tingling with anticipation?

Fuming, she followed him to the galley, then took the plate of food he handed her and sampled. His boasts hadn't been idle. The eggs, potatoes—even the coffee were good.

"Not bad, Sloane," she said somewhat reluctantly. "Who taught you to cook? Your mother?"

"Hardly. She took off when I was ten and my brother was eight. Said she needed space and she'd come back in a couple of months, but she never did. Last I heard she was in Italy somewhere."

"That's a lot of space," Sophia said quietly, wondering how a mother, any mother, could do such a thing.

He shrugged. "We got by. My old man bought a tavern on the south side, and my brother and I worked there. Short-order, bus boy, waiter. I pretty much did it all.''

"And bartending," she added. ''Is that why your department chose you to work at Steam?''

"Actually it was more of a punishment.'' He bit into a piece of bacon. ''I had a disagreement with a lieutenant and his nose sort of stepped in front of my fist."

The bite of egg Sophia had just scooped up stopped halfway to her mouth. ''You hit a superior officer?''

"He sent a team in to raid an auto body shop before I gave the okay. Two months undercover work down the drain, and in the chaos, two officers were shot. If anyone had died, I would have done more than broke the guy's nose.''

She studied him for a long moment. ''That's some job you've got, Nick.''

"It's no cakewalk.'' His gaze met hers. ''Hard as hell on a relationship. My last girlfriend moved in, then out again in a space of six weeks. I'm still pissed she took my toaster.''

"Trying to make me jealous?'' She *was* jealous, dammit, and she knew it was ridiculous. ''Shall we compare notes?''

His eyes narrowed, then he set his fork down and reached out to take her chin in his hand. ''Bad idea, babe, unless you want to see someone's nose broke. Everything before this happened doesn't exist. From now on, there's just you and me. If you don't see it that way, this is your chance to say so. I don't share.''

His grip on her, the intensity of his gaze, his statement of ownership, all of it was brutish and barbaric and absolutely thrilling. ''That goes both ways.''

He nodded, then released her chin and traced the line of her jaw with his knuckles. ''You are so soft.''

Sophia felt the floor shift under her. He'd gone from fierce to tender in a heartbeat, and she simply didn't know how to respond.

''I want you,'' he said, making her heart trip, but then he dropped his hand. ''But I've got something I have to go do.''

''What do you mean 'I'? You're not leaving me here.''

''You distract me, Sophia. I can't afford to be distracted.''

''Get over it.'' She lifted her chin. ''I'm going with you.''

He shook his head, then sighed. ''Has any man ever said no to you?''

Smiling, she simply sipped her coffee. Some questions were better left unanswered.

Going to the Savannah Police Department in the middle of the day was risky but necessary. Because he worked there, Nick knew how to circumvent the security. He knew what cameras were where, who would pay attention and who wouldn't. And even if someone did notice him, all they would see was a bucktoothed, nearsighted pizza delivery guy with a blond ponytail.

And besides, with Sophia dressed the way she was, no one would be noticing him, anyway.

Walking behind her on the sidewalk was sheer torture. She had the best pair of legs he'd ever seen. The skirt she wore was black and tight and short enough to be illegal in twenty-six states. Her heels were black, too, strappy and so damn high he'd have thought she'd need an oxygen mask to breath in the thin air up there.

Hell, if he kept watching those hips of hers swing back and forth, he'd be the one who needed oxygen.

He had to be insane, letting her talk him into coming with him. But with the disguises they'd put together from the prop room, his plan just might work. He was fairly certain that Kurt hadn't put out an APB on Sophia yet, but even if he had, between the makeup, fake mole beside her mouth and short red wig, no one would recognize her.

They would *notice* her, he thought, letting his gaze drift down to her bottom again, but he doubted her own mother would know who she was.

One block away from the station, she stopped in front of the display window of a jewelry store and appeared to be studying a diamond necklace. He stopped beside her, pretended to study an address on a slip of paper.

"Just making sure you're still back there," she said over her shoulder without turning around.

"Oh, I'm back here all right." He caught her reflection in the mirror while he shifted the pizza box in his hand. "Watching the trail of devastation you're leaving in your wake. One guy walked into a mailbox and another guy in a Lexus nearly rear-ended a delivery van."

She tugged on the hem of her pink halter top, exposing a little more cleavage. "I guess the plan is working."

"Oh, it's working all right. A little too good. You pull that top any lower or hike your skirt any higher and *I* won't remember what I came here for."

One corner of her glossy red mouth tipped up

while she ran a finger over the strand of pearls at her throat. "You ready?"

That was certainly a loaded question. "You can still back out, Sophia. It's not too late."

"Yeah, Nick, it is," she said softly. "The second I walked into that alley, it was too late. I'm not backing out, and I won't stand idly by, either. Let's do it."

He'd thought nothing and no one could ever surprise him. But Sophia did. He hadn't seen it when he'd first met her, had thought that because she was beautiful and working upstairs in a cozy office that she was spoiled or lazy. All he could think now was, where the hell had she been all his life?

"I'll be right behind you." He slung the pizza box up on his shoulder. "If anything goes wrong, anything at all, don't wait for me. Just walk out calmly and go back to the boat. Got it?"

"Got it."

He followed her down the block, then through the entry doors of the police station. The lobby and security check-in point were unusually busy, but the front desk was clear. Every head, male and female, turned when Sophia walked up to the young desk clerk, a sergeant named Pete Stubbs.

"Excuse me, Officer, can you help me?"

Oh, she was good, Nick thought. Not only was

she using some kind of European accent, her voice had just the right touch of breathlessness and frailty. What man wouldn't want to help this woman?

Pete swallowed visibly and smoothed a hand over his tie. "That's—" the man's voice cracked, then he cleared it and spoke more deeply "—that's what I'm here for, miss."

Nick headed for the security checkpoint, which was a two-part process, the scanner and the walk-through metal detector. The line was long today, which worked in Nick's favor. All he had to do to bypass the system was get by the guard, a lieutenant named Lyle Cross.

"Pepperoni, pineapple and anchovy for Whistle-meyer," Nick said loudly, moving to the front of the line. Everyone in security and on the third floor knew that Detective Lieutenant Dave Whistle-meyer ordered the obnoxious pizza at least three times a week.

"You're new." Lyle looked Nick over. "I'll have to scan you, then check you out."

"Fine by me," Nick said with a bored shrug. "But can you make it quick? I got two more deliveries."

"Ohmigod!" Sophia's shriek echoed through

the station lobby. "My pearls! My grandmother's pearls!"

Tiny iridescent pearls rolled and bounced across the polished floor. To the pleasure of every man in the room, Sophia dropped to the floor on her hands and knees. His bulging eyes on Sophia, the guard didn't even notice Nick move past.

It took him exactly one minute to get up to the third floor, then casually stroll through the office. Several agents, DEA and Savannah police, were gathered around a corner desk eating lunch. Nick spotted Iris, Captain Emmet's secretary, coming out of Emmet's office, but the attractive redhead didn't even glance up from a file she was reading.

He was nearly across the room when one of the female officers, Linda Rodman, looked up.

"Hey, pizza guy."

Breath held, Nick slid her a bored glance.

"Whistlemeyer's in the john—just leave it on his desk."

With a wave of his hand, Nick kept walking. When he rounded the corner, he ducked into his own cube, then opened the bottom drawer of his desk and pulled out the false back.

Every undercover cop in the department had a "stash," which usually consisted of weapons, sometimes drugs that would buy information, some cash and a bug or wire for those times when a court order took too long.

Nick had never been a patient guy.

He retrieved what he needed—a Beretta, a couple hundred dollars and a wire tap. He tucked the cash in his pocket, the gun in the waistband of his jeans and tossed the wire tap and a bug in the pizza box. Two more minutes had passed.

Three minutes after that and a trip to Kurt's office, Nick was on his way back downstairs. All he had to do now was collect Sophia and get the hell out of here.

When he came around the corner, he spotted her. She was smiling up at a man, openly flirting. Nick's heart slammed in his chest.

Kurt.

Chapter 6

"You are so kind to help me." Though her insides were shaking, Sophia managed to flash Kurt a brilliant smile. "How can I ever thank you?"

"Your name and phone number would be a great start."

When Kurt pressed three pearls into Sophia's hand and let his touch linger there, her stomach rolled. He'd come up behind her out of nowhere several minutes after she'd staged her performance with the broken necklace. The other men who'd assisted in retrieving her pearls had moved on after she'd thanked them, but Kurt had stayed.

This can't be happening, she thought. The man who'd tried to kill her two nights ago was now trying to pick her up.

"I do not know you." She laid her family's Hungarian accent on heavy, was equally disgusted and relieved that Kurt was not looking at her face. *Dammit, Nick, where are you!* "My mother would not approve."

"Kurt Matthews. Detective Matthews," he added, as if to impress her. "I assure you, you're safe with me."

Safe? Sophia nearly choked. She could still hear Marcos's moans after Kurt had shot him, then the sound of bullets exploding just inches over her head. It took a will of iron not to lunge for this man's eyes.

"A detective. That is so fascinating."

Her heart lurched when she spotted Nick come around the corner. His step faltered when he saw Kurt, then his mouth pressed into a hard line.

"My name is Ava Kovak." Sophia held out her hand quickly, releasing the pearls in her palm. They dropped to the floor and bounced. "Oh, how clumsy I am."

While Kurt bent to retrieve the pearls, Sophia looked at Nick and shook her head, then quickly turned her attention back to Kurt when he straightened.

"Do you have a pen?" she asked, smiling at Kurt as she dropped the pearls into her shoulder purse. "I will write it down for you."

From the corner of her eye, she watched Nick walking closer, pretending to read a flyer he'd picked up off a counter. She was on the verge of hyperventilating when he stopped no more than three feet away.

"Why waste time? Let's pretend I already called and go to lunch now." He leaned in closer and lowered his voice. "I live close by. We could go to my place for the afternoon."

Between Nick inching closer and Kurt's revolting invitation, Sophia struggled to hang on to her last thread of composure.

"I would love to, but I must pick up my twins from preschool." As she'd figured, the mention of children dimmed the spark of interest in Kurt's gaze. Batting her fake eyelashes, she dug in her purse for a pen and scrap of paper, then quickly scribbled the number for her dry cleaners and handed it to him. "You will call me tonight?"

"Sure." He tucked the number in his shirt pocket. "Tonight."

"I will sit by the phone," she purred, then waggled her fingers and walked off. She prayed that Kurt would keep his eyes on her as she strolled out of the police station. When she passed through the doors into the heat of the afternoon, the breath she'd been holding rushed out.

She didn't look back when she crossed the street, prayed that Nick would be right behind. Halfway down the block she felt his hand on her elbow. He pulled her off the sidewalk, across a patch of grass, then behind a large stone statue of an angel.

She realized that they were in Colonial Cemetery. How appropriate, she thought, then whirled on him.

"Are you *crazy?* What the hell were you doing in there?"

"Me?" His eyes narrowed with anger, then he yanked the fake teeth out of his mouth and shoved them into his pocket. "What the hell were you doing coming on to Kurt like that? What would you have done if he'd made you?"

"He was too interested in my cleavage to even look at my face. And he would have been more suspicious if I'd just walked away from him. Men like Kurt expect women to fall all over them." Sophia felt her knees give out, and she sagged back against the statue. "All you had to do was walk

out and I would have been right behind you. Why
did you take a chance like that?''

"I wasn't about to leave you there with him.
Dammit!'' A muscle jumped in Nick's jaw, then
he sighed and leaned next to Sophia. "He
shouldn't have been here for another couple of
hours. Something's going on.''

Having Nick beside her, his arm touching hers,
calmed Sophia's raging nerves. "What?''

Nick pulled a small tape recorder and what
looked like a hearing aid out of the waistband of
his jeans. "Let's see if we can listen in and find
out.''

While Sophia walked to a corner hot dog vendor,
Nick settled on the grass with his equipment. He
had the recorder ready to go and the earpiece
hooked up by the time she got back. She handed
him the bag of food and two bottles of water, then
pulled off her heels with a sigh of pleasure and sat
beside him in the shade of the statue. When she
stretched out her long legs in front of her, his throat
turned to dust.

"A picnic in a cemetery.'' She dug a hot dog
out of the bag. "You're quite the romantic,
Sloane.''

"Is that what you want?'' He couldn't resist her,

couldn't keep himself from touching her. He ran a fingertip up her bare arm to the knot of her halter top. "Romance?"

She leaned into him, shivered when he slid his finger along the base of her neck. "Every woman wants flowers and candlelight. Maybe a little music. I'm no different."

He lifted a brow. "You're different from any woman I've ever met."

"The situation is different, Nick." She glanced away, stared across the cemetery at a young woman laying flowers on a grave. "Maybe that's all this is between us. The situation."

"Is that what you think?"

"I don't know what to think. I only know that when you went upstairs without me, I felt like I'd lost my lifeline. Then you were walking toward Kurt and—" She looked back at him and he saw the moisture in her eyes. "I wanted to hit you, I was so mad."

Not exactly what he'd expected her to say, but with Sophia, there was no predictability. He grinned at her. "You're not the first woman who's said that to me."

Shaking her head, she smiled. "I'm sure I'm not."

"But it is the first time it's meant something."

He cupped her chin in his hand. "The first time it's really mattered."

They stared at each other, understood the line they'd stepped over. Knew that there was no going back.

He moved toward her, lowered his mouth to hers, then snapped his head back up at the sound of a phone ringing in his ear.

"Matthews."

"You were supposed to be in my office an hour ago. I want to know what the hell is going on and I want to know now!"

"Who is it?" Sophia was practically climbing in his lap, a pleasant distraction, but a distraction just the same. He pressed his hand to his ear and listened.

"Captain Emmet. Shh."

"I told you—" Kurt lowered his voice *"—I've got it under control."*

"The hell you do," Emmet yelled. *"My ass and yours are on the line here, dammit. Get this resolved now!"*

"Yes, sir. Consider it resolved."

When Emmet slammed down the phone, Nick swore.

"What?" Sophia grabbed his arm. "What is it? What did they say?"

"Nothing that proves anything." Or disproved anything, he thought. "Just that Emmet wants something resolved."

"Do you think your captain's involved?"

"I don't know." He shook his head. "There's no love between us, but it's still tough to swallow that he's part of smuggling drugs. Until I have proof, I—we—can't go in."

"God." She closed her eyes. "I'm tired."

"It'll be over soon," he said quietly. "I'm not going to let—" He stopped, pressed his hand to his ear again. "There's another call coming in."

"Who is it?"

"Iris, Emmet's secretary..." He listened for a minute then said, "She wants to know what time they're on for tonight. She says she's got a present for him."

"So he was hoping for an afternoon quickie with me and a hot night with Iris, too." Sophia shook her head in disgust. "Why am I not surprised?"

Nick listened until Iris hung up, then frowned. "He's making a lot of dates for a man who should be worried about being exposed as a drug smuggler and murderer. That tells me he thinks he's covered his tracks pretty well."

"Thanks for sharing that little bit of uplifting information. I'll just sleep so much better tonight."

"You'll sleep tonight," he said, then pulled her close and kissed her hard. "We both will. That's a promise."

With a sigh she laid her hand on his waist as if to steady herself. Her eyes widened and she glanced down. "Gosh, Nick, is that a gun in your pants or are you just happy to see me?"

"Just in case we need it." His sober expression shifted into a smile. "It's a gun, but I'm happy to see you, too."

"Maybe we should stop by the drugstore on the way back to the boat." She ran a fingertip down his chest. "Just in case."

He dropped a kiss on her lips and murmured, "My thoughts exactly."

It was dark by the time they got to the *Savannah Sweetheart*. Sophia headed straight for her room, stripped off her wig and outfit, then stepped into the shower. After sitting on the grass in the heat and humidity all afternoon, Lord knew she needed it.

With a sigh, she turned the spray on and lathered off the day's grime and perspiration. The hot water eased the tension and frustration of the long day, and the muscles knotting her neck and shoulders slowly relaxed. It seemed like years since she and

Nick had left the boat this morning, a lifetime since she'd stepped out into that dark alley.

Fighting the threatening tears, she dumped shampoo on her wet hair and scrubbed at her scalp.

Other than the phone call from Nick's captain to Kurt, they'd come up with a big, fat zero. There'd been a few other calls that had come into Kurt's office phone, but nothing that suggested collusion from anyone else in the department. The only good thing they'd come away with today was the fact that Nick had a gun and more cash.

As much as Sophia hated guns, she had to admit, she felt just a little bit safer now.

She lingered a while longer, but when her skin started to wrinkle, she turned off the water and stepped out of the tiny shower. After she'd dried off and tugged a comb through her hair, she rooted through her gym bag for the extra pair of shorts and T-shirt she always carried, then pulled them on.

Now all she needed was something in her stomach. On the way back to the boat, she and Nick had stopped at a deli and brought back sandwiches, but they hadn't eaten anything since the hot dogs for lunch.

With her mind on a turkey sub, Sophia stepped out of the bathroom.

And gasped.

Chapter 7

A white votive candle flickered on the nightstand, another on the floor at the foot of the bed. Light rippled across the room. Sophia lifted her gaze to Nick, who stood, arms folded, leaning back against the deckside door. He wore the same jeans he'd had on earlier and a black T-shirt they'd bought on the waterfront this afternoon. He was barefoot, his hair still wet from his shower, his face freshly shaved.

"What's this?" she asked, struggling to keep her voice calm.

He shrugged. "I found them in a drawer in the galley."

And you brought them up here. To me. She pressed a hand to the flutter in her stomach. Careful, she warned herself. Don't make too much of this.

But then she spotted a red plastic rose on the bed, and the flutter in her stomach moved up to her heart.

It was that moment, that very instant, she knew she was in love.

Swallowing the thickness in her throat, she moved toward him. "And the rose?"

"That was in the prop room."

She stopped in front of him, bare toes to bare toes, and lifted her face to his. Her entire world had turned upside down and gone crazy, but this, being with Nick, was the only thing that felt right to her. The only thing that felt sane.

"Thank you," she whispered. "It's beautiful."

"You're beautiful."

Men had told her that before, but the words had never mattered. Her looks had nothing to do with who she was inside, what she felt or what she thought. But hearing Nick say the words, watching his eyes darken with desire, thrilled her. For him, she wanted to be beautiful; she wanted to be everything he'd ever wanted and more. There were no pretenses, no games here between them. She felt vulnerable, and for the first time in her life she would give herself completely to a man. If there was pain later, so be it.

"Your shoulder?" she asked.

"My shoulder is fine."

Keeping her eyes level with his, she reached for the hem of her T-shirt, lifted it over her head and dropped it to the floor. Her pulse skipped when he looked at her.

On a shuddering breath, he reached for her, slid his arms around her waist and dragged her to him. Her arms came around him, and he dropped his mouth on hers. He tasted like mint, smelled like soap and man, and she couldn't get close enough. His chest was hard against her softness, and even the thin cotton fabric separating them was too much.

His hands slid down from her waist to cup her behind and pull her closer, more intimately against his hardness. She moved against him, felt the deep rumble in his throat, a half moan, half growl.

He yanked his mouth from hers. "You keep doing that and this is going to be over quickly."

She slid her hands back down his chest, then yanked his shirt upward. "Good. We've got time for slow later."

She'd already waited too long for this man. A

lifetime. Every minute was precious to her, every second.

When bare skin met bare skin, she moaned. Her breasts tightened and ached to be touched, and when he brought his hands around to do just that, she moaned again.

As one, they moved backward to the bed, tearing at their clothes, stumbling over each other. Her skin was on fire, her blood rushing, every nerve ending deliciously sensitive to every stroke of his large, callused hands.

By the time they tumbled onto the mattress, they were both naked, both breathing hard.

''Now,'' he said raggedly, then rolled her underneath him and entered her. ''Now.''

''Hurry.'' She arched upward to meet him. ''Please, hurry.''

There was nothing gentle about their joining, nor did she want there to be. They strained against each other, her nails digging into the rippling muscles of his broad back, his hands clamped tightly on to her hips as he drove himself into her again and again.

Desperate, wild, mindless, they raced to the finish line together, reached it at the same time. The climax exploded through her and she cried out, wrapping herself more tightly around Nick. His moan was harsh and guttural, his shudders cresting with hers.

There were aftershocks, little ripples of pleasure still coursing through her even after he collapsed on top of her. Closing her eyes, she let her arms drop, felt like a cork on the ocean, bobbing and floating, letting the current take her where it would.

When he finally moved, she protested, but was too helpless to stop him. He rolled to his back, bringing her on top of him.

"Nice," she murmured, resting her head on his shoulder.

"Nice?" He frowned at her. "Just nice?"

She snuggled into the crook of his arm. "I meant lying here like this. I can't think of a word to describe everything else."

"How 'bout amazing?" He pressed a kiss to her temple. "Incredible. Unbelievable."

"Definitely unbelievable," she agreed. When he stroked his hand lightly over her head, it seemed as if even her hair had feeling. She crossed her arms on his chest and looked down at him. "But I guess that pretty much fits into our lives at the moment."

"You think?"

"Nick, this—" she dropped her gaze "—nothing like this has ever happened to me before."

"You've never been shot at, framed for drug smuggling, then barely escaped in a speeding car?" He looked at her with surprise. "What a sheltered life you've led."

His sarcasm earned him a smile and a pinch on his chest. "You know what I mean."

"Yeah." He ran a fingertip along her jaw, then lifted her chin. "I know what you mean."

He didn't know how to say it, that he'd never felt so…connected, with any person before. He'd never been good with words, didn't know the right ones, and even if he did, wouldn't know how to use them. Instead he lifted his mouth to hers and kissed her, a mere brush of his lips against hers, yet so much more.

When he laid his head back down, she dropped her chin on her crossed arms and smiled down at him. "And for the record, I did lead a sheltered life. My father had the eyes of a hawk, the nose of a bloodhound, and I swear he was psychic. When I was growing up, it was nearly impossible for my sisters or me to pull anything past that man."

"If I had daughters, I'd do the same."

"Do you have any?" she asked quietly.

"Kids?" He shook his head. "I've never been married."

"You don't have to be married to have kids."

"I do."

She ran a fingertip across his collarbone. "An honorable man."

"Realistic." He loved the way her breath caught when he brushed his hands along the sides of her breasts. "It's tough on a kid to just have one parent."

"I'm sorry about your mom," Sophia said softly.

"Don't feel sorry for me." Lifting his head, he kissed her nose. "I had it a hell of a lot easier than most kids with one parent. And what about you? How come you aren't married to some wealthy doctor or lawyer, living the life of luxury, with 2.3 kids in the back seat of an SUV?"

"I thought about it once," she admitted. "I was twenty-three. He was a stock broker. Very successful, very handsome."

"Is that so?" Jealousy, unexpected and sharp, reared its ugly green head. "What happened?"

"It was too easy." She rolled a shoulder. "Even my father liked him, which was unheard of. But I realized that I was in love with the idea of being in love. Once that faded, there was nothing else there."

"Good." He moved his hands down her sides and cupped her bottom, laying claim. He realized how quickly everything was moving between them, was surprised that it didn't bother him in the least.

Even making love had moved too fast, he thought. They'd both wanted—needed—it to be that way. The next time will be slow, he told himself, then slid his hands up her back and through her hair. He wrapped his fingers around the still-damp strands.

"I won't be easy, Sophia," he said roughly.

"I won't be, either."

He tugged her mouth to his. "We'll see about that."

She held his gaze in a challenge, then they met each other halfway. Instantly the kiss turned greedy. Thoughts of moving slow and taking his time flew out of Nick's brain. Sophia's hands and mouth seemed to be everywhere at once. His heart slammed against his ribs; his blood burned.

When she lifted her hips, then dropped back down and took him inside her, they both moaned. Candlelight rippled over her pale, smooth skin. Her lips were parted, her eyes half-closed as she moved, setting a pace that drove him wild. He reared up, desperately needing his hands on her breasts. Her nipples hardened when he took her inside his mouth and sucked. She gasped, lost her rhythm for a moment, then quickly found it again.

He moved to her other breast, gave it the same attention, bringing them both closer to the edge.

"Nick—"

Clutching his shoulders, she cried out. They held each other, shuddering, then sank back onto the mattress, hearts beating wildly.

He gathered her close, pressed his lips to her temple, listened until her breathing steadied and she drifted to sleep.

He no longer cared what happened to himself. His only need was to protect this woman in his arms. He glanced at the gun on the nightstand, knew without hesitation, without question, that he would do whatever he had to do to keep her safe.

Chapter 8

Sophia dreamed of tropical islands, clear, aqua-blue water and soft, warm sand. While an ocean breeze skimmed over her bikini-clad body, gentle waves crashed on the nearby shore. Lying on a towel, not a care in the world, she stretched out on her stomach under the shade of a tall palm tree and sighed with contentment. Nick sat beside her, rubbing suntan lotion on her back while he murmured sweet nothings in her ear. She could lie here like this with him forever, no place to be, not a care in the world, not a single—

"Rise and shine, sweetheart. Time to get a move on."

The slap on her behind was anything but gentle. Her eyes flew open just long enough to look over her shoulder and glare at Nick. He stood beside the bed, already dressed. Sinking back down into the mattress, she pulled her pillow over her head. "You interrupted a beautiful dream, Sloane. Come back in an hour."

"No can do." When she sank deeper under the sheet covering her, he sighed. "Don't make me come in there and get you."

If she hadn't wanted to sleep so badly, she would have dared him to make his threat good. But they'd been up until two, and it couldn't have been much more than six right now.

Sophia had never cared for women who whined, but under the circumstances, she felt completely justified. "I'm tired. Leave me alone."

He sat on the mattress beside her and pressed his mouth to her bare shoulder. "Were you dreaming about me?"

"No," she lied, bit back a moan when he brushed his lips back and forth on her skin. "I was dreaming about George Clooney. He was rubbing suntan lotion on my back."

"Liar."

In spite of the exhausting night they'd had, and the fact that her body was still sore, Sophia felt her blood heat up as Nick moved systematically up her neck. Maybe she wasn't so tired, after all.

Still, maybe she'd make him work a little before she dragged him into bed with her. "You're pretty sure of yourself, buster."

"Any reason I shouldn't be?"

She turned her face toward him and smiled. That was one lie she couldn't tell. "No."

"Good." He grinned back. "Now let's get going."

"Hey!" When he snatched the sheet off her, she yelped, then grabbed her pillow and covered herself as she flipped to her back. "You are no gentleman, Nick Sloane."

"Never claimed to be, darlin'." He laid a quick kiss on her lips, then yanked her out of bed and tossed her sweatpants and tank top to her. "Get dressed."

"I'll bet you were the playground bully when you were a kid," she groused, reaching for her sweatpants. "So where are we going, anyway?"

"Marcos's apartment."

She glanced up sharply. "You've got to be kidding."

"If we can find a connection there between Kurt and Marcos, we just might stack a few more chips on our side of the table."

"But wouldn't Kurt have already gone there?" she asked. "He's covered himself everywhere else so far, surely he wouldn't have left anything to incriminate himself."

"Sooner or later everyone makes a mistake. I'm hoping his will be sooner."

Sophia was fully aware of Nick's eyes on her as she tugged her tank top on, considered torturing him a little, then thought better of it. "So how do we get in?"

His gaze lifted from her breasts and he smiled. "How else? We break in."

Marcos's apartment was on the bottom floor of a two-story brick building on the south side. Nick had done enough undercover work to know that if you acted like you belonged somewhere, most people wouldn't give you a second look. Though Sophia had donned her red wig again, Nick didn't bother with a disguise today. From listening to Kurt's phone calls yesterday, he knew that his partner—his *ex*-partner—had a hearing in front of Judge Watkins at 9:00 a.m.

Nick glanced at his watch. It was 8:45 now, which gave him at the very least an hour before Kurt would be out of court. Plenty of time to get in and get out again.

"Are you going to pick the lock?" Sophia asked after Nick knocked twice on Marcos's door. There was no sound from the other side, but upstairs someone was playing Led Zeppelin at full volume.

"Something like that." Nick stepped back, then kicked the door in with one solid hit just below the doorknob. He waited a moment, listening, but Led Zeppelin never missed a beat.

Wide-eyed, Sophia stared at him.

"Come on." He pulled her inside and closed the door behind them, then swore at the mess in the living room. Sofa cushions pulled out, pictures crooked, every drawer open in a corner desk.

"Looks like the maid hasn't been here in a while," Sophia said dryly.

Nick checked the bedroom and kitchen, then swore again. "Kurt was thorough, I'll give him that."

"What was he looking for?"

"Insurance, most likely." Nick pulled on a pair of black knit gloves he'd found in the prop room, then picked up a stack of unopened mail. "If Marcos had half a brain, he would have kept something to use as leverage in case Kurt didn't play it square. But if he kept it here, Kurt would have found it."

Folding her arms, Sophia watched him sort through the mail, then pick up the phone lying on the floor and make a sweep through the directory. "What if he didn't keep it here?"

"Kurt would have checked Marcos's car and work space, too."

"If I could get into the security tapes at Steam, maybe we could—hey, wait." Sophia looked at the speed dial buttons on the phone. "This one says 'mom.' Marcos told me his mom died when he was a kid."

"You don't say." Nick pressed the button and held the receiver between his ear and Sophia's. It rang twice on the other end.

"Captain Emmet's office," Iris said cheerfully.

Nick hung up the phone, then met Sophia's surprised gaze.

"Well, well." He grinned at her. "Looks like Marcos's got a friend."

An hour later, from a pay phone in the back of Churchill's Pub, they called Captain John Emmet's office again. This time Nick not only didn't hang up, he told Iris who was on the line. It took Emmet exactly two seconds to pick up the phone.

"Sloane! Where the hell have you been?" Emmet bellowed. "I've been covering for you, but dammit, I—"

"Kurt's dirty." Nick kept an eye on his watch,

knew how quickly his captain could not only trace the call, but have a patrol car respond, as well. "He was in on the drug smuggling with one of the bartenders at the nightclub, Marcos Cooper."

"Well, isn't that a coincidence," Emmet drawled sarcastically. "Kurt said the same about you. Only reason I haven't put out an APB is I wanted to hear your side before it's all over the *Savannah Morning* headlines. Tell me where you are and I'll have someone pick you up."

"Can't do it, Captain." Nick looked at Sophia, who was worrying her bottom lip, then at his watch again. They didn't have much time. "There's someone inside the department involved, too. I'll have the proof I need by tomorrow."

"What proof? If you have proof, then you come to me, dammit. How do you expect me to—"

Nick hung up the phone.

"Come on." He took hold of Sophia's arm. "We've got to get out of here."

"Where are we going?"

"To wait."

They crossed the street to a corner deli and took a seat in a window booth. They'd barely ordered coffee when Kurt pulled up, alone, in an unmarked car and went into the pub. He came out two minutes later, scowling, looked around, then jumped in his car and screeched his tires when he drove off.

"Oh, God." Sophia drew in a slow, shaky breath and closed her eyes. "So they are in on it together."

"Maybe." He stared at the steaming cup of coffee the waitress put in front of him. "Maybe not."

"Gosh, that helps."

He saw the moisture in her eyes when she opened them, wanted to tell her it would be all right, that they would be all right, but the truth was, he didn't know. And the one thing he couldn't do was lie to her.

"It's only three blocks to my parents' bakery from here," she said quietly and stared out the window. "They're in the middle of the lunch rush right now. My sister Tina will pick up the slack for me, but I imagine my mom is cursing me, blaming my lack of responsibility on my gypsy blood."

He reached out and covered her hand with his. "Gypsy blood, huh?"

"On my father's side, so my mother says whenever she disapproves of my behavior, which is most of the time." She wiped at a tear that slid down her cheek. "She drives me crazy, but, God, I miss her. And my father and sisters. Did I tell you my sister Rachel is pregnant?"

"Rachel?"

"I'm the oldest, then Tina, then Rachel. Rachel and Tina both got married this year, which makes me the spinster."

He laughed at that, then settled back in the booth and sipped his coffee. "Boy or girl?"

"What?" She furrowed her brow.

"Is she having a boy or girl?"

Sophia smiled. "A girl. My mother's first grandchild. She's already carrying a picture of the ultrasound to show everyone."

"When's she—Rachel—due?"

"Eight weeks. Good job distracting me, Sloane. Does the sight of a woman's tears frighten you?"

"Terrifies me. Usually I run the other way."

"Not this time?" she asked carefully.

"Not this time."

They stared at each other for a long moment, then Nick said, "So what about your dad?"

"What about my dad?"

"You think he'll like me?"

Sophia arched one delicate brow. "Are you asking to meet my parents?"

"Yeah." He set the coffee cup down so she wouldn't see his hand shake. "I guess I am."

"That bullet you took might be easier," she said. "My father will scowl at you all night and

my mother will interrogate you on everything from
how much money you make to how many children
you want. Most men can't handle it.''

"I'm not most men, Sophia," he said simply.

"No." She smiled slowly. "That you're not."

They sat quietly for a long moment, then she
wrapped her hands around her coffee cup and
sighed. "So what now, Nick?"

"Now—" he gestured to the waitress "—we
call Kurt and set up a meeting."

Chapter 9

"This is insane. You're insane." Arms crossed, Sophia paced the length of the *Savannah Sweetheart's* dining area, then back again. Nick stood at the mahogany bar several feet away, assembling a silent security alarm he'd purchased that afternoon at an electronics store. "There's no way Kurt is going to let you walk away alive."

In two hours Nick was meeting Kurt in front of the Crab's Net on River Street. Sophia's biggest complaint was that he refused to let her come with him.

"He won't kill me in the middle of a very public, very crowded tourist spot, especially if he thinks I have evidence against him.'' Screwdriver in hand, Nick opened the lid of a white plastic dome. "Hand me those batteries inside that bag, will you?"

"You don't know that.'' Frustrated, she pulled the package of batteries from a brown paper bag and slapped them on the bar. "If you'd let me go with you, I could cover your back.''

"We've been over this. You're not going, and that's that.''

Resisting the urge to stomp a foot, Sophia moved closer, hands on her hips. "You have got to be the most stubborn man I've ever met.''

"I'll just take that as a compliment.'' He popped the batteries in and ran his hand over a sensor. The alarm screeched like a banshee, then Nick pressed a remote control and the alarm went silent.

When Sophia started to argue again, he pointed the remote at her. She snatched it from him and tossed it back on the bar. "Dammit, Nick. This isn't funny.''

"Sophia.'' He took her by the shoulders and sighed. "I'm not going to do anything stupid or foolish. I just need to flush Kurt out into the open, and unless I miss my guess, whoever's in on this with him will be there, too. Once I know who and what I'm dealing with, I can make a move.''

She dropped her head on his chest. ''I'll go crazy if I stay here.''

''You'll be safer.'' He smoothed his hands over her shoulders.

''And if something goes wrong?'' she asked softly. ''If you don't come back?''

''Call your sister Tina. With the Danforths' influence, she'll be able to get you a good lawyer and protection.''

She shook her head. ''Abraham Danforth is running for senator. If the news media picks up a story that his son's sister-in-law is involved in drug smuggling, it won't matter that it's not true. The scandal will hurt his campaign. And my parents. Oh, God, I can't imagine what this will do to them.''

''Stop it.'' Nick cupped Sophia's chin in his hand and tipped her head up. ''None of that is going to happen, dammit. Don't even think it.''

There were times when a woman needed a man to be comforting and tender, but there were times, like now, when a woman really just needed a man to be strong and reassuring. How Nick seemed to know which one she needed when was a mystery,

but she knew he was right. She couldn't think
about him not coming back. Couldn't bear it.

"Okay," she said, sighing. "But so help me, if
you don't come back, I'll kill you myself."

He smiled at that, then lowered his head slowly.
When his lips touched hers, she leaned into him.
This time she sighed, not with exasperation but
with longing.

"How much time do we have?" she murmured,
pressing her body closer to his.

"An hour." But when her hands slid up and
under his T-shirt, he drew in a breath. "Maybe an
hour and a half."

It wasn't enough, she thought. An hour. A day.
A lifetime. But she'd take what she could get, and
right now she wanted it all.

She felt his heart jump when she slowly moved
her fingers over his muscled chest. His skin was
warm, slightly damp from the heat and humidity of
the day. He tensed when her fingertips skimmed
tiny circles over his flat nipples.

He took hold of her arms and held her still, his
gaze intense as he stared down at her. "Don't think
you can change my mind about coming with me."

She lifted a brow. "Sounds like a challenge."

"No." He grinned, then released her arms. "But
you're welcome to try."

"Maybe I will." She slid her hands down to the snap of his jeans. She lingered there, brushing her knuckles lightly back and forth on his skin above his waistband. Smiling, she dropped her hand and stepped back. "Or maybe I'll just go take a cold shower."

On a growl, he snatched her back. "Or maybe you won't."

When his mouth swooped down on hers, Sophia felt the kiss sizzle through her limbs. She wrapped her arms tightly around his neck, lifting herself up on toes that surely had smoke curling out of them. She understood that the danger she was in intensified everything she was feeling, but still, this kiss was different. This kiss had more than an edge of desperation. More than raw, piercing need. This kiss was charged with promise. Not just that he'd come back to her today, but that he'd come back to her every day.

He reached down and cupped her behind, pulled her closer to him. When she moved her hips against him, he moaned.

"Wrap your legs around me," he said, his voice ragged and hoarse.

He lifted her higher, and she wound her legs tightly around his waist. He kissed her again and again, and she met every thrust of his tongue with her own. She was already aching for him and the intimate joining of their bodies. He had her gasping for breath and impatient.

"Too many clothes," she managed between gulps of air.

His mouth never left hers as he moved the few feet to a booth in the corner of the dining room. When he bent and lowered her onto the tabletop, she lay back, offering herself to him, wanting him to know that she was his.

He stood between her legs, his gaze dark and glinting with desire. She refused to think about later, refused to waste these precious moments with doubt or worry.

Without a word, his gaze still on hers, he hooked his thumbs into the waistband of her sweatpants and inched them past her hips, down her thighs, then slipped them off her legs. Her heart slammed in her chest as he stared at her. She gripped the table edges, waiting, breath held, trembling with anticipation.

She thought it might be possible to die from a need this acute, this staggering, and when he slid his hands ever so slowly up her bare legs, she was certain of it.

"Nick." His name rushed out on a breath. "Please…"

He ignored her plea, content with caressing the outside of her thighs with his callused palms. The rough texture on her skin left her breathless, incredibly aroused and thoroughly frustrated.

"You're so soft," he murmured. "Like silk."

When he slid his hands to the sensitive skin on the inside of her thighs, Sophia sucked in a sharp breath, then reached toward him, needing to touch him, to bring him closer to her.

"No." He shook his head. "Not yet. I want to watch you."

She started to complain, but then he lightly brushed the vee of her thighs with the tips of his thumbs and it was impossible to speak. When he lowered his head, she couldn't think.

Oh, but she could feel.

Her body pulsed with sensation, and when he pressed kisses to the inside of her thigh, she moaned. Instinctively, she arched upward, gasping when he slipped her panties off in one quick move. He teased her with soft bites and hot kisses, until she was pleading with him. His tongue found her, stroking, sliding over her until she was crazed with desire.

"I want you inside me," she sobbed. "Now, please."

He rose, lowered the zipper of his jeans and

shoved them down, then slid his hands under her
hips and lifted her to him. She gripped the sides of
the table on a moan when he entered her, moaned
again when he seemed to grow harder and larger
inside her. Raw need consumed them both, and
when he began to move, nothing else existed but
the overwhelming, primitive pleasure between a
man and woman. The pleasure grew like flames,
rising higher and higher, hotter and hotter, sweeping over them both.

She cried out, shuddering. On a groan, deep and
guttural, pure male, he followed her.

It was seconds, minutes perhaps, before either
one of them could move. She finally managed to
lift her arms, then slide her hands over his shoulders, down his back. He trailed kisses, light, feath-
ery, warm, on her neck and shoulder. The *Savannah Sweetheart* swayed in rhythm to the river's
flow, a constant, gentle rocking that reassured and
calmed.

"You'll come back," she whispered, her voice
thick with conviction and the aftermath of desire.

"Yes."

Closing her eyes on a sigh, she barely noticed
when he finally picked her up and carried her to
the bed, when he laid her down on the soft mattress. She lost herself in the strength of his hard

body, the taste of his salty skin, the musky scent of man and woman. What she couldn't say with words, she told him with her mouth and her hands, with her body.

I love you.

For one moment she allowed herself the possibility that he might not come back. In that same moment she realized if something happened to Nick, she was capable of violence. With every resource and by any means, Kurt and John Emmet would pay.

Nick placed the alarm at the top of the gangplank. The device had a fifteen-foot radius of detection, and if anyone tried to board the ship, the alarm would sound.

He handed her the remote, then pulled his Beretta out of his waistband. "I want you to have this. Just as a precaution."

Eyes wide, she stared at the gun, then emphatically shook her head. "I haven't a clue how to shoot a gun, and besides, you're the one walking into a hornet's nest."

"Sophia, if Kurt, or someone working with him, finds this place and—"

"They're out looking for you, remember? And, anyway, if I did shoot at someone, I'd not only miss, I'd most certainly piss them off and they'd shoot back.''

She had a point, but dammit, he hated leaving her alone without some kind of protection. Still, he felt it was more dangerous to take her with him, so he kept the gun.

"Go to the upper deck and watch for me. I should be an hour, no more than two. Take your cell phone. If I'm not back in two hours, use it.''

Sophia hadn't time to answer before Nick's arm snaked out and grabbed her, pulled her close. His kiss seared her, left her breathless and wanting yet terrified at the same time.

Just as quickly he released her, then turned away.

She watched him walk down the gangplank, felt her chest and throat tighten when he moved across the dock, then disappeared around the corner of the boat. Moving quickly out of the alarm's radius, she pressed the button on the remote, then hurried up the stairs to the top deck, hoping to catch a glimpse of him walking across the wharf.

She frowned when she couldn't see him. He couldn't have gotten away that quickly, she thought. From her vantage point, she could see all the way to River Street.

Where had he gone?

Frowning, she walked back to portside and searched the dock. It was empty. When she glanced across to the parking lot, she spotted him standing beside a green van.

What was he doing down there? she wondered. He had no reason to be in the parking lot.

Then Kurt stepped out from behind the van, pointing the barrel of his gun directly at Nick's chest.

Chapter 10

"I know you've got a gun under that shirt, Nick." Kurt gestured with the barrel of his Glock. "Nice and easy, lay it on the ground and step back."

Nick gauged the distance between himself and Kurt, knowing that the odds of jumping the man and dodging a bullet at this close range were between slim and none.

Gritting his teeth, Nick silently swore. How could he have been so careless? He'd been thinking about Sophia, worrying about leaving her alone, and his carelessness may very well cost them both their lives.

"I won't ask you again, Sloane," Kurt growled. "Lay your gun down or I'm going to shoot your goddamned foot off."

A muscle twitched in the corner of Nick's eye as he reached under his shirt, then laid his Beretta on the ground and stepped back. "How'd you find me?"

"The gift basket Sophia's real estate agent delivered to her apartment. All it took was a phone to the agent's office, and the woman was more than willing to share Sophia's new venture with me." Kurt picked up the gun and stuck it in the waistband of his slacks. "I know Sophia's on the boat. Why don't we go join her?"

When Nick hesitated, Kurt raised his gun. "Now. And get your hands up high. For all the trouble you've caused me, Nick, I'd just as soon shoot you."

Nick didn't dare look up and give away Sophia's location, but he prayed she was watching, prayed he could buy them both a little more time.

"Have it your way," Nick said with a shrug, then turned and moved toward the boat. "So where's Emmet?"

"You plant a bug in my office and think you've got it all figured out." Kurt laughed. "By the way,

I will admit that was pretty good. I'd like to know how you got in.''

His hands in the air, Nick moved slowly up the gangplank. ''Give me my gun back and I'll tell you.''

''How 'bout you give me your so-called evidence that I'm involved in the deal with Marcos?'' Kurt poked the barrel of his gun into the middle of Nick's back to move him along. ''Maybe, just maybe, I'll let you and the girl live.''

Nick knew the second Kurt found out there was no hard core evidence against him, both he and Sophia were dead. And there was no way in hell Nick would let that happen.

''Call her out.'' Kurt cocked his gun when Nick didn't respond. ''Now, dammit, or I'll blow out your shoulder.''

''I'm here.'' Sophia stepped out from behind the stairs on the bottom deck. ''Don't shoot.''

''Dammit, Sophia,'' Nick snarled at her. ''Get back.''

''Do what he says, Nick.'' Sophia moved to the railing. ''Let's just give him the tape and video.''

''So she's smart and gorgeous,'' Kurt said with a chuckle. ''I'll bet she's good in the sack, too. I'd always intended to find out for myself.''

When Nick started to turn, Kurt shoved the gun

in his back again. "Ah, ah. Be a good boy. Now how 'bout we go aboard and talk this over?"

"He's right, Nick." Sophia locked her gaze with Nick's. "Let's hear what he has to say."

Nick knew what Sophia was trying to do, but he didn't like it. She was in the line of fire now. Later he'd yell at her. Right now he needed to stay focused on Kurt.

"Tell you what," Kurt said goodnaturedly. "I'm in such a good mood, I'll not only let you both live, I'll give you a million bucks to disappear. What do ya say, partner?"

"I think—" Nick nodded at Sophia, then prepared himself for the next step "—that I'd tell you to go to hell."

When Nick moved forward one more step, the alarm screamed. Startled, Kurt glanced away, only for a millisecond, but it was all the time that Nick needed. He swung around and grabbed the other man's arm, then snatched the gun from his hand and jumped back.

"I'd also say—" Nick pointed the gun at Kurt's chest '—that you're definitely not my partner anymore."

"Look, Nick, let's talk about this." Kurt held up a hand. "Two million. You could go live like a king somewhere with that kind of money. You know how to disappear, how to make sure you won't be found. Two million dollars can buy you anything you want.''

''What I want is a full confession from you and to see you locked up for good,'' Nick said in disgust. ''But, like you said, for all the trouble you caused me, I should just shoot you. Lord knows it would save the taxpayers a lot of money.''

''Nick!'' Sophia shut off the alarm and leaned over the railing. ''Are you all right?''

''Call 911,'' Nick said over his shoulder. ''Tell them you heard gunshots.''

''You move, bitch, and you're dead.''

At the sound of the woman's voice from the other end of the dock, Nick snapped his head up.

Iris. Emmet's secretary.

Nick saw the fury in the redhead's eyes, the angry grimace on her mouth. She'd removed the jacket of the navy pantsuit she wore every day and rolled up the sleeves of her white shirt. The gun in her hand was aimed at Sophia.

Sonofabitch.

''Hey, Iris, welcome to the party.'' Nick kept his gun on Kurt. ''Why don't you put that gun down before someone gets hurt?''

''Don't be stupid, Nick.'' Iris moved closer, never taking her eyes off Sophia. ''I haven't come this far, risked everything, to let you or Kurt's incompetence get in the way now.''

"You're calling me incompetent?'' Kurt glared at Iris. "All you had to do was lay on your back and get information out of Emmet. That was easy for you.''

"You would think that,'' Iris spat back. "Your brains are all below your belt. And since I'm the one with a gun here, not you, why don't you shut up and quit wasting time?''

"How sweet,'' Nick said dryly. "A lover's spat. Hey, Kurt, did you know that Iris here was making a deal with Marcos on the side?''

It was a shot in the dark, but based on the look of surprise on Iris's face, Nick's guess hit its mark.

Kurt's eyes narrowed. "What the hell's he talking about?''

"She wasn't just sleeping with you and Emmet.'' Nick's smile was flat. "She was working Marcos, too. Marcos had a direct line to Iris's office phone on his speed dial.''

"Don't listen to him, baby.'' Iris sweetened her tone. "He's lying. I wouldn't do that to you. You know I wouldn't.''

"You lying bitch, you were playing me?''

"Can we talk about this later, for God's sake?'' Iris moved beside Kurt but kept her eyes and gun trained on Sophia. "Now put your gun down, Nick, or I swear I'm going to put a neat little hole in the bimbo's head."

He couldn't chance it, not with Iris pointing her gun directly at Sophia. Ignoring Sophia's plea not to listen to Iris, Nick slowly lowered his gun to the ground, and Kurt picked it up.

"That's a good boy." Iris took her attention off Sophia. "Now let's all just go inside and—"

Nick wasn't certain exactly what happened next, but he heard a whoosh, felt the movement of air past his head, then saw the explosion at Iris's feet. The woman's skirt burst into flames. Screaming, her arms flailing, Iris ran to the edge of the dock and jumped into the water.

"What the hell—" Kurt stared wide-eyed at Iris, who was thrashing in the water, then at Sophia, who stood at the railing with a flare gun in her hand. She was reloading when Kurt raised the gun at her.

Nick didn't think, he didn't need to. He ran at Kurt, felt the burning pain when the bullet grazed his temple, heard Sophia scream, then the *flap-flap-flap* of a helicopter overhead and a man's booming voice on a bullhorn.

But none of that mattered. All that mattered, all he could think about, was keeping himself between

Kurt and Sophia. Nick lunged at the other man and they both went down, grappling for the gun. It was a life-and-death struggle, and both men knew it. But his need to protect Sophia gave Nick the edge. He slammed Kurt's arm against the wooden dock, and the gun dropped. Kurt reached for it, but Nick kicked it away, then slammed a fist into Kurt's nose, felt the crunch of bone under his knuckles. Kurt hollered in pain, reaching for his blood-covered face, giving Nick the opportunity to rear back and drive a fist into Kurt's gut. Air rushed from his lungs, then he crumpled.

Dazed, Nick stood on shaky knees and swiped at the blood blurring his vision, watched the helicopter blow dust and debris as it landed in the parking lot beside the dock. Police cars swarmed the area, lights flashing and sirens blaring. Nick tossed the gun in his hand several feet away and identified himself to the officers rushing forward.

"Nick!" Sophia ran down the gangplank, then grabbed hold of the sides of his head. "Ohmigod, your head. Sit down."

"I'm fine." He circled her wrists with his fingers and pulled her hands away. "That was one hell of a chance you took."

"She had a gun pointed at you." There were tears in Sophia's eyes. "I had to do something."

"And you just happened to have a flare gun in your back pocket?"

"I found it in the emergency trunk on the top deck. I figured it was a long shot, but it was the best I could do."

Nick glanced at Iris, who was being pulled from the water by two officers. "I'd say your best was pretty damn good, sweetheart."

Sophia scowled at the woman. "She called me a bimbo. I was aiming for her head."

Laughing, Nick pulled Sophia into his arms and dropped a kiss on her temple. "Remind me never to make you mad."

"Sophia!"

Nick watched a pretty woman with light brown hair come flying down the wharf. A man was at her side, and Nick recognized him immediately. Everyone living in Savannah knew who Reid Danforth was.

"Tina!"

Sophia flew out of his arms and rushed toward the other woman. They hugged, then both started to cry.

While the women hugged and cried, Reid walked up and held out his hand. "Reid Danforth."

"Nick Sloane."

Reid nodded at Nick's head. "You okay?"

"Just a scratch." He glanced at Sophia. "Thanks to your sister-in-law."

"You want to tell me about it?"

"Later." Nick saw his captain come storming down the dock. "I'm going to need a few minutes here."

The sunset that night was breathtaking. Stripes of pink and silver against a sky of deep blue. The tangy scent of salt and brine hung heavy in the cooling evening air, and in the distance another riverboat, ablaze with lights and the sounds of a live blues band, slowly floated past the *Savannah Sweetheart.*

The chaos of the afternoon seemed more like a bad dream than reality. Sophia leaned against the railing, watching nature's stage production of changing color, finding comfort in the simplicity of a setting sun and the knowledge that same sun would rise again the next morning.

After everything that had happened, she needed that reassurance.

The last detective had left an hour ago. Iris and Kurt had been handcuffed and hauled off, statements had been given, Nick's head had been bandaged.

She could still see that moment in her mind, playing over and over. Kurt swinging his gun toward her, Nick jumping into the line of fire, the blood running down his face. Shuddering, she closed her eyes and forced the image from her mind.

"Cold?"

She turned at the sound of his voice behind her. Just looking at the bandage on his temple made her stomach drop and her pulse lurch. She couldn't think about what might have happened. He was fine now. They were both fine.

He moved behind her, slid his hands up her arms. "Beautiful."

"It is, isn't it?"

"I meant you," he said, wrapping his arms around her.

His words made her blood warm and her bones soft. With a sigh she leaned back against him, thinking—wishing—she could stand here like this forever. "What happens now?"

Nick rested his chin on top of Sophia's head. "The department, especially Emmet, will take a lot of heat for a while. The media will be drooling over the combination of a bad cop, sex and drug smuggling. We'll be called in to testify, but the way Iris spilled her guts after they pulled her out of the water, including the location where Kurt dumped Marcos's body in the river, it's pretty much a slam dunk.''

"That's not what I meant, Nick." She turned in his arms and looked up at him. "I mean, what now?"

He looked down at her, his blue gaze intent. "I've been working DEA for almost ten years, Sophia. It's all I know. My undercover work will be blown when this story gets out, but I'll still be on the task force. The hours are long, the pay marginal, and I'm not the easiest person to live with."

"You trying to scare me off, Sloane?"

"Actually," he held her gaze, then swallowed. "I was asking you to marry me."

If he hadn't been holding on to her, she might have slid to the floor. Now it was her turn to swallow. "*What* did you say?"

"I thought at first that we might live together for a while, you know, just so you'd be sure." Nick's voice was a bit shaky, his grip on her arms tight. "But then I realized I don't want to give you an out. I figure we'll just get married and you're stuck with me. You know, for better or worse. Maybe have a couple of kids and cinch the deal."

"Let me get this straight," she said carefully,

her heart pounding so loudly she could barely hear herself. "You want to get married and have kids?"

"Are you trying to make this harder for me?" He frowned at her. "I love you, dammit. I'm not letting you walk out of my life."

Her heart swelled with joy at the less than romantic confession of love. *He loved her, dammit.* She'd never heard sweeter words.

"Well, my stars," she laid her Southern accent on thick while she twirled a fingertip on the front of his shirt, "since y'all put it like that, I guess I'll just have to accept."

She saw the wave of relief roll across his face, then he swooped his mouth down on hers. The kiss wasn't demanding, but it certainly was possessive. She locked her arms around his neck, lifted her body to his, couldn't imagine anything more perfect than standing on the bow of the *Savannah Sweetheart,* kissing the man she loved.

The man she was going to marry.

Her head spun at the thought. Marriage. Children. She hadn't realized how much she wanted all that. But she did. Because of Nick, she desperately wanted it.

When he lifted his head, she was breathless and more than a little shaky.

"Well?" He stroked her back, kept her body

snug against his, as if he never wanted to let her go.

"Well what?" She laughed when he lifted a brow. "Oh, yeah. I love you, too, dammit."

Smiling, he kissed her again…tenderly, a kiss filled with promise and love.

"It's been a rough few days," he murmured against her lips. "I should take you home."

"Don't you know, Nick?" She touched his cheek, felt the love in her heart overflow, wondered how she'd ever lived without his man. "We *are* home."

* * * * *

Look for Barbara McCauley's
Silhouette Desire,
MISS PRUITT'S PRIVATE LIFE,
available in July 2004.

WITH A TWIST

Maureen Child

To Amy J. Fetzer,
for all your help with details on Savannah—
and just for being you.

Chapter 1

"How to feel out of place in one easy lesson," Michael "Mad Dog" Connelly muttered into his beer glass.

"Chill, brudda." Danny "Hula" Akiona, a proud, full-blooded Hawaiian, deliberately threw Island slang into nearly every conversation—just to remind people of his heritage. At home wherever he happened to find himself, Danny lifted his beer in a half-assed salute and grinned at his friend.

Mike shook his head. "Man, we should have stuck to the bars down near the harbor."

"Nothing wrong with letting a little class into your life."

''Eight bucks for a beer is more 'class' than I'm interested in.'' Mike hadn't counted on spending his first night of leave in the ultrahip new jazz club, Steam. But after hearing how Mike's sister, Colleen, had raved about it, Hula had been determined to give it a shot. Since Mike hadn't had any plans that were more interesting, here they were.

''Hell, man,'' Hula said, taking a gulp of his beer, ''we're just back—in one piece—live a little.''

Mike thought about it, then nodded. His friend had a point. He and the rest of their SEAL team were just back home after a dangerous hostage rescue mission in the Middle East. Hell, they'd been lucky to get the whole team—and the hostage—out alive. Eight bucks for a beer seemed like nothing when it was put into perspective. He smiled. ''You're right, man. Let's have a few, and toast the boss.''

Hula grinned. ''The boss is celebrating fine right now, he don't need our good wishes.''

True. The boss, or their team leader, Zack Sheridan, had gotten married a few months back and was no doubt cuddled up to his new wife, Kim Danforth, while Mike and Hula looked for company. But, Mike consoled himself, at least they had a good place to look.

Steam was everything the gossips had made it out to be. The restaurant/bar/jazz club was packed. A dark, mahogany bar took up one whole wall. Behind the bar, more dark, gleaming wood, interspersed with mirrors and glass shelves were lined with liquor. Wrought-iron light fixtures provided the dim glow that settled over the quiet crowd like a blessing. Several high tables were clustered around the floor, with shadowy booths lining another wall. The seats and backs of the chairs were upholstered in red velvet and looked as if they belonged in a high class bordello. Dark red roses filled small vases that sat atop each table, and the scent of something wonderful drifted from the kitchen. The whole place felt…intimate—which was, most likely, just what the owners had been shooting for.

Strange being back in-country after six months of active duty. It was always a culture shock to come back to a world where he wasn't walking around armed to the teeth at all times. He loved his job, but being a SEAL made being a civilian a little more difficult. It always took a few days to acclimate himself to "normal" life. And then by the time he was used to it, his leave was over and he was back on active duty.

He took a drink of his beer and enjoyed the icy

froth sliding down his throat. Just a week ago he'd been chugging warm, sandy water and had been grateful for it. Now, thanks to his sister's insistence, he was in the bar of a trendy club, feeling out of place. Still, at least no one was shooting at him.

Mike and Hula hadn't been able to get a table for dinner. The place was booked weeks in advance, or so the cute hostess had told them. So they were making do with bar food and a few drinks. The snacks were delicious, the drinks overpriced, and the two of them stood out like a couple of hounds at a poodle contest.

Hell, he could practically *hear* money reproducing in the leather wallets of the people surrounding him. A couple of Navy SEALS couldn't compete in that category. No military man was going to have a bank balance that would impress anyone. But then, he thought with a smile, none of the guys in expensive suits would've made it in *his* world, either. A fat wallet wouldn't have bought their way out of a desert.

Still, Mike would have been more comfortable down at one of the taverns they usually went to when in town on leave. Colleen, though, had said he owed it to himself to splurge a little. And he had to admit she'd been right. The bar food was excellent, the place was loaded with atmosphere, and at nine there'd be some good jazz—which was one of the reasons he was willing to hang around. Well, that and the view.

Like everything else at Steam, the cocktail waitresses were things of beauty. One of them, a blonde, had already caught his eye, her black dress skimming a figure that could make a grown man weep. And while he was waiting for her to come back from wherever she'd disappeared to, there was the redheaded waitress in the corner to appreciate.

Hula talked and Mike nodded occasionally, but he wasn't listening. Instead, he was focused on the redhead, just ten feet away. Unusual, since he normally avoided redheads—and at that thought, he winced a little. Memories of one specific redhead, six years before, filled his mind. Back then he'd been too young and too stupid to know what he'd had when he'd had it.

But that was then and this was now. And *this* redhead had his complete attention. With her back to him, he could only tell that she was tall and curvy with legs that went on forever. She wore black stockings and red high-heeled shoes and red ribbons were entwined in the mass of short, auburn curls that dusted across her shoulders. The black skirt of her uniform just barely covered the curve of what looked to be an excellent behind, and he couldn't wait for her to straighten up and turn around so he could get a look at her face.

"Yo, man," Hula said, with a short, sharp laugh that caught his attention. "She's *way* outta your league."

Mike shot his friend a quick, confident grin. Hell, he'd never been able to resist a challenge. "Ten bucks says I get a date."

"With her?" Hula laughed, dug in his pocket and came up with a handful of bills. Pulling a ten out, he slapped it onto the tabletop and said, "You're on."

"Watch and learn," Mike said, dropping his own ten on top of his friend's. Taking Hula's cash would only make meeting that redhead all the sweeter. Then speaking louder, he said, "Excuse me. Miss?"

The redhead turned with a smile on her face that quickly dissolved into a mask of stone.

"Oh, hell," Mike muttered.

Balancing a tray that held four drinks ready to be delivered, the redhead stomped across the floor and didn't stop until she'd reached Mike's side. Ignoring Hula, she glared at Mike for a full, heart-stopping minute before saying tightly, ''You son of a bitch.''

Then she dumped her tray of drinks in his lap and stalked off, head high.

People gasped, Hula laughed and grabbed up the bet money, and Mike Connelly sat there dripping, watching the woman he'd once loved walk away.

Back in the kitchen, Kelly O'Shea trembled with the collision of fury and passion warring inside her. But then, it had always been that way between them.

Fire and gasoline.

Dynamite and matches.

Mike and Kelly.

She lifted one hand and rubbed her forehead with her fingertips. For God's sake, she'd be lucky if Clay didn't fire her for this. Clay Crawford owned Steam and he probably wouldn't appreciate one of his waitresses dumping drinks in a customer's lap. On the other hand, he was a man who understood women—which was more than she could say for Mike.

''Why is he here? And why'd he have to come into *my* place?'' Oh God, she sounded like an old movie...*Of all the gin joints in the world...* She leaned back against the wall and tuned out the subdued roar of noise created by the chefs, their assistants and the waiters coming and going through the swinging doors.

Mike Connelly, Navy SEAL and the love of her life. Well, he used to be the love of her life.

Kelly stared at the ceiling, but all she could see was Mike's face. Damn it. She closed her eyes, but that didn't shut off the image of him. It was ingrained in her mind. Just as it had been from the moment she'd first met him.

Funny, but you'd think that six years would be a long enough time for her to have gotten him out of her system. But like a slow-moving virus, Mike Connelly just slipped from one spot to another in her mind and body. Never really leaving, only hiding until he could attack her at her most vulnerable moments.

Dark hair, deep blue eyes and a mouth that used to do some amazing things to her more than willing body. Oh, my. She trembled and she was pretty sure she actually sighed.

Quickly, she opened her eyes, straightened up and gave a guilty look around—as though everyone in the kitchen were mind readers. Thank God for small favors, no one would know what she was thinking.

Well, except for everyone in the bar who'd witnessed her little outburst. She groaned and slapped one hand to her forehead. And here she'd been so sure that she'd conquered her whole flash-fire temper thing. Apparently not when it came to Mike.

"Kelly?" Donna Tucker, a small blond working the bar with her, stepped into the kitchen, still clutching her empty serving tray. "You okay?"

"Terrific."

"Who was that guy?"

"Would you believe me if I said I didn't know?"

Donna grinned. "No."

"Didn't think so."

"So why the alcoholic tsunami?"

"Long story."

Donna nodded. "Okay, but are you gonna come back out there soon? I can't work the whole room alone—I might run screaming into the night."

Kelly gave her a tired smile. "Sure. I'll be out in a few minutes, okay?"

Donna laid one hand on her arm and gave it a squeeze. "I'll hold the fort."

Alone again, Kelly thought, if six years hadn't been enough, standing in the kitchen for another fifteen minutes wasn't going to help. God. He was here. Back in Savannah. Back in her life. No, not her life. Just her world. Big difference.

Back to work, she told herself. Straightening up, she silently gave herself a little pep talk. She would *not* let Mike blunder back into her life. She would *not* give in to the urge to walk into the bar and smack him. She would *not* lose her job along with her temper.

Beside her, the swinging door flew open, nearly slapping her with an enthusiastic punch. Before she could complain however, Mike Connelly stepped through, his narrow-eyed gaze sweeping the busy kitchen. In his soaking wet jeans and button-down red shirt, he looked huge and mad and, damn it, *gorgeous.*

Why couldn't he have gotten ugly?

Briefly she thought about cringing back and keeping out of sight, but that instant of cowardice disappeared almost as quickly as it had blossomed. Why should *she* hide?

Instinctively she went on the offensive. Why wait to be attacked? Go out and meet it head-on. She wouldn't let him see that she was still shaken. "What are you doing?" she demanded, pushing away from the wall.

His head whipped around and she felt pinned by his gaze as if she were under a hot light being interrogated.

"You're asking *me* that?"

"Fine." Her gaze dropped briefly to his soaking-wet blue jeans and maybe she felt an ounce of guilt. But she squashed it flat under gallons of self-righteousness. After six years of both mourning and cursing a man, a woman was allowed a little leeway, wasn't she? "You're not allowed back here."

"Ask me if I care."

"Of course you don't," she snapped, still feeling the sizzle of temper dancing through her veins.

"Man, you haven't changed a bit," Mike muttered, ignoring everyone around them and concentrating solely on her.

Damn. That had been one of his best traits, Kelly remembered. How he could make her feel as if no one in the world existed except her. Of course, in this instance that wasn't exactly a good thing.

"Kelly!" the head chef shouted from across the room, "Get that guy out of my kitchen or I'll start sharpening the knives."

"Relax Rick," she said, automatically defusing the cranky but incredibly talented chef. "He was just leaving."

"Like hell I am," Mike interrupted.

"You don't belong here," Kelly said.

"He's not leaving!" Rick shouted, then asked of

no one in particular, "How can I be expected to create in an atmosphere of chaos?"

"Keep your shorts on," Mike told him, unimpressed with the short, round man quickly turning purple beneath his chef's hat.

"My—" Rick blustered, slammed the business end of his carving knife into the butcher block counter top and demanded, "Kelly…"

"He's already gone," she said, and sailed past Mike, headed back to the bar, knowing that he'd follow her and prevent Rick's imminent heart attack.

Once through the kitchen door, Mike grabbed hold of her arm and Kelly told herself to forget all about the quicksilver punch of electricity that jolted her system and sparkled behind her eyes.

To help in the whole ignoring process, she pulled her arm free and spun around to face the man—and her memories. She looked up. Way up. Why hadn't she remembered exactly how tall he was, she wondered. Could it be because she usually pictured him lying down beside her, or on top of her or under her or…

Oh, for heaven's sake.

It was dark in the bar area, but still Mike's eyes seemed to glitter at her. He was mad. Well, who wouldn't be after having a Mai Tai, a scotch and soda and two beers dumped in his lap?

And if she expected to keep her job, she'd better start by soothing the irate customer.

"I'm sorry about the drinks, okay?"

His mouth twisted. "No, you're not sorry and it's not okay."

"Fine." She lifted her chin defiantly. "I'm not sorry. Sue me."

"Kelly, damn it..."

"Don't you start on me, Mike Connelly," she said, keeping her voice low enough that only the customers closest to them could overhear. She couldn't believe this was happening. For years she'd imagined running into Mike again. After all, his only family, Colleen, still lived in Savannah, so he was bound to be here sooner or later. But always, *always,* her daydreams involved her looking fabulous and spurning a dejected, preferably *homeless* Mike who was groveling at her feet, begging for forgiveness.

This meeting was not going according to plan.

He glanced around, intimidating a few of the more curious people into turning their gazes away, then he looked back at Kelly. "We need to talk."

"No, we *needed* to talk six years ago," she countered, surprised at the sting of unexpected tears in her eyes. She would not give him the satisfaction of knowing that he could still get to her. Well, except for the whole dumping-drinks-in-his-lap thing. "Now, I need to get back to work, and you need to leave me alone."

He flinched. She could see it in his eyes. Maybe that was a low blow, she thought, but didn't he deserve it? After all, *she* wasn't the one who'd walked out just a month before their wedding.

"Kelly." He reached for her, then changed his mind and let his hand drop to his side. "I don't want to just walk away again."

The tone of his voice, the shadows in his eyes, even the way he held his mouth all got to her. Why he could still turn her insides into syrup, she didn't know. What she *was* sure of though, was that she couldn't afford to get pulled into Mike Connelly's orbit again.

Six years ago the pain had crippled her.

She couldn't go through that again.

Nodding encouragement to herself, Kelly sucked in air like a drowning woman, held it for a long moment, then slowly let it slide from her lungs. "You don't have to. This time I'll do the walking."

Chapter 2

Sitting in a bar all night should have been more fun.

But watching Kelly ignore him wasn't Mike's idea of a good time.

He should leave.

But he couldn't.

Hula had finally packed it in a couple of hours ago, but Mike stayed where he was as though his butt was glued to the chair. He watched Kelly work the room, balancing heavy trays of drinks, chatting, laughing, smiling at her customers. And he wished to hell she'd smile at him.

But she wouldn't even look at him.

Didn't seem to matter, though. He could still see the expression on her face just before she'd dumped the drinks on his lap. Fury, yes. But there'd also been pain in her eyes, and for that he could have cheerfully kicked his own butt if he could have figured out just how to accomplish it.

Six years was a long time.

Not long enough to erase the memories of how he'd left it with Kelly, though. He'd handled it badly; he knew that. And if he had it to do over again, he'd sure as hell do it differently. But life didn't give you do-overs. You made your mistakes and then you paid.

And sometimes, he thought, the payments just kept coming.

From the lounge on the other side of the building came the low, soft wail of a saxophone, sounding like liquid tears. A piano kept time and the soft brush of drums and a bass fiddle added enough to the mix that the four-piece band sounded like a well-tuned symphony. Around Mike, people tapped their fingers against the tabletops. The cocktail waitresses dipped and swayed in unconscious rhythm with the beat, and once more Mike's gaze fixed on Kelly.

He reached for his cup of coffee—he'd stopped

drinking beer as soon as he realized he would be staying till closing time—and took a long swallow in a futile attempt to ease the fire burning inside. It wouldn't help, of course, but what choice did he have? For six years the memory of her had stayed with him, taunting him. There'd been other women over the years—hell, he was no saint. But not one of them had ever meant what Kelly had. Not one of them had ever touched him as Kelly had.

She'd left her mark on his heart—his soul.

And now she wouldn't even *look* at him.

Damn it, she could at least argue with him some more.

"You just gonna sit here all night?"

He surfaced out of his thoughts slowly, like a diver trying to avoid the bends. Shifting his gaze to the blond waitress, he gave her a tight smile. "Any reason why I shouldn't?"

She tucked her empty tray under her arm and then followed his gaze as he watched Kelly delivering yet another round of drinks across the room. Shifting her gaze back to him, she said, "Not if all you want is coffee."

Mike glanced at her. "Meaning…"

"Meaning," she said, "that Kelly doesn't do one-nighters, so if that's what you're after, you're really wasting your time."

"Who says that's what I'm looking for?"

She laughed shortly and shook her head. "Honey, all you Navy guys are alike. You come into town looking for a good time, and then you disappear."

Shaking her head, the blonde went back to work and Mike found himself wondering just how many Navy guys hit this club every night? And how many of them were hitting on Kelly?

Damn it, and was she hitting back?

"Idiot." He'd given up the right to question anything Kelly did when he walked away six years before. He spun his coffee cup on its saucer and watched the inky liquid slosh back and forth like a tiny, choppy sea. None of his business who Kelly saw or what she did. He knew that. But it didn't stop his guts from churning.

Was Kelly thinking that's what he wanted, though? Did she figure he was just looking to recapture old times in one long night of tangled sheets and sweaty bodies? And if that *wasn't* what he was after, what the hell *did* he want?

Forgiveness?

He laughed to himself. Judging from the way Kelly had greeted him, he doubted she'd be big on forgiving him anything.

Then, what?

Simple, he thought, as he watched Kelly throw her head back and laugh at something her well-dressed, male customer had said.

He wanted what he'd wanted six years ago.

What he'd been stupid enough to let go of.

He wanted Kelly.

Kelly stepped out into the black, warm summer night and took a deep breath. Savannah smelled of jasmine and the river and a thousand other wonderful scents that she'd never found anywhere else. On a clear June night, the stars shone like thousands of tiny penlights, and a cool sigh of breeze drifted in from the river, easing back the humidity that would only get worse over the summer.

The city was dark but for the streetlights and a few lit storefronts. Bars were closed, and even the hardiest of customers were on their way home. Kelly's feet hurt, her back ached and her purse jingled merrily with plenty of tips. One good thing about working at Steam…the clientele were generous tippers.

She glanced around, inspecting the nearby shadows and swallowed back the twinge of nerves that always assaulted her when she left work this late. Savannah was a nice place, but like any city, it could be dangerous. And a woman alone, late at night, stayed safe by staying aware of her surroundings.

Heading for the parking lot, she wished momentarily that she'd had one of the bouncers walk her to her car, but she hadn't wanted to wait. After an entire evening of feeling Mike Connelly's eyes boring into her back, all she wanted to do was escape.

"Colleen should have warned me," she muttered, already planning on what she'd say to her old friend. She and Mike's sister had been friends before Mike and Kelly had become a couple and they'd stayed friends when it was over. But Colleen hadn't said a word this time about Mike being in town. The happily married mother of two sweet kids had been keeping Kelly up-to-date on Mike over the years whether she wanted to hear it or not.

Colleen made no secret of the fact that she'd like Mike and Kelly back together again. Kelly usually let Colleen's inclination to interfere slide, but if she was behind tonight's little "coincidence" of Mike showing up at Steam, there was going to be trouble.

Kelly stopped short when a shadow moved at the corner of the building. Backing up a step, she fought the tiny fingers of fear already clawing at the base of her throat. Her car keys, held in her fisted right hand, speared up through her fingers, a handy little weapon. And she cocked her arm, ready to throw a punch and scream her head off.

Then the shadow took shape.

Kelly blew out a breath as anger slipped past her fear and took charge. She should have known he'd be waiting for her. "Damn it, Mike. You scared me."

"You should be scared. What the hell are you doing walking through a parking lot at night by yourself?" He stepped away from the building and faced her, a wall of living, breathing outrage.

And, oh, boy, even furious, Mike Connelly made a heck of a picture. The parking lot lights were bright enough to define every plane of his face. In the past six years, he'd hardened up some, she thought, as her gaze drifted over his squared jaw and a nose that had been broken at least once. His dark blue eyes were shadowed by the overhead lights, but it didn't take a psychic to know that they were flashing with the impatience that was vibrating around him.

Between his impatience and her hot temper, they'd had plenty of memorable fights during the two years they were together. They'd also shared some world-class making up sessions. Until that last fight, of course. When Mike had joined the Navy and shipped out instead of marrying her.

Well, he could just deal with his impatience this time. She hadn't asked him to sit in the bar all night staring at her as if she was the last steak at a banquet for starving men.

"I'm going to my car, not that it's any of your business."

"You shouldn't be alone."

She gave him a cold, scathing look as she passed him. "Since you're obviously here, I'm *not*."

He grabbed her upper arm and stopped her in her tracks. Instantly warmth blossomed, her knees went weak and her blood boiled. What was *that* about, she demanded silently of whichever gods were listening. Six years, and he could still turn her on with a touch?

So not fair.

Why was it that over the last six years she'd never met another man who had the same effect on her? She'd tried to get over Mike. To put him behind her. But every time she felt as though she was getting close, his memory sneaked up on her and made any man she happened to be seeing at the time pale in comparison.

"Let me go." She said it coolly, calmly and congratulated herself silently on her self-control.

"I want to talk to you."

"I don't think so." Not quite as calm and cool. She tried to jerk her arm free, but his long fingers only tightened their grip until she felt the press of them on her skin like five individual branding irons.

"Why're you riding me so hard?" he demanded, looming over her in a lame attempt at intimidation.

She cocked a hip, tapped the toe of her shoe against the asphalt and glared at him until he released her arm. "Hmm. Let me think." Brightening dramatically, she said, "Oh, yes. I remember now. Aren't you the one who left a month before our *wedding?*"

His jaw clenched tight and she could practically *see* steam coming out of his ears. Good. No point in her being the only one angry around here.

"That was six years ago," he finally said in a voice that was lined with steel.

"Six years and four months," she corrected, then added as she stepped around him, "but who's counting?"

"Damn it, Kelly," he said, coming after her in long-legged steps she would never be able to beat in those three-inch heels.

"What we had was a long time ago. It's over. Go away, Mike."

"I did that once before."

She smiled tightly. "I remember."

"I know. Look," he said, grabbing her arm again and then releasing her before she could open her mouth to demand he do it. "I know I screwed up. But you played a part, too."

Stunned, absolutely stunned, Kelly stared at him openmouthed for what felt like an eternity. "We had a fight," she reminded him.

"And you told me to get out."

She laughed shortly. "I didn't mean *forever.*"

He shoved one hand across the top of his head and dug his fingers through his closely cropped dark hair. "I didn't mean it to be forever, either," he said, his voice suddenly less fierce and more tired.

"Then why'd you join the Navy?"

"Too many beers piled on top of too much mad."

"And going to boot camp looked better than marrying me?"

"Damn it, Kelly, we were too young. *I* was too young. I got scared."

"You think I wasn't?"

"I don't know. I only know I couldn't go through with it. Not then."

"So you walked away."

"Seemed like the best thing to do at the time."

The best thing? Joining the Navy and walking away from what they could have had was the "best thing"? Her mouth moved, opening and closing. She felt it, but couldn't seem to stop it. Words rushed through her brain and clogged in her throat, each of them trying so hard to be the first one uttered that none of them could make it. Finally, she did the only thing a speechless, furious woman could do.

She kicked him.

The toe of her red, three-inch, come-and-get-me pumps slammed into his shin just below his knee, and Kelly had the satisfaction of hearing his quick intake of breath.

"Man," he muttered, reaching down to rub his leg, "you really haven't changed at all, have you?"

"Not. One. Bit."

He straightened up and moved in close, backing her up against the side of her car until Kelly felt as if all the air in the world had suddenly evaporated. His chest was too broad. He was too tall. His hands too big. His mouth too...close, as he bent down until they were eye-to-eye.

"Still shooting first and asking questions later, huh?"

"You bet," she said, and wished her voice

sounded just a little firmer. But she was doing well just to keep her knees locked and stay upright. A nonshaky voice was just a little too much to ask for at this point.

Had it gotten hotter? The air felt steamy, and so close it was like trying to breathe water. Her lungs strained and her heart crashed painfully against her ribs.

Mike reached out and grabbed a handful of her hair, letting the dark-red curls sift through his fingers until she felt each tender caress. Her heartbeat thundered in her ears and her blood rushed through her veins, as thick and hot as the Savannah night.

"I always liked that about you," he said, his breath dusting her cheeks as he moved in closer, closer.

"Damn you, Mike," she whispered, just before his mouth came down on hers. And in the next instant she knew *she* was the one in trouble here.

Chapter 3

Kelly knew she should stop him.

Her brain kept screaming at her to do just that.

Her mouth, however, was otherwise occupied.

She couldn't breathe.

Didn't care, either. Instead, all she could focus on was his touch. The way his big hands cupped her face. The way his broad, muscled chest felt as it always had, like an impenetrable wall, protecting her from the rest of the world. So tall, she thought, going up on her toes, instinctively moving in closer to him, pressing her body along his length as though they'd never been apart. As if the past six years hadn't happened.

That thought rattled through her brain and then dumped a metaphorical bucket of ice-cold water over her head, ruining the cocoon of sensation Mike wove around her so skillfully.

Planting both hands on his chest, she gave him a shove. It was sort of like trying to shove an SUV, but she gave it her best shot. Mike reacted instantly.

He let her go, then took a step back, scraping one hand over his face. Sucking in a gulp of air, he blew it out again, then folded his arms across his chest and looked at her. "That was better than I remembered," he said softly, his voice a low rumble of sound that rippled along her already raw nerve endings.

Oh, boy, was it, she thought. But she wasn't going there. If she admitted to him what he could still do to her, it would open the door to too many possibilities she wasn't ready to deal with yet. "What do you want, Mike?"

"Cup of coffee?"

She looked at him and laughed shortly. *So* not what she'd been expecting. She'd thought for sure he'd give her a long, slow look out of those dark blue eyes and say something sexy...something designed to pump her blood just a little faster, hotter.

But then Mike never did the expected. Never had, probably never would.

"What do *you* want, Kelly?" he countered.

Too much of what she shouldn't have, she thought but didn't say. Instead of getting into some deep, meaningful conversation in the middle of night while standing in a dark parking lot, she quipped, "World peace and three-inch heels that don't hurt."

"Tall order."

She forced a smile. "Shoot for the stars, that's me."

"Always was," he said. "So why are you working in a nightclub? As I remember it, you wanted to be a school psychologist."

He did remember. Did he, she wondered, ever think about her? Did he remember, as she did, how it used to be between them? Instantly memories flooded Kelly's mind. Images of the two of them, sitting out under the stars, talking about their dreams and what their lives would be like. They'd had it all worked out right down to the house they'd build in the countryside. Even the number of children they'd have—three, two boys and one girl. By now, at least one or two of those children would have been born. She'd have been a mother—and at that thought, she actually felt her uterus contract painfully. Well, the future hadn't exactly worked out as they'd planned, had it?

But she was doing her best to see to it that her own career plans stayed on course. Even though she'd had to take an extra year or so to finish college.

"Still do," she said shortly, half turning to unlock her car door. She opened it, tossed her purse inside and leaned her forearm across the top of the door. "I'm getting my Master's during the day and working here at night pays the rent and buys groceries."

He unfolded his arms and jammed his hands into his jeans pockets as if trying to keep from reaching for her. She appreciated it. Because she wasn't at all sure she'd fight him if he moved in for another kiss. Her lips were still burning and her knees were still weak from the last one. So she was pretty sure her defenses were shot.

And, oh, boy, did she need defenses.

People made mistakes all the time, but making the *same* mistakes was just stupid. She wouldn't allow herself to count on Mike Connelly again only to lose him to the Navy one more time.

Another soft breeze ruffled past them, and at the back of the club, a door opened. "Kelly?"

She turned to look at the man standing on the

verandah alone. Clay Crawford leaned both hands on the porch railing, watching them. The parking lot lights illuminated him like a man on a stage. He wore a long-sleeved white dress shirt, open at the collar and sharply creased black slacks. Tall and muscular, he had dark brown hair and blue eyes even darker than Mike's, and right now those sharp eyes were fixed suspiciously on Mike. "Everything all right?"

Kelly smiled. Clay was everything a true Southern gentleman should be. Tall, dark, gorgeous and fiercely protective of his friends. "I'm fine, Clay, thanks."

He didn't look convinced. "I'll be around if you need...*anything.*"

"I appreciate it," Kelly said.

"She won't," Mike said at the same time.

"That'll be up to the lady, now, won't it?" Clay countered.

"Oh, boy." She looked from one man to the other, and each of them looked dangerous. Mike bristled like a bear being challenged and Clay was ready to defend his territory. She didn't know whether to laugh or scream. She was too tired to be dealing with *one* cranky man, let alone *two.* "A testosterone standoff. What fun," she muttered. "And me without my popcorn."

"Kelly…"

She held up one hand toward Mike. "Just let it go," she said quietly. Then she turned to face her boss again. "It really is okay, Clay. Mike's an old—" she nearly choked on the word "—*friend.* Good night."

"All right, then, if you say so. 'Night, Kelly." But Clay made no move to leave. Instead he eased one hip onto the railing and settled in as though sinking down into a comfortable recliner.

Kelly sighed and reached up to rub the spot between her eyes. A headache was brewing and it was going to be a real pip.

"Your watchdog?" Mike muttered.

"My friend," she corrected.

"Yeah?" His eyes narrowed. "You just told him *I'm* your 'friend.'"

"Different kind of friend," she said, and she was definitely enjoying the snarl in his voice. What? Had he expected that she'd been sitting home alone for the last six years? Okay, so most of the time, she *had* been alone, but he didn't have to know that. "Besides," she said, "Clay's also my boss."

"*Clay?* What the hell kind of name is that?"

"Keep your voice down," she muttered, and realized that when she next reported for work, Clay was going to be damn curious about this.

"Is he anything else to you?" he asked tightly, sliding the man on the porch another look.

Okay, fun's fun, but enough already. "Not that it's any of your business, but no."

"Looks like he's interested to me."

"Well he's not." She shot Clay a quick look herself, embarrassed to be still standing in the middle of the parking lot under observation. "Now I'm going home."

"Kelly," Mike said, catching hold of the car door as she slipped into the driver's seat, "I want to see you."

Her ridiculous, slow-to-learn heart, did a quick two-step. She paid no attention. "You *are* seeing me, right now."

She was going to leave. Mike tightened his grip on the door's edge and kept her from closing it in his face. He looked in at her, and everything in him came to life, as though he was just waking up from a long coma. Her green eyes were shadowed, and in the pale dashboard light she looked tired and even more beautiful than he'd remembered.

He couldn't let her drive out of his life.

"One date," he blurted.

"What?" She looked at him as though he'd lost his mind. Well, hell. Maybe he had.

"One date." He said it again, liking the sound of it.

She shook her head slowly and chewed at her bottom lip for a long minute. "For old-time's sake? No, thanks."

A rush of adrenaline pumped through him. Think fast, Mike. And talk even faster. "This isn't about the past, it's about now."

She sighed, shoved the key into the ignition but didn't turn it. Then she grabbed the steering wheel in both hands and held on as if it were a life preserver tossed into a churning sea. "We don't have a 'now.'"

"Yet."

Her hands fell from the wheel and she glanced up at him, stunned. "You're amazing."

He risked a grin and hoped she'd react like she always used to. "Thanks."

Her lips twitched into a reluctant smile, and Mike felt like the same buzz of satisfaction he'd had the day he'd won his team's underwater swim challenge.

"So how about it?" he asked.

"It's not a good idea."

"That's not an answer."

"I don't know, Mike..."

"Is that a yes?"

"It shouldn't be."

Maybe not. Maybe he was being an idiot. Maybe he was hoping for too much. Pushing too hard. But finding her as he had tonight seemed like a gift from the fates, and he wasn't willing to turn his back on it. Instead he wanted to snatch at this unexpected second chance and run with it. "But it *is* a yes." It wasn't a question.

Her hands tightened on the wheel until even in the dim light, he could see her knuckles whitening. "Okay, yes."

"Atta girl." The words slid from him on a quietly exultant breath.

"I have school during the day, and I work most nights. But I'm off on Thursday."

"That's three days from now."

"In a hurry?"

"Guess I am."

"I'm not," she said, keeping her gaze focused on his. "So—Thursday?"

"I'll be there."

"Pick me up at my house around seven."

"Where do you live?" he asked as she closed the door and fired up the engine.

She rolled the window down and looked up at him. "My folks' place. You remember how to find it?"

He could have found the old house in the dark, blindfolded. He'd spent so much time with her there, on the porch swing, in the backyard, in her room when her parents were gone. His body jumped to life and it took all his willpower to step back from the car as she gunned the engine, and the old four-door coughed and sputtered reluctantly.

Then she put the car in gear and drove out of the parking lot without looking at him again. Mike watched until her taillights disappeared, then he shifted his gaze to the man still sitting in the shadows of the verandah like a sentinel.

A spot between his shoulder blades itched—like it did every time he was in the field. It was a feeling that had saved his life more than once. He could tell when he was being watched, and Mike didn't care for it in civilian life any more than he liked it when on a mission. "She says you're a friend," he said, his voice loud and clear, carrying easily in the otherwise still night air.

"I am."

He tipped his head to one side and stared at the man who looked as relaxed as a coiled spring. "How close a friend?"

A match flared in the darkness as Clay Crawford

lit a cigar. In seconds, the rich scent of tobacco smoke drifted across the parking lot toward him.

Clay held the cigar out and studied the glowing tip of it. Then, casually he stood and walked toward the back door of his place. Before he stepped inside, though, he turned and said, "Looks to me as though I'm a better friend to her than you are."

Then he was gone, and Mike was alone again, forced to admit that the son of a bitch was right.

Chapter 4

Just after the crack of dawn, Mike headed down the stairs from the apartment over his sister's garage. As a SEAL, Mike was accustomed to waking up in the predawn hours. As a mother of two boys under the age of two, so was Colleen. So he knew he'd find her up and moving around already.

The small neighborhood outside Savannah was quiet, and Mike's stealthy footsteps on the creaky wooden stairs did nothing to disturb it. Birds sang in the trees, and from somewhere far down the block, a door slammed, the sound echoing in the silence like a gunshot.

God knew he was *way* more familiar with gun-shots than suburban living, but at the moment, he wasn't thinking about any of that. All he wanted right now was a few minutes of his sister-the-buttinski's time.

Whenever he was in town, he stayed at the ga-rage apartment, since Colleen insisted it was stupid for him to stay in a hotel when there was family nearby—and it didn't make sense for him to own his own place. Hell, he'd be lucky to see it for more than a few months every year.

Ordinarily, he was glad for the setup. Gave him a chance to see his only family and a rent-free place to drop in and out of. But just now, he was thinking that he'd have been better off camping out down by the river. At least then he wouldn't have been maneuvered into a surprise reunion with Kelly. Not that he minded seeing her again. Hell, that was the one up side to this mess. But a little warning might not have been out of line.

At the bottom of the stairs, he stepped into a slice of light thrown through the kitchen windows to banish the early-morning shadows. He didn't even bother glancing in the windows, he just headed for the back door and walked inside. Col-leen always unlocked the door as soon as she was up and moving, so Mike could come and go as he pleased. Today, she just might regret that move.

"Unca Mike!" T.J., short for Tom, Jr., grinned and waved an empty spoon at him. Perched on his booster seat at the table, the little boy grinned at his favorite uncle.

"Hey, shrimp." Mike reached out to ruffle the boy's soft, dark brown hair, feeling his heart do a slow bump and roll, as always. "Making trouble?"

"Not yet, but it's early," Colleen said, smiling up at her brother as she set a bowl of oatmeal in front of T.J. "Want some coffee?"

He shot her a narrow-eyed look. "Does it come with answers?"

She hid a smile…badly. "Thought you liked yours black."

"Colleen…"

"Hand this to Danny, would you?" she cut him off by giving him a tiny plastic plate holding a piece of toast, minus the crust, sliced up into several smaller wedges.

Half turning, he set the plate decorated with cartoon characters on the high chair tray and grinned when the baby grabbed for the food. "Geez, this kid can eat."

"Takes after his uncle."

"Uh-huh," he said, turning back to his sister,

who was purposely keeping her back to him. "Don't think compliments are going to get you out of this."

"Who, me?" She reached down two mugs from a cabinet, then grabbed the coffee carafe and filled them both. Handing one to her brother, Colleen took a sip herself and watched him over the rim of the cup. "So you saw her."

"Yeah. Right before she dumped a tray of drinks in my lap."

She winced. "Yikes."

"You should have told me."

"How did I know she'd throw a tray of drinks at you?"

"You know what I mean."

"Fine. If I'd said something, you wouldn't have gone to the club."

"*My* decision."

"And your decisions have always been so *good* when it comes to Kelly."

"Damn it, Colleen..."

"Damn it," T.J. echoed, grinning while oatmeal dribbled out of his open mouth.

"Nice going," Colleen muttered, then looked at her son. "We don't say that word, T.J."

"Mike does."

"*Uncle* Mike shouldn't,'' his mother said, shooting her brother another look.

The boy shrugged and returned to shoving his spoon through the thick cereal as if it were a ship plowing through an ice floe. His baby brother was happily tossing toast around the kitchen floor to be gobbled up by the family Schnauzer, hiding under the table.

"So…?" Mike prompted a minute later.

Colleen sighed and pushed her long, dark brown hair back from her face. "Okay, so I didn't want to tell you Kelly works at Steam. I wanted you two to see each other. To talk.''

"We talked," he admitted, leaning one hip against the countertop. He'd been going over their happy little reunion in his mind all night. He'd tried to figure out what he could have done differently. How he might have handled the surprise of facing those green eyes again in a better way. Nothing had come to him. Nothing except the fierce need to see her again. "It wasn't pretty.''

Colleen sighed, then reached out and punched his upper arm.

"Hey!'' He frowned at her.

T.J. laughed, and the baby threw more toast.

"Well, honestly, Mike. You're hopeless.''

"And you're nosy," he countered, setting his now empty coffee cup on the fake butcher block.

"I tell her that all the time," Tom said as he stepped into the kitchen in a navy blue three-piece suit.

"Some help you are," Colleen muttered as her husband bent to kiss her cheek just before snatching her coffee and helping himself.

"Hey, blame it on the Y chromosome," Tom said, smiling. "I'm on Mike's side in this."

Mike grinned at his brother-in-law. "And it's appreciated."

"I'm on his side, too," Colleen said, glaring at both of them.

"Daddy!" T.J. crowed and kicked out of his booster chair to slide to the floor. Running toward his father with outstretched, gooey hands, the boy was intercepted just in time by his mother.

"There are just too damn many Y's around here," Colleen muttered as she marched T.J. off to clean him up.

"Damn!" T.J. howled.

Mike and Tom clinked their mugs together in a halfhearted toast as silence reigned in the kitchen again.

Kelly spent the next few days trying to concentrate on her classes. Not an easy thing to do when your brain wasn't cooperating. It wasn't just simple exhaustion. She was used to being tired. Working until two in the morning and then arriving at school by seven-thirty didn't make for much sleep. But these days things were different.

The sleep she'd managed to get at night was now absolutely ruined by recurring dreams of Mike. And not the ordinary, run-of-the-mill, based-on-the-past dreams, either.

These were Technicolor, the-hills-are-alive, feel-the-hormones-spring-into-life dreams. It didn't help that Mike was showing up every night at Steam. He'd sit in the bar, nurse a single beer all night long and keep her involved in snatches of conversation.

He made her laugh, made her furious. He invaded the comfort of her world, getting to know her co-workers, making friends of the bouncers and the bartenders. Oh, he and Clay still bristled at each other, but everyone else at Steam was now convinced that Mike was a hell of a guy.

Now she walked across the campus, and as beads of sweat rolled down her spine beneath her peach-colored tank top, she shivered. Her dreams had left her not only exhausted but hungry. Hungry for what she'd once known. Hungry for what she'd been looking for ever since Mike left town.

"Pitiful," she murmured, then said, "Sorry," as she absently bumped into another student, hustling along the same path winding through the trees.

She'd tried to get over Mike, but his memory continued to linger. There hadn't been many men in her life since Mike...but every single one of them had been compared to him and inevitably came up short. No one's smile was as wicked. No other man's touch was as electric. No other man had the ability to turn her on with a look and melt every defense she'd ever possessed.

Kelly sighed, stepped off the path and dropped to a grassy patch beneath the closest tree. The temperature in the shade was a good five or ten degrees cooler than under the direct sun. She leaned her head back against the rough bark and stared up at the sky through the leafy umbrella overhead. Leaves danced lazily in the slow breeze and cast a nearly hypnotic spell over her.

Mike.

It always came down to Mike.

How could she move into her future if her present kept getting cluttered with her past?

"I can't," she said, shifting her gaze to the dozen or so students she could see wandering around the campus. Everyone here seemed to have their lives on a direct path. They knew where they were going and knew just how to get there. In comparison, Kelly felt as though she'd been wandering lost in the woods for years.

She reached for the bottle of water stuffed into her dark blue nylon backpack. Taking a long drink of the lukewarm liquid, she sighed and told herself that she had to find a way to get past the hopes and dreams her subconscious had obviously been clinging to all this time. She had to find a way to put Mike where he belonged.

In her past.

And as she sat beneath the gnarled oak tree, a plan began to take shape.

"I'm not speaking to you." Kelly glared at the phone receiver in her hand, then slapped it up against her ear again.

"You and Mike both," Colleen said, then shouted, "T.J., don't push the truck across your brother's head."

Kelly smiled, then told herself to not be charmed. Her best friend had set her up and she was mad, darn it. She'd even avoided talking to Colleen for the past few days. But she couldn't avoid her forever. Leaning in toward the bathroom mirror, she waved the mascara wand over her eye-lashes again and said, "You shouldn't have set us up like that, Colleen."

"Yeah, yeah," her friend said. "I already had the lecture, thanks. Both from Mike *and* Tom."

"Did you listen?"

"No."

"Didn't think so." Kelly shifted the phone to her other hand and did the same with the mascara wand.

"When I'm concerned about the people I love, I have to act. I can't just sit by and—"

"—let us run our own lives?" Kelly finished for her.

"That seems a little harsh."

"But true?"

"Fine. I'm a terrible human being. I should be shot at dawn. No wait," she said quickly. "Not dawn. If I'm going to be shot, I want to at least be able to sleep in *once* before I die."

Kelly chuckled and put the mascara away. As she gave herself the once-over in the mirror, she asked, "Kids still getting you up way too early?"

"Concern!" Colleen said quickly. "Does that mean I'm forgiven?"

"Almost." How could she be angry at Colleen for trying to help, when for the past six years, her best friend had had a ringside seat to see how much Kelly had missed Mike?

"Good. So what are you wearing for your date?"

"It's not a date."

"Mike's picking you up, taking you somewhere and bringing you home again. Unless there's a Taxi sign on the roof of my car—which he's borrowed—that's a date."

A date.

With the man who'd walked out on her six years ago. She was an idiot. A moron. A fool, setting herself up to be flattened again.

And butterflies were swarming in her stomach.

She slapped one hand against her abdomen in a feeble attempt to regain control. "Fine. A date. But its not the start of something new, Colleen, so don't get your hopes up."

"Huh?"

Kelly stood back from the mirror and gave herself another good look. Dark green dress with a deep vee neckline and a hip-hugging skirt with a hem that stopped just before illegal. Oh, yeah. She was ready. If she knew Mike, her plan would be put into action with no problem at all.

"I finally figured it out today," Kelly said, then

stopped herself. "This is between you and me, Colleen. No leaks to the other side."

Her friend laughed shortly. "Believe me, after this morning, this double X has no interest in being kind to the Y's of the world."

"What?"

"Never mind. What're you up to?"

"Just this," Kelly said, hitting the light switch, then walking from the bathroom. "It occurred to me this morning that the reason I never got over your brother was simple."

"You still love him?"

Kelly winced and picked up her purse from the end of the couch. She didn't even want to *go* there. "I didn't say that. I had no closure, that's all. He walked out, joined the Navy and pretty much disappeared from my life. *That's* why I can't move on. I need closure."

"Uh-oh," Colleen said, and in the background Kelly heard one of the boys crying. "Look, I gotta run, so make it fast. What's going on?"

"Very simple," Kelly said, stepping into her best pair of oh-baby black, high-heeled sandals, "I have to have sex with Mike again."

"What?"

"You heard me. The only way to get him out

of my system once and for all is to sleep with him again.''

"Kel…''

"Trust me,'' Kelly said, and smiled to herself as Mike's headlights flashed through the living room sheers. "This is gonna work.''

Chapter 5

Angelini's, an Italian restaurant on the outskirts of Savannah, was quiet, elegant and romantic. Which would have made it perfect if Mike hadn't felt as nervous as a teenager on his first date.

Stupid, maybe, but it couldn't be helped. He'd faced down mortar fire without flinching, defused bombs seconds from exploding without batting an eye and yet…sitting across a candlelit table from Kelly weakened him in ways he didn't even want to consider. She was more beautiful every time he saw her. The dark green dress she wore did great things for her grass-colored eyes. And the dress's neckline did amazing things for her breasts—which in turn did some damn fine things for his hormone levels. Her skin looked creamy and smooth in the dim light, and the candle's flame seemed to sparkle in the depths of her dark red hair. Six years ago Kelly had been a beauty, today she was so much more. She'd become a woman while he was off running around the world. A hell of a woman.

He'd watched her at Steam. Seen her laughing with her co-workers, using that fabulous smile to defuse impatient customers and working her amazing behind off without a complaint. She had a goal and she was doing everything she could to reach it. She'd taken the same steps in her life that he had in his own. She'd found her own path and she'd done it without anyone else's help.

There was a self-assurance about her now that went bone deep. She carried herself with confidence and poise and she hit him hard on so many levels he couldn't even count them all.

But could the woman love him as the girl once had?

She took a sip of merlot and then ran her tongue across her bottom lip, chasing down a stray droplet of wine. His gaze locked on that action, and his body tightened, sending what felt like stray shots from an M16 ricocheting through his blood stream.

"Mike?" she said softly, calling him back as if he'd wandered off—as, actually, he had.

In his image-filled mind, they were no longer seated in the quiet, upscale restaurant. They were instead rolling around on a big bed, naked, sweaty and locked together. And no way did he want to leave that image for the stilted reality of the present situation.

"Yeah," he muttered thickly, reaching for his cup of after-dinner coffee. He took a quick gulp, set the cup back down on the table and forced a smile. "Sorry."

"Where'd you wander off to?" she asked. "Nice place?"

"I think so."

She smiled, slowly, slyly, as if she knew exactly what he'd been thinking. Mike's blood pumped even harder as he asked himself what the hell was going on. One day she's ready to fry his ass for the mistakes made years ago—and the next she was looking at him like she wanted to lap him up.

Well, hell. Did it really matter what was happening here? Wouldn't he rather have her smiling than shouting at him?

Oh, yeah.

"I was just asking you about being a SEAL," she prompted.

"Right." A SEAL. His job. The one mainstay in his life. His gaze locked on her full lips again, and coherent speech died a quick death. "It's good."

She laughed, and the sound was silky, draping itself around him in a tantalizing web that only strengthened the need rippling within.

"Could you vague that up for me?"

He smiled. "I like it. I'm *good* at it."

"I bet you are."

"How'd you know about me being on a SEAL team, anyway?"

"Colleen's kept me posted," she said, with a small shrug, "at times, whether I wanted her to or not."

"Yeah?"

She took another long sip of her wine, and Mike's gaze locked on her mouth again. Couldn't seem to look away.

"So why the SEALs?"

He sucked in a deep breath, and prayed that there was enough blood left in his brain to keep it working for a while longer. And prompted by Kelly's question, Mike's thoughts turned to the Navy. The SEALs and his team members—his family.

Smiling, he said, "I wanted the SEALs because they're the best. Because you have to work your butt off to prove you deserve to be one of them. And once you're in…''

"Yes?"

''You're a part of something that's bigger than anything you can imagine.'' He fought for a way to explain the incredible sense of worth that being a SEAL had given him. But there were no words important enough. So he kept searching as he said, ''It's tradition. And honor. And respect—for the service and for your team members.''

She watched him, and he saw understanding flash in her eyes and he was grateful for it. The Navy would always be a bone of contention between them, since he'd walked out of their last argument, had one too many beers and signed up. But he had to believe it had been the right thing to do. For both of them.

He studied her eyes. The eyes that had haunted him and were with him still. Those cool green depths looked fathomless. Like staring at the surface of the sea—he knew there were wonders hidden, all he had to do was dive in and find them. But to do that, they had to clear up the past first. Taking a chance, he followed his gut and splintered the easy feel between them.

''I joined the Navy looking for—''

"Escape?" she asked and her gaze flickered brightly with a flash of old hurt and anger.

"No," he said, reaching across the table for her hand. His fingers closed around hers, and he held on when she would have pulled free. He had to make her understand that he hadn't been running *from* her, but *toward* something else. "No, I was looking for *purpose,* I think. We were so young, Kel." He shook his head and shrugged at the mistakes of the past. "I didn't have a clue about what to do with my life beyond loving you."

She flinched, but recovered quickly. "And that wasn't enough?" Her voice sounded small, as if the words had escaped her throat before she'd had the chance to cut them off at the pass.

His answer would hurt her, but damn it, wasn't it time they said everything they should have said six years ago? "No, it wasn't."

Again she tugged at her hand, but he held her fast. Her shoulders stiffened and she lifted her chin in the patented Kelly O'Shea fighting tilt. Hell, he'd missed their arguments almost as much as he'd missed loving her. And now that he'd started, he had to finish.

"I loved you, Kelly. Always did. From the first time I saw you."

Her mouth worked, and he thought he caught the

shine of tears in her eyes before she blinked them back.

"But it wasn't enough—not for either of us. Hell, I didn't even have a good enough job." Back then he'd been working at a friend's auto repair shop and wondering what the hell to do when he grew up.

"We could have made it."

"Maybe," he conceded, though he'd often wondered if hard times would have cemented them together or shattered what they'd had, "by giving up everything we wanted."

"I wanted *you*," she pointed out.

"You also wanted college," he said, his words hushed but hurried. "You wanted to help kids. It's a good dream, Kelly."

"And I'm making it happen."

"Yeah, but if we'd got married then, maybe you wouldn't have."

She laughed shortly, harshly. "Oh. So you dumped me for *my* sake."

"I didn't dump you."

"No? What was joining the Navy, then?"

"Looking for a future for myself."

"Not for us?"

It was hard to say aloud what he'd finally realized himself years after leaving Savannah. "There couldn't *be* an us until there was a *me*."

She yanked her hand free and leaned back in the padded, black leather booth. Her pale skin and dark red hair stood out against the dark fabric like a match struck in the shadows. She was all fire and light and, God, he wanted her back in his life.

He'd lived without her for six long years, figuring that she'd never be willing to see him again, talk to him again. He'd gotten occasional updates on her from Colleen but hadn't tried to see her. Not after that one and only time.

A cowardly thing from a man who made his living bravely facing down dangers that most people never had to deal with. But Kelly had always been both his weakness and his greatest strength. She could bring out the best and the worst in him, and sometimes the two of them together were more flammable than anything else.

But then, what was life without a little excitement?

A damn boring proposition.

Kelly folded her arms across her chest, obliterating his view of her cleavage, and scrubbed her hands up and down her upper arms as if fighting a chill. "Okay, Mike, if you were off building a future so we could be together, why did you never come to see me?"

He rested both forearms on the tabletop and leaned in. "I did, once. About two years after I joined up, I was in town and I went to see you at your folks' house."

She frowned.

"You were sitting on the porch with a guy. You looked…" Damn cozy he wanted to say, remembering the flash of pure jealousy that had nearly swamped him as he watched that man drape an arm around her shoulder. "Like you'd moved on," he said instead.

"What guy?"

"You want me to describe him?"

"Yes."

"No problem," Mike said. After all, the guy's image was burned into his brain. "Tall, blond, thin moustache, beady eyes, weak chin."

Kelly laughed and shook her head. "Nice."

"It's how I remember him." He also remembered wanting to get out of the car and plow his fist into the guy's face.

"Jerry Soper."

"What gave it away," he asked, "beady eyes or weak chin?"

"Blond," she said with another shake of her

head that sent those dark, soft curls into a dance around her face. "He was a friend. From school."

"Looked like more than friends to me."

"Is that now, or was it then, any of your business?"

"No," he admitted, and the single word tasted bitter to him.

"So you tried to see me once in six years."

He shifted on the seat and squinted across the room at their waitress. If this was going to erupt into one of their legendary "conversations" it'd be better to pay the bill and talk outside, away from innocent bystanders. But the waitress simply refused to look his way. Practicing her flirting skills on a busboy, the girl didn't even notice Mike scowling at her.

Sighing, Mike turned back to face Kelly. "Every time I talked to Colleen, she'd tell me about this guy you were seeing or some other guy. I figured you were done with me. So I did you a favor and stayed clear."

"Some favor."

"Yeah, I'm battin' a thousand."

"You should have come and talked to me."

"You wouldn't have wanted to see me then any more than you did now."

"Probably not," she admitted, "but I deserved the chance to turn you down, didn't I?"

"Yeah, you did," he said, leaning back and scraping one hand across his face. "I should have come to see you, Kel. I wanted to."

"That doesn't make it okay that you didn't."

He looked at her, his gaze steady. "I'm here now."

"Because Colleen sent you to Steam."

"Okay, I give you that much. That first night was because of her. But I'm not here tonight because of Colleen."

"I know," she said, and sat forward, reaching for her coffee cup. "I just don't know what to do about it. What to feel about it."

He grabbed her hand again and turned it over, stroking the center of her palm with the tip of his thumb. So smooth. So soft. He knew her body well. Knew her every reaction. Knew where to touch her to make her moan. Now Mike watched as her eyes slid closed and her lips parted on a sigh.

"Why don't we just let it play out?" he suggested. "See what happens."

She opened her eyes and looked directly at him. "If we keep seeing each other, Mike, you know *exactly* what will happen."

He stroked her skin a little harder and was

pleased to see her gasp. "I'm counting on it, babe."

His eyes were deep and dark and more tempting than anything Kelly had ever seen before. Mike himself was more…*everything* than he had been all those years ago. He was more sure of himself. There was an air of quiet confidence about him. He was taller and stronger and more imposing than she remembered, too. When they'd walked into the restaurant tonight, every woman in the place had turned to get a look at him.

Kelly couldn't blame them. His voice was a low-pitched rumble that rolled across her defenses and flattened them. His touch was heat and silk and gentle strength. And when he smiled, it was all she could do to keep from leaping across the table at him.

Maybe this hadn't been such a good idea after all. But the minute that thought blasted through her mind, she found herself defending the plan. She needed to be with Mike again. How could she ever hope to fall in love with someone else, if Mike was still haunting the corners of her mind and heart?

Answer…she couldn't.

He'd etched himself into her memory and continued to linger there long after she'd wished him gone. And even when she managed to avoid thinking about him during the day, her subconscious tortured her in her dreams. There was no ignoring the impact he'd had on her life. There was no escaping the fact that he had been her first love—the love she'd thought would last a lifetime.

And the only way to convince herself it was over was to sleep with him again. To let reality crash down on her time-fogged memories and show them for what they were...a broken heart's embellishment.

He pulled her hand close and bent his head to kiss the inside of her wrist. The tip of his tongue ran over her skin, and Kelly felt heat pool deep within her, making her want to squirm uncomfortably on the bench seat.

She managed to stop a shiver before it swept completely up her spine, but there wasn't a darn thing she could do about her blood pressure. With every stroke of Mike's thumb against her skin, with every tiny, nibbled kiss, she felt it climb. Her pulse pounding, heart racing, she tried to seriously rethink her excellent plan of seduction.

She'd wanted closure. She'd needed it. But every minute spent with Mike felt less like "goodbye" and more like "hello, big boy." She listened to him talk about his work—what he could tell her, at least, and she saw the pride in his eyes. The satisfaction he felt in doing a job that was important—to everyone. And she couldn't help thinking about the other sides of his job...the parts he skipped over—the dangerous parts. And she knew that long after he'd left Savannah again, she'd still be thinking about him, praying for his safety.

And she wondered, just *who* was seducing *whom?*

Chapter 6

Mike pulled into her driveway, threw the car into Park and shut off the engine. The air-conditioning died instantly, and the heat in the car built with every passing second.

He reached for her, but Kelly must have sensed what was coming. She opened her car door and stepped out. A moment later Mike did the same. Slamming the car door, he braced his forearms on the roof of his sister's four-door compact and stared at Kelly. In the moonlight she looked even better than she had by candlelight. The soft, pale glow of the moon washed over her, illuminating her features and making her eyes shine as if lit from within. His breath caught in his chest and he wondered how in the hell he'd ever walked away from her.

Oh, he'd done the right thing—for both of them—he was sure enough of that. He'd found himself in the Navy. Found his place in the world. The past six years had shaped him, molded him, given him a sense of duty and pride he might never have found otherwise.

But the price had been high.

Kelly lifted her face into the soft breeze and inhaled deeply. "Smell that?" she whispered. "Jasmine."

"Never smells the same anywhere else," he said softly. The simple truth had an explanation that was just as simple. The scent of jasmine would forever be locked into memories of Kelly. Memories of soft summer nights, young passion and the flavor of kisses full of promises. Jasmine without Kelly was just…empty.

As she looked up at him, Mike felt the power of her gaze slam into him like a bunched fist to his midsection.

"What's it make you think of?"

He knew what she was talking about. "That last summer," he said, memories crowding his mind.

"You and me. Down by the river. Or on your porch swing."

She inhaled sharply and let the air slide from her lungs in a sigh. "Me, too."

"I've missed you." Never more than in the past few days, when he'd been so close to her and yet separated by years of hurt. He'd watched her work, seen her with her friends, and wished that she was as easy with him as she was with them. But he'd had his chance. Was it too late now to try again? Or would he be a fool *not* to make an attempt to win her back?

"Me, too," Kelly said, giving him a fast shot of hope.

"So what do we do about it?"

"I'm not sure." She lifted one hand and pushed her hair back from her face, and all Mike could think was that he wanted to do that. Wanted to fist his hands in her hair, drown in its silkiness.

"Kelly…" He came around the end of the car and stopped at her side. Reaching for her, he cupped his hands over her bare shoulders, concentrating on the smooth, soft feel of her. Everything in him urged him to pull her close, to wrap his arms around her and hold on until the rest of the world fell away. Until the past no longer hung like a thick fog between them, obliterating the present and shrouding the future that could still be. But caveman tactics wouldn't work with Kelly. Never had.

He smiled to himself, remembering all the times she'd gone toe-to-toe with him, never backing down, giving as good as she got. There were guys in the SEALs who would never go up against Mike Connelly—but Kelly O'Shea would take him on in a heartbeat.

God, he loved that about her.

"Take a walk with me," he said, letting one hand slide down the length of her arm to capture her long, slender fingers.

"Now?" she asked, a smile peeking at the corner of her mouth. "In this heat?"

"You're a Southerner, Kelly. Heat never stopped you before."

She looked up at him and he held his breath. He didn't want the night to be over yet. He wanted to be with her. To walk beside her the way he used to. To feel her hand in his and know that sweet rush of satisfaction he'd only felt when he was with Kelly.

"Okay," she said. "Where?"

"You know where," he countered, already turning for the sidewalk, drawing her along with him.

"The river."

"*Our* river."

She smiled, he could hear it in her voice when she said, "You realize that the city of Savannah thinks the river belongs to them."

"Everybody makes mistakes," he quipped, then waited to see if she was going to throw his six-year-old error back at him. But she didn't.

"Yeah, they do," she said quietly, and tightened her grip on his hand.

At the river walk, they fell into step between clusters of locals and tourists, all looking for a little breeze and coming to the water to find it. Apparently, no one wanted to stay inside on a beautiful June night—even if they had air-conditioning.

Kelly breathed deeply, letting the warm, flower-scented air engulf her. But along with the sweet perfume of the magnolias and jasmine, she also caught the scent of Mike's aftershave, and the fresh, citrusy aroma slapped her hard.

That hadn't changed, either, she thought. So much was the same between them, and yet the differences were blatant, too. He was no longer the eager young lover—he was strong and quiet and sure of himself in a way he hadn't been before. And she felt herself drawn to him more inexorably than ever.

Which clearly made her nuts.

His hand on hers was callused and rough and brushed against her smooth palm with an erotic slide that made her blood rush and her head swim. His voice rumbled around her as he told her about his life in the Navy. With his words he painted vivid pictures for her, and she felt almost as though she could feel the swell of a ship beneath her feet. As though she, too, were jumping out of an airplane in the darkness and waiting lifetimes before opening a parachute. It was a world so different from her own—yet now it was Mike's world.

"You've done so much," she finally said, and he glanced down at her. "And I'm still here." She laughed shortly. "Heck, still in *school.*"

"Colleen told me you took a couple of years off in the middle of college."

"I did," she said, turning her gaze out to the moonlit surface of the river as it rushed through the city.

"She didn't tell me why."

"My mom was sick." Kelly felt his hand tighten on hers, and she felt a rush of gratitude for his silent support.

"What was it?"

She shifted a quick look at him. "Breast cancer."

He stopped dead and pulled her around to face

him. Surprise, sympathy and frustration darted across his features in quick succession. "Man, Kelly, you should have told me. Colleen should have told me."

She shook her head and reached her free hand up to cup his cheek. "There's nothing you could have done, Mike."

He caught her hand in his, linking them completely. "I could have *been* here. Damn it Kelly...I'm so sorry I wasn't."

Kelly stared up into his eyes, and heat dazzled through her in response to what she saw there. His emotions, once so hard to judge, were there, written plainly in his eyes. Regret was uppermost, and just for a moment she let go of the past and the pain she'd clung to so desperately for so long.

And it was good to be with him. Good to have him to lean against. "I was, too," she admitted. "But we got through it and Mom's fine now, Mike. She and Dad gave me the house, bought an RV and took off to see the country."

He grinned, relief shining in his eyes. "*Your* mom? Camping? Wish I'd seen that, too."

Kelly laughed. Her mother had never been the back-to-nature type. But her brush with cancer had awakened a need to experience more of life than she had before. Kelly started walking again and said, "Mom insists it's not really *camping* as long as you're cooking on an actual stove and sleeping in an actual bed."

"Bet your dad's loving it."

"Are you kidding?" Kelly laughed. "He's in heaven."

"Right now," Mike said softly, "so am I."

She sucked in a gulp of air and held it. "Mike…"

"Don't say anything," he said quickly. "Not yet."

She smiled. "Then when?"

"After."

He bent his head and kissed her. Gently at first, the smallest brush of his lips across hers. And Kelly's insides lit up like a fireworks display.

Gently, relentlessly, he coaxed her into the rush of sensation that only he had ever been able to make her feel. This was what her life had been missing for years. This is what she'd searched for in the men she'd been dating.

He pulled her close, folding his arms around her, molding her body to his and keeping her there with a viselike strength. Kelly stared up into his eyes and felt caught.

A kid on a skateboard roared past, his wheels howling on the asphalt. Somewhere in the distance a cranky toddler screamed, and all around them tourists snapped pictures of their kids, the trees or anything else that caught their fancy, while their camera flashes lit the night like high-tech fireflies.

And none of it mattered.

All that mattered right now was Mike and how she felt being in his arms again. Slowly he lowered his head, keeping his gaze locked with hers as if trying to keep from breaking the spell locking them together. But there was nothing to worry about there, she thought mindlessly. The spell hadn't been broken in six long years—it couldn't be broken now.

When his mouth touched hers, she leaned in to him and took all he offered. She sighed into him and opened her mouth to his relentless invasion. His tongue swept past her lips, and the intimate caress sent ribbons of want and need spiraling throughout her body. She reached up, locking her arms around his, and wished the rest of the people on the riverbank into oblivion.

An instant later, though, Mike lifted his head, looked down at her and whispered, ''Let's get out of here.''

Her brain was fuzzy, and her lips were still buzzing. Her knees were ready to fold, and something deep inside her was on fire.

He wanted to go home with her.

And, oh, boy, she wanted that, too.

Here it was.

What she'd planned.

But given the way she was feeling at the moment, she wasn't at all sure of her plan anymore. What if, instead of getting over him, she only fell deeper into the feelings and desires she'd known before?

That thought was enough to put a steel rod down her spine. She straightened right up and stepped out of his embrace, swallowing hard, trying to make her brain override her hormones. No easy trick. The fact that she felt suddenly and completely cold without his arms around her only proved to her that she was in big trouble.

"Yeah," she said, turning back the way they'd come. "I think I should get home. Good idea."

"Kelly—"

Plan, schman, she thought. What she needed was time enough to convince herself that she could survive Mike touching her and leaving her again. A couple of years ought to be enough. "Mike, we're not going to do this."

"Oh, yeah," he said, oblivious to the tourists now watching them as intently as they would a stage play. He took her arm and turned her to face him. His eyes were on fire, and need was etched into his features. "We *are*."

Hunger reached up and clawed at her. Amazing what the look in his eyes could do to her. Reason went out the window. If she listened to her brain, she'd say no way. After all, he'd been back in town—in her life, for only a few days. If she slept with him now, did that make her a sucker? Easy pickings?

Or just destined to be in Mike Connelly's arms?

Oh, time wasn't going to help, she thought absently, losing herself in the flash of Mike's eyes. Her plan might be risky, but at least it would get her one more night with Mike. One more night to feel the wonder, to surround herself with the magic that was only created when they came together.

Was it all as beautiful as she remembered?

She had to know.

"Yes," she said, forgetting about second thoughts. Forgetting about the plan, about anything beyond the feel of his hands on her. "I guess we are."

Chapter 7

Kelly didn't even remember the walk home.

Her elegant, three-inch heels hardly touched the ground throughout the trip. Mike's long legs made short work of the few blocks between the river and her house. Like an aircraft carrier leading a dinghy, he towed her in his wake so quickly her hair flew out behind her like a dark red flag.

He didn't stop until they were on her front porch, surrounded by ferns, and she was fumbling in her too-small purse for her house keys.

"What's the holdup?" he muttered, his voice thick and rough with a need she recognized and shared.

She blew out a short breath. "I can't find the darn keys."

"It's a small purse, how hard can it be?"

Pretty darn hard when your hands were shaking, and Mike's big body was blocking the porch light—not to mention hovering close enough to make her blood boil and hum in her veins. Impatience screamed inside her as she pushed her compact, wallet and tin of mints aside.

"Got 'em!" She yanked them free of her purse and held them up like an Olympic champion holding her medal up for the world's approval.

"Thank God," Mike muttered, snatching them out of her hand. Turning quickly, he shoved the key home, unlocked the door, then threw it open. Reaching back, he grabbed Kelly's hand and pulled her into the house behind him. Then he slammed the door shut again, flipped the dead bolt and leaned back against the door, yanking Kelly close.

"Can't wait," he murmured, bending his head to kiss her neck, the line of her jaw. "Not another damn minute."

His desperation fed her own.

As if it needed any help.

"Me, too."

His tongue traced a damp, hot line down the column of her throat, and Kelly gasped. "Oh, boy."

"Oh, yeah."

His breath dusted her skin, caressed her in a soft, barely there sort of way that teased as it seduced. His hands slid up and down her spine, feeling for the zipper at the back of her dress, and Kelly squirmed against the rock-solid wall of his chest, willing him to hurry up and find it already.

He did, an instant later. The silky sound of the zipper sliding free invaded her senses almost as much as the feel of the icy, air-conditioned air touching her bare skin. Then *he* touched her, skimming his palms up and down her bare back, and Kelly closed her eyes, giving herself up to the wealth of sensations coursing through her.

His work-roughened hands scraped against her flesh, awakening every cell in her body. She leaned in closer still, wanting more, wanting everything. He shifted his kisses, moving back up her throat to her cheeks, her eyelids, the tip of her nose and then, at last, her mouth.

He took her lips, pushing past them with a wicked swipe of his tongue that stole what was left of her breath. Her mind shut down. At least, she was pretty sure that was the reason she was suddenly blind to everything but this man's hands on her body. This man's mouth on hers. His breath rushing into her lungs, her sighs feeding his hunger until the air around them pulsed with the nearly electrical flash of desire erupting between them.

"Mike..."

"Shut up, Kel," he whispered against her mouth, and she felt his smile. That seriously sexy half smile that had always had power over her.

"Right," she whispered, nibbling at his lower lip. "Shutting up now."

"Atta girl," he said, and, shifting, he bent, scooped her up in his arms and held her tight against his chest.

"Whoa..."

He smiled again and Kelly's heart slammed against her rib cage hard enough that she wouldn't be surprised to find a bruise there in the morning.

"You said you were shutting up," he teased.

"Yeah, but when Tarzan picks a girl up, she's got the right to comment."

"Tarzan, huh?" Both dark eyebrows wiggled.

"Don't let it go to your head." She laughed up at him and realized how much she'd missed this. Not just his kisses, his touch, his heat, but the laughter. The arguing, the making up, the little jokes that only they shared. This was what had been missing. Not just the romance, but the *connection.*

Something she hadn't found with anyone else.

"Tell you what," he said, letting one hand slide up her thigh until she shivered, "How about tonight…me Mike, you Kelly?"

She took a deep, shuddering breath before releasing it on a moan. His fingers kept sliding higher and higher on her leg until he was close, so close to the heat pooling at her center. His gaze caught hers, and the blue of his eyes churned with emotion. Deep waters, Kelly thought, and wondered absently if she would sink or swim. But an instant later she realized it didn't matter—she was neck deep now, so she might as well enjoy the ride. "Okay," she finally said, "that works for me."

One corner of his mouth tipped up into that half smile again, and this time she felt *way* more than her toes curl. She didn't have time to react, though, before he started across the living room, headed for the stairs.

She'd left two lamps on when they'd gone out for dinner, and now they produced two wide pools of golden light that fell across the well-worn, comfortable room.

Mike's gaze was focused and his steps long and sure. He took the stairs at a dead run, holding her close to his chest, and a wild thrill erupted in Kelly. He carried her as if she weighed nothing, and the sensation of the big, strong man holding her close raced through her. Oh, boy. Maybe there was something to be said for the Neanderthal routine after all.

He reached the top of the stairs and ground out, "Where?"

She blew out a breath. "I'm in my parents' old room. End of the hall on the right."

"I remember." He was already moving, apparently not willing to waste a moment of their time together.

He walked into the big, square room, and when Kelly reached for the light switch, he twisted her away from it and looked down into her eyes. "No. I want to see you in moonlight."

She met his gaze and relished the swirl of excitement and arousal spinning through her. "I don't remember you being this romantic, Mike."

"I don't remember you being this beautiful," he whispered, and kissed her, locking their lips together as he crossed the room to the queen-size bed on the far wall.

The brightly colored but faded rag rug muffled his footsteps until they sounded like a rapid heartbeat. Air-conditioning kept the room pleasantly cool, and moonlight speared in through the frothy white sheers hanging at the bank of windows on either side of the room. Unlit candles dotted the surfaces of her dresser and the nightstands and even without lit wicks, the sweet scent of honeysuckle and jasmine pervaded the room.

"I want you bad," Mike said as he reached down with one hand to grab the flowered quilt bedspread and toss it to the foot of the bed.

"Back atcha," Kelly muttered, and clung to him when he laid her down on the mattress. She kept him with her and when his mouth came down on hers, she gave herself up to the moment. The moment she'd dreamed about, and hungered for, for six long years.

Everything in her came alive as it hadn't since he'd left. Every cell in her body jumped up and shouted *hooray* as his right hand swept up beneath the hem of her skirt. His long fingers dragged across her skin, sending tingles of expectation racing along her nerve endings. When he met the flimsy barrier of her black silk thong panties, he groaned tightly and nestled his head in the curve of her neck.

"Oh, man, if I'd known you were wearing these under that incredible dress, I never would have made it through dinner."

She laughed, a deep, throaty roll of amusement. "Maybe I should have told you."

He grinned against her neck. "The surprise was better."

"Happy to help."

"Now it's my turn," he said, and flicked off those panties with one quick move of incredibly strong fingers.

She gasped, then held that small breath and hoped it would be enough to sustain her as he slipped one finger into her depths. Kelly arched into his touch as if reaching for light after a lifetime of darkness. Her hips moved into his hand as his thumb stroked the tiny bead of flesh at her center, and exquisite sensations rocketed through her body.

"I've missed you," Mike whispered, lifting his head long enough to plant a deep, soul-searing kiss on her mouth. When it ended, he left her gasping— for air or for more, she wasn't sure.

And it didn't matter.

He touched her more deeply, caressing, stroking, pushing her toward a climax that had been years in the making. Kelly kicked off her heels, planted her feet on the mattress and rode his touch fiercely. It was good. It was right. And it wasn't nearly enough. She wanted Mike inside her. She wanted his hard length buried deep within her body, lock-

ing them together as they used to be, as they should
have been…always.

"Now." She squeezed the one word out past the
knot of need lodged in her throat.

"Soon."

She grabbed hold of the jacket he was still wearing and yanked him even closer. "Now, Mike. I
need you inside me, *now*."

He groaned, stared down into her eyes and said,
"Okay, yeah. Now."

Moving together, they tore at each other's
clothes, hands stroking, taking, giving. And then
there was nothing but skin on skin, heat on heat.

Mike rolled across the bed, holding her tight,
keeping her with him, loving the feel of her long,
lithe body aligned with his. He couldn't seem to
touch her enough. He wanted to explore every inch
of her body and learn its curves all over again.
They'd been apart so long that it was all new—all
encompassing.

How had he lived so long without her? How had
he made it through years of days and nights empty
of her scent, her sighs, her touch?

And how could he ever go back to that emptiness?

At the thought, he stopped thinking. Now wasn't
the time to worry about tomorrow or the days to

come. All he wanted to think about now was Kelly. And having her in his arms again.

He kissed her, taking her mouth in a gentle invasion, sweeping his tongue into her warmth, staking his claim again, branding her with his heart and his body. Her tongue brushed against his in an erotic dance that caused his heart to race and his brain to shut down. She was everything. Everything and more.

He caught her in the splash of moonlight, rolled her over onto her back and levered himself above her. She reached for him, dragging her short, neat nails down his chest, scoring his skin lightly with her touch. He shivered, and as she moved to welcome him, open for him, he paused long enough to reach for the condom he'd tossed onto the bedside table. And when he'd done his best to protect her, he slid himself home and stopped, luxuriating in the glory of being surrounded by her.

"Mike." His name came on a sigh as she lifted her legs to wrap them around his hips. She reached beneath his arms to hold him, splaying her palms against his back. Arching into him, she took him deeper, higher and it was all he could do to maintain...hold himself back from the edge.

"Take me, Connelly," she whispered.

"Take me, O'Shea," he countered as he rocked his hips against her.

She inhaled sharply, deeply, digging her head back into the mattress beneath her. Moving with him, she kept pace, hurrying along the edge of madness, racing toward completion, toward oblivion. Together they made the climb, higher and higher, locked together, hands and bodies joined, mouths mating eagerly, desperately.

In moments they found what they had lost so long ago, and together they tumbled over the edge.

Chapter 8

"I think I'm paralyzed." Kelly's voice came in a strangled groan.

Mike laughed shortly, and his rolling chuckle rumbled from his body into hers.

"Mmmm…" A hum of renewed desire washed through her as he shifted inside her. His incredible body was already growing, filling her again, and she savored the sense of completion dancing through her veins.

He moved again, as if to roll off her, and she stopped him, slapping her hands on his upper arms. "Don't. Don't go away. Not yet." She just didn't want to lose this link with him. She wasn't ready yet to give it up. To become separate individuals again.

He nodded, then pushed up onto one elbow and looked down into her face. "I'll crush you into dust."

She smiled. "It's a soft mattress."

"You're softer."

She squirmed and gave him a self-satisfied grin. "And you're *not*."

"So true."

Kelly studied his features, burning them into her mind. It wasn't as though she needed to—Mike's face was as much a part of her as her own reflection in a mirror. In twenty years she'd be able to conjure his image in her brain, and it would be clear enough, sharp enough to make her blood run hot and thick.

She reached up, stroking his cheek, the line of his jaw, with her fingertips. He turned his face into her touch and kissed her hand.

"That was…" he said softly.

"…amazing," she finished for him.

"In a word." He dipped his head to claim a kiss, and as he moved, his body shifted within hers again and a gasp slipped from her lips. Changing position slightly, he was able to drift tiny kisses along her throat and down her chest.

She held him, her hands sliding up and down his back, her palms defining muscles on muscles. So familiar and yet so different, she thought through a thick haze of passion that was already building again. There were new scars on his skin. Marks of his life without her. Old wounds, long since healed, that she knew nothing about. And she wondered how he'd been hurt and if there'd been anyone to take care of him. Close on the heels of that thought were new and terrifying ones as she realized that once he left her, he would be going back into a dangerous world.

A world where she had no place.

Her fingers moved again, to the biceps of his right arm. Her thumb slid across the edge of raised skin that snaked in a long, thin line. "What's this?" she asked, her voice quiet but filled with the need to understand some small portion of his life.

He smiled against her chest. "Stingray. Off the coast of California. I guess I pissed him off."

"One of your many gifts," she said, still smiling as she tried to imagine him, alone in the dark of the ocean.

"They don't call me Mad Dog for nothin'," he

boasted, dropping another line of kisses along her chest as he headed for her right breast.

"Mad Dog, huh?" She squirmed as he neared his goal.

"Tenacious, babe," he murmured. His breath swept hot against her flesh. "I never give up."

But he'd given up on *them* six years ago, she thought. Had he changed that much? Did he dig in now and fight for what he wanted? Would he fight for *her?* Would he *want* her for more than an hour in bed?

And if he did, what then?

Could she forget about old betrayals and pain for the chance at something more?

His mouth closed on her nipple, and Kelly stopped thinking for a minute. His tongue stroked the sensitive, pink tip until she arched beneath him, groaning. He tasted her, suckled her, and she felt lightninglike strikes erupt within.

She was in deep trouble.

Thoughts crashed through her mind like bumper cars, colliding into each other and smashing the truth into her brain whether she wanted it or not.

Her memories of Mike's lovemaking hadn't even come close to the reality.

Mike slid up her body again, kissing her chin, her cheeks, her eyes and then finally her mouth.

"You're thinking," he chided.

"Just barely," she admitted, licking her lips as if to savor the taste of him.

"No thinking allowed."

"Guess you'd better distract me."

One dark eyebrow lifted. "A challenge?"

Kelly laughed, and it felt so good. Felt good to be with a man who understood her, who knew her body even better than she did. Who was confident enough to make her laugh during lovemaking.

Oh, no, she was in love again.

Her laughter died as she looked up into his dark blue eyes and actually *felt* herself falling. And this time it was deeper and richer and so much more than she'd felt as a girl of twenty. This was more because *she* was more. A girl couldn't feel what a woman could.

There was no help for it. The plan ruined, heartbreak on order, she was jumping into the deep end with rocks tied around her feet. Too late to worry about it now, she thought, because truth to tell, even if she'd seen this coming, she wouldn't have missed this night for anything.

He swept one hand down the length of her body and then slipped it between their still-joined bodies.

A gulp of air whistled between her teeth as he touched her sensitive center, stroking her softly, gently until the first ripples of need began to build again.

"Mike, I can't..." Too much, she thought wildly, even as her body prepared for another on-slaught of sensation.

"You can," he murmured, watching her eyes go glassy. "*We* can."

Her body trembled, and Mike absorbed every gentle ripple into his heart. Being with her, watching her take him into her body, feeling the two of them joined again, filled the emptiness inside him. For the first time in six long years, he felt whole again. As if he'd found the missing part of his life.

His heart.

"Mike..." She called his name and it sounded like music to him.

"Take it all, Kelly," he whispered, stroking her center, watching passion jump in her eyes. "Take everything."

"You, Mike," she said, struggling to focus on him. "Let me take you."

She caught him with her words and held him with her touch. His brain shut down and his body took over. He buried himself even deeper inside her, and with a few long, smooth strokes, pushed her to the brink—and when she called his name, he eagerly followed after.

A few days later Kelly realized she'd become a heck of a good liar.

Oh, not that she was running around Savannah telling tall tales to unsuspecting tourists. In fact the only person she was lying to was herself.

And they were beauts, she thought, as she helped set up the bar at Steam. She kept insisting to herself that nothing had changed. That the plan was still good, still working. It didn't matter if she was in love, she lied to herself. She would still let Mike go. She couldn't risk everything again to watch him walk away. This time she'd do the walking.

And yet…every night now for the past three nights, Mike had taken her home and spent the night driving her body into heaven and her mind into turmoil. How would she be able to walk away from him when she couldn't seem to stop wanting him? She should be stopping this. She should have found her closure and moved on. Instead she kept sinking deeper and deeper, and now she wasn't sure at all what to do about any of it.

All she knew was that Mike's leave would be up in another week and he'd be leaving again. Going off to God-knew-where to do God-knew-what.

He would walk away from her again, and this time she didn't think she'd survive it.

But damned if she knew what to do about it.

She worked on automatic pilot, straightening the wide array of liquor bottles lined up behind the polished mahogany bar. She dusted, arranged and in general spruced up the joint in preparation for opening. Rows of finely cut glassware stood ready and twinkling in the soft, elegant lighting. A smooth mix of old standards and cool jazz piped through the overhead speakers, setting the mood and scene that the club had become known for.

Everything was as it should be. At least in this little corner of her world. It was just her personal life that was once more in the middle of a whirlwind.

"Problem?"

The deep voice behind her startled a jump out of Kelly, but in the next instant, recognition set in and she turned to smile at Clay Crawford.

"Evening, boss," she said, flipping a clean white bar towel over her left shoulder.

He grinned, a tall, dark-haired man with eyes as deep a blue as Mike's. Funny, she could see the resemblance, but looking into Clay's eyes didn't send her into a weird little spiraling dance of need and confusion. What was it, then, that made one pair of eyes magical and another simply kind?

Clay slid onto a bar stool, leaned his forearms on the bar top and studied her. "How's it going, Kelly?"

"In general," she said with a shrug, "okay."

"And less generally?" he asked, a smile still hovering on his lips.

"Less okay," she admitted and leaned forward, propping her elbows on the bar and cupping her chin in her hands.

"I thought so." Then he made a show of looking behind her.

She shot a look over her shoulder, though she knew darn well there was no one there. "Who're you looking for?"

"Your shadow."

"Ah." She nodded.

"Yeah. The guy who's become my best customer in the last week or so."

She smiled sadly, glancing at the empty table in the corner. The spot she'd come to think of as Mike's table. And she knew that long after he'd left town again, she'd be seeing him there, smiling at her. Oh, God, the haunting of Kelly O'Shea had already started. Turning her gaze back to Clay, she

said on a sigh she hadn't meant to allow to escape,
"He'll be in later."

"Problem?" Clay asked.

"Sort of." *Sort of?* How about, *Oh boy, howdy?*
Straightening up, she snatched the towel off her
shoulder and unnecessarily wiped off the already
gleaming bar top as she spoke again. "Clay, let me
ask you a hypothetical question."

He nodded. "My favorite kind."

"Let's say there was someone in your past.
Someone you once loved more than anything."
Kelly stopped, pulled in a breath and let it slide
out again. "Someone you wanted to spend the rest
of your life with."

"Hypothetically speaking, of course," he said,
giving her a small, encouraging smile.

"Yeah." She swallowed hard. "The question is,
should you leave the past buried…or should you
try to bring it back? Recapture what you had?"

He took the cloth from her and wiped a spot off
the edge of the bar before tossing it back to her.
"Never go back, Kelly," he said. "You'll never
see the future if you keep staring at the past."

True. But, "How can I risk it again, Clay? Last
time the pain was so bad, I thought I'd die. This
time I know I would."

He took her left hand in his and gave it a pat.

"What makes you so sure there'll be pain this time?"

She laughed shortly, sharply. "Luck of the Irish?"

His lips curved, but his eyes were suddenly filled with regret. Shaking his head he said softly, "If you get the chance at love, don't pass it up. You just never know if it'll ever come around again."

For the first time since she'd known him, Clay Crawford's elegant, laid-back attitude had changed. He looked like a man who had his own ghosts dogging his footsteps. Instantly Kelly's heart twisted in sympathy. "You speaking from experience?" she asked quietly as the music pouring from the stereo system shifted to a slow dance song from the forties.

Clay's eyes clouded briefly as if he were staring at a scene only he could see. "There was someone once," he admitted, his deep voice barely audible over the music.

"What happened?"

"Nothing. She was *way* out of my league," he murmured, almost as if he'd forgotten Kelly's presence entirely.

In defense of her friend, Kelly bristled. "If that's what *she* thought," Kelly said, giving his hand a squeeze, "then she was nuts."

He snapped back to the present, shrugging off the burden of his past like a man slipping out of an ill-fitting jacket. Then he gave her a sly smile. "Now, that's just what I told myself."

Better, Kelly thought. The shadows hadn't entirely lifted from his eyes, but she didn't want to think of her friend being unhappy. Better to see Clay with his smile in place and his eyes filled, as usual, with wry amusement.

"Hey, everybody," a woman called out as she stepped into the lounge.

"Sophia," Clay crooned, holding out one hand toward her. "My right hand—and I use the term *very* loosely—man."

"Ha-ha-ha." Sophia Alexander, Clay's assistant and the club's manager, pushed her long blond hair back from her face and stuck out her tongue at her boss. Then, turning to Kelly, she said, "We still on for shopping tomorrow?"

She'd forgotten, actually, but since the day had been planned three weeks ago, she'd just tell Mike she had plans. It'd be good for them to spend a few hours apart, anyway. Best to start preparing for the inevitable separation.

"You bet."

"Good." Sophia followed Clay as he headed for

the back stairs leading to his office. "I need a dress for Saturday night."

"We'll find one," Kelly called out, then caught her own reflection in the mirror over the bar. Clay's words ran through her mind again and again, and she asked herself one more time just what she was going to do about this situation with Mike. Nothing came to her, though. "Dresses I can find," she told her reflection in the mirror. "Answers? Not so much."

Chapter 9

Days slipped past, and in his head Mike could almost *hear* a ticking clock counting down what little time with Kelly he had left. Soon he'd be headed back on duty. He'd catch up with Hula, Three Card, Hunter and the boss, and the team would be sent off to…who-knew-where this time.

He punched the steering wheel of his sister's car and felt pain shoot up his arm. Well, hell, at least that was a tangible thing. Physical pain was something he knew how to deal with. He'd been shot and stabbed and bitten, and it hadn't slowed him down. But this thing with Kelly had him torn up inside—not sure if he was coming or going. And he was a man who didn't like feeling lost and unsure of himself.

Ordinarily, after just one week of leave, he was champing at the bit to get back to work. To put his skills to the test. To do what he did best. Usually he couldn't wait to get back into the field. Into the thick of things. To follow the action and do his duty, whatever the hell it might be on any given day. Now, though, all he could think about was Kelly.

He wasn't ready to leave her yet.

Because, damn it, he knew he hadn't convinced her that now was any different from six years ago. She was keeping a part of herself back from him. He felt it, saw it in her eyes, sensed it in her touch.

Especially the past few days. It was as if she was already pulling away from him.

Oh, the sex was great. Hell, better than great. But if all he was looking for was a bed partner, there were easier women to deal with than Kelly O'Shea. Yet despite what he might want, Kelly seemed determined to keep whatever they had together in the bedroom. She wasn't yet willing to let him into the other areas of her life—her hopes, her dreams—her *future*. Not that he could blame her any, but how in the hell was a man supposed to win her over if he was being shipped out?

He pulled his sister's car to the curb in front of a tiny house and threw the too-small sedan into Park. Setting the brake, he stared out the passenger-side window at what looked like a doll's house. There were flowers everywhere. A rainbow of color splashed across the white clapboard front of the place and tumbled from window boxes. The tiny front porch looked like an Amazon rain forest, with hanging plants and tubs of yet more flowers marching up and down the steps and crouching on the railing.

Last February he'd seen this place for the first time, and right now it looked like a life preserver floating on a choppy sea. Here was safe harbor.

Mike climbed out of the car, slammed the door and headed for the walkway. Only halfway up, he breathed a sigh of relief. The shade beneath the ancient oak guarding the Sheridan-Danforth house cooled the temperature a good ten degrees. Yet it couldn't help the hot, steamy feel of air thick enough to chew, fighting its way into his lungs.

Nothing like the South in summer.

Mike skipped the steps and jumped to the shady overhang of the porch. Then he leaned on the doorbell and listened to "Anchors Aweigh" echo inside the house.

The door flew open and Mike was still grinning. Keeping his gaze fixed on the man standing in the doorway, Mike hit the doorbell again and laughed as the tune repeated itself. "Making a few changes around here, boss?"

Zack Sheridan, Mike's SEAL team leader, leaned on the doorjamb and grinned himself. "Kim's a little pissed, but personally, I think she likes it."

"What's not to like?" Mike asked with a dramatic shrug.

"Exactly what I said." Zack stepped back and said, "Come on in, Mad Dog, wanna beer?"

"Oh, yeah, sounds good." Mike stepped into the small living room and saw that a few things had changed since Zack had married Kim Danforth. The walls were still a cool blue, but parts of Zack's past dotted the room now. A pair of fatigues were draped across a chair in the corner and the bookcases were crammed with Zack's collection of military history books. Framed photos of his SEAL team were hung on the walls along with pictures of Zack's and Kim's wedding and their families.

Overall, the place looked a little less rigid than it had before and a little more lived in. Just a few months ago Zack had been assigned to protect Kim Danforth, the snooty fish geek as Zack had called her then. And now, Zack was happily married to the geek—er, Kim.

"So where's the better-lookin' half of your family?" he asked as Zack came into the room, carrying two bottles of beer.

Zack dropped onto one of the blue-and-white-checked sofas and propped his bare feet up on the coffee table. His jeans were threadbare and his Go Navy T-shirt was frayed at the collar. The boss looked comfortable and happier than Mike had ever seen him. Smiling, Zack said, "Kim's off teaching dolphins to ride bikes or some damn thing."

"If anyone can do it, she can," Mike said, lifting his beer in silent salute.

"Damn straight." Zack smiled to himself, and Mike wondered if he looked as sappy as the boss did now when he thought of Kelly.

"So what've you guys been doing?" Zack asked, dragging Mike's thoughts back to the here and now. "Haven't seen one of you this leave."

Mike shrugged and took a sip of his beer. "We just figured you and Kim'd like some time alone."

"And I thank you," his friend and superior officer said with a mocking incline of his head. "But now that you're here, catch me up. Everybody ready to go back to work?''

"I don't know." Mike stood up suddenly and stalked over to the brick fireplace on the far wall. Leaning one hand on the hand-carved mantel, he stared down into the cold hearth as if looking for answers to the questions stumbling through his brain. "Haven't seen the guys myself this trip. Well, except for Hula, the first night in."

"Yeah?"

Mike shifted a look at Zack, wondering how he could ask what he wanted to ask without sounding like an idiot. Hell. Guys just didn't talk about stuff like this. But, after studying the other man for a long minute, he asked, "How's Kim handling being married to a SEAL?"

Zack's dark brown eyebrows lifted. "She's good. Says that if anyone should marry a SEAL, it should be a marine biologist."

"I'm not kidding around."

"Yeah, I see that." Zack balanced his beer bottle on his flat stomach and looked at his friend. "So what's going on?"

He wasn't really sure why he'd come to see the boss—except for the fact that talking to him had always helped Mike straighten out his own mind. And, hell, maybe it was just as simple as knowing he needed a friend. Whatever the reason, Mike started talking, and when he was finished, he scraped one hand across his face as Zack said, "So basically, you want to marry her."

Mike blew out a breath. There it was. Out in the open. And damn it, it sounded good. Right. This is what he'd been aiming for since that first night when she'd dumped a tray of drinks in his lap. This is what he needed. Even as a confused kid, he'd known in his heart that Kelly was the one for him—even if he hadn't been able to claim her then. Now he knew what he wanted. He just didn't know how he was going to be able to convince Kelly.

"Yeah," he said. "Guess I do."

"Before we ship out?"

"Oh, yeah." Mike couldn't imagine leaving her again, for months maybe, without having their relationship sealed and locked down. He wanted to go off knowing she'd be there when he got back. He wanted to make sure that this time she knew he'd *be* back.

"Then, my friend," Zack said as the front door opened and his wife walked in, "you'd better get busy. You're running out of time."

"Who's out of time?" Kim asked, dropping her backpack by the door and walking into the room. Her waist-length, midnight-black hair swung in a ponytail as she walked, and her green eyes sparkled. "Mike! What a great surprise! You staying for dinner?" she asked, crossing to give him a kiss on the cheek before going back to drop onto her husband's lap.

"Can't tonight, Kim, thanks," Mike said.

"You kiss him first?" Zack asked, pretending to be insulted.

"Yeah, but I kiss you *last*," Kim teased. "So, somebody want to tell me what's going on?"

Zack shot a look at his friend. "Mad Dog's getting married."

Kim shouted, jumped off Zack's lap and ran to Mike, giving him a huge hug of congratulations. And Mike could only hope that getting married would be as easy as Zack made it sound—but knowing Kelly, he highly doubted it.

The next day Kelly was dressed and ready to walk out the door to work when Mike arrived unexpectedly. Usually, he simply showed up at the club and stayed until her shift was over. She watched him climb out of the too-small car and unfold his long legs, and her heart fluttered a little just at the sight of him.

"What are you doing here?" She held the front door open.

"I have to talk to you," he said, catching her before she could step out onto the porch.

She laughed but shook her head. "I can't wait, I'm already running a little late and—"

But Mike was a man on a mission. After talking to Zack the day before, he'd been shopping. He had a plan, he had a ring—now all he needed was his woman. He grabbed her upper arms, set her back from the door, then stepped farther inside himself and closed the door behind him.

"What's going on?" she asked, staring up at him. Her grass-green eyes caught him and held him and he knew he wanted to be looking into those same eyes for the rest of his life.

He only hoped she'd be willing to take another chance on him.

"My leave's up in a few days," he said, and watched as the light drained out of her eyes. Good sign? Or bad? Hell, he wished he knew. Wished he could tell what she was thinking. Feeling.

"When?"

"Sunday."

She inhaled sharply and blew the air out of her lungs as she nodded. "Fine. Thanks for the warning."

He frowned, confused. "That's not why I'm telling you."

She pulled free and took a step back from him, as if already keeping a distance between them. To protect herself? To lock him out? Who the hell knew?

"Then why?" she asked.

"Because I don't want to leave with things…unsettled between us."

One finely arched red eyebrow lifted. "Times have changed, then."

"Yes. And so've I."

"Me, too," she said and her features stiffened along with her spine. "And I'm not going to do this with you again, so I'm just going to go to work now. If you still want to come by tonight—"

"Of course I'll be here tonight," he said, grabbing her upper arms and holding her so she couldn't bolt before he'd had a chance to say what he had to say. "That's my whole point. I want to be here with you every night. Every night I can be, I want to be with you."

"You have been," she said, and her voice sounded small, anxious. "Let's just leave it there, okay?"

He held her tighter, as if fighting for her already. "Damn it, Kelly, no. I don't want to 'leave it there.' I want more."

She pulled away from him again and swiped one

hand across her face but not before he saw a single tear escape the corner of her eye. "I wanted more six years ago, Mike. I thought you did, too."

He sighed heavily and pushed both hands along the sides of his head as if trying to hold his skull together despite the pounding going on in his brain at the moment. "We've been over this. I thought we settled it."

"We have," she said, steadying herself with an effort he could see. "This isn't about the past anymore. Honestly, Mike. This is about me."

"What do you mean?"

She hitched her black purse strap higher on her shoulder and clutched it tightly in one fist. "This last week, our time together, was about me getting over you, Mike. That's all. I needed closure. So I could move on with my life. Find someone who loves me enough to marry me."

"Closure?" He shook his head as if he hadn't heard her right. "What the hell do you need closure for? *I* want to marry you."

"No, you don't." The words were squeezed out of a tight throat as she lifted her chin into that defiant tilt he knew so well.

"Now you know me better than I do?"

"Doesn't matter," she said softly. "What does matter is that the last couple of weeks have given me time to come to grips with what I feel for you, Mike.''

Man, this was *not* going as he'd planned. In his little scenario, Kelly said yes, told him she loved him, then called in sick to work so the two of them could spend the night setting a lovemaking record for how many times in one night.

What the hell had happened?

''I needed to get you out of my heart,'' she was saying, and each word stabbed at him like the tip of a bayonet. ''So that I could *finally* move on and love someone else.''

''Kelly, damn it—'' He reached for her again, but she held up both hands, warding him off. He let his hands drop to his sides, but still he tried to reach her with the words that had been in his heart for years. ''I love you.''

She flinched, as if the words had actually *hurt* her. Then she looked up at him and said, ''You told me that six years ago, too. It didn't stop you from walking out.''

His back teeth ground together, and his heart felt as if it were being squeezed in a cold, tight fist. ''This is different.''

''Yeah,'' she agreed sadly, stepping past him to open the door. ''It is. This time *I'm* the one walking out.''

And in a heartbeat—an eternity—she was gone.

Chapter 10

He loved her.

Kelly groaned tightly and threw the car into Park. Shutting off the engine, she sat in Steam's parking lot and stared out at the trees just beyond the windshield. A hot wind was blowing, and the line of trees surrounding the lot dipped and swayed as if dancing.

And watching the leaves twist and turn in the breeze wasn't doing a damn thing to take her mind off Mike.

She slapped her hands to her face and groaned again. He loved her. He'd proposed. He'd offered her everything she'd wanted for six years, and she'd left him standing in her living room.

"What is wrong with me?" she muttered, and thanked heaven no one was there to answer. She was fairly certain she wouldn't like what they had to say.

She'd told Mike this wasn't about the past—but was that the truth? Wasn't there still a part of her that wanted to make him pay for hurting her so desperately? Even though her rational mind had accepted the fact that just maybe he'd been right when he said they'd been too young? Wasn't there still a small, wounded part of her still looking for payback?

Hadn't that been what the plan was all about?

"Oh, God, the *plan*." Her hands dropped to the steering wheel and squeezed it tightly. "Yeah, that worked out really well. Closure. God, what an idiot." Shaking her head, she stared blindly at the trees again and realized what she should have known all along. There was *no* getting Mike Connelly out of her heart. He was there to stay, having carved out his place in her soul so many years ago.

No wonder she hadn't been able to move on.

It wasn't a lack of closure, it was the simple fact that she'd never stopped loving him.

And now it was all over. In her own panic and

fear, she'd turned him down as he had her so long ago, and they'd finally come full circle.

Was it all about pain, then? she wondered as a knife blade of agony pierced her heart and left her gasping. Were she and Mike destined to be two ships crashing in the night? Had she really turned away from another chance at love just to prove a point? She wasn't that stupid, was she? No, she wasn't. Couldn't be. But how could she be sure that Mike meant his proposal now when he hadn't then? And why didn't she have any darn answers?

A knock on her car window startled her, and Kelly turned to look into Sophia's concerned gaze. Automatically she rolled the window down and let in a blast of hot air that slapped at her.

"You okay?" her friend asked.

"No," Kelly admitted, feeling the sting of tears prickle at the backs of her eyes. Oh, great. Just what she needed. To start her shift with tears streaming down her face. Lots of pity tips tonight.

"Want to talk about it?" Sophia's features softened in sympathy.

"Not really." She so didn't want to have to explain to her friend just how big an idiot she was. Kelly opened the car door, rolled up her window, then climbed out and locked up the car. Swinging her purse onto her shoulder, she took a deep breath of the damp air and blew it out again. She felt...*empty*. And, oh, God, she wondered if she'd *always* feel that way. "Maybe later, okay?"

"Sure," Sophia said and wrapped an arm around Kelly's waist as they headed for the back door of Steam.

It was good to have friends, Kelly thought. Because now that she'd chased Mike off, she was going to be exploring whole new levels of loneliness.

The club was crowded, as it was every night. In Savannah, it seemed, people didn't wait for the weekend to have a good time. Even on a Wednesday night, there was a long wait for dinner, and the bar was practically standing room only.

Mike eased into the lounge and let his gaze scan the mob of people, searching for one face in particular and coming up empty. His regular table was taken, so he pushed through to the end of the bar and leaned his forearms on the glossy wood finish.

The bartender, recognizing him, sent him a smile and a nod and automatically filled a tall crystal glass from the tap. Delivering Mike's drink, the man went back to work, and Mike concentrated on the task at hand. How to get through Kelly

O'Shea's hard head to make her understand they belonged together.

He'd been so stunned at Kelly's reaction to his proposal it had taken him a while to realize that she'd actually said no. But there was just no way Mike Connelly was going to take that no for an answer. Not now. Not after finding her again.

He already knew what life without Kelly was like—and it wasn't acceptable.

Not anymore.

"Closure," he muttered darkly, his eyes narrowing on the crowd. He noticed Donna, one of the cocktail waitresses, laughing with a customer, and his scowl deepened. Kelly wanted to put him behind her so she could move on? To some other guy?

"Oh, I don't think so." Just imagining Kelly with some other man made his blood boil and the top of his head threaten to blow off. He'd never let another guy have a shot at her. Not when he loved her so much his chest hurt with it. Kelly was his, damn it. His heart. His soul. The very best part of him—and he wouldn't lose her.

Not now.

Not ever.

"You say something?" the woman on the stool next to him asked.

''Nope,'' he said, and moved farther down the bar, ignoring the sparkle of interest in the woman's blue eyes.

There was only one woman he wanted smiling at him. And, by God, he wasn't going to settle for less.

At the other end of the bar, the swinging door from the kitchen opened and Kelly swept through, carrying a tray of appetizers. Mike's heart galloped in his chest as he forgot about his beer and moved away from the bar.

Stepping into the middle of the room, he watched her work the crowd. She delivered her order and smiled as though she didn't have a care in the world. Unless you were looking at her eyes. And there, Mike saw everything he needed to see. Misery.

Good, he thought, hope leaping into his chest and digging into his heart. If she was miserable, maybe she'd listen.

She spotted him, and her face froze over. A shutter dropped over her expressive eyes, locking him out. But it was too late. He knew she loved him, damn it, and he wasn't leaving this place until *she* knew it, too.

He took a step toward her, but she shook her head and held up her now-empty tray in front of her like a warrior's shield. "Go away," she said evenly.

"Not a chance." He didn't bother to keep his voice down. Hell, if he had to, if it was what she needed, he'd go up onto the roof and shout his love for her.

A couple of people turned to watch, caught by the tension humming between them. Mike didn't care who watched. His gaze was fixed on Kelly. His muscles bunched, preparing to run after her if she made a dash for it.

But she stood stock-still, as if rooted to the spot. Around them, conversations slowly dwindled to a studied hush as more and more of the crowd became aware of the drama playing out in their midst.

The music played on though, a soft, sweeping saxophone that rose and fell as if the room was breathing.

"You walked out." He braced his feet wide apart and folded his arms across his chest.

"You noticed."

She was trying for glib, but Mike heard the pain in her voice.

"Why?" he demanded.

"Don't do this, Mike."

"Oh, yeah, we're doing this."

"Not here."

"*Right* here, babe." He wasn't moving. Not an inch. Not until they had this settled, and Kelly admitted she belonged with him.

She blew out a frustrated breath that ruffled the dark red curls that had fallen across her forehead. "You are unbelievable."

"Thanks."

"Wasn't a compliment."

"Depends on your point of view."

"Mike—"

Several people had now twisted around in their chairs, watching avidly, not even bothering to pretend otherwise. Candlelight flickered on the table-tops, and the music shifted to something a little jazzier.

"I asked you to marry me."

A woman sitting close by gasped and clutched both hands to her chest, giving him a warm smile. A better response than he'd gotten from the woman he loved, Mike thought, grimly focusing again on Kelly.

"And I gave you your answer," Kelly said quietly, pushing the words through gritted teeth.

"Not the right one."

"It's the right one for me."

"Liar."

Her head snapped back, her mouth dropped open

and her eyes narrowed. She glanced around at the people staring at her, awaiting her response, then turned to Mike again. She looked as if she wanted to throw something. Or scream. He didn't give her a chance to do either.

"You *love* me, O'Shea."

Kelly looked wildly around the room again, as if searching for help from the interested crowd. None was offered. Instead, the place went even quieter, except for the jazz combo playing through the stereo system.

Seconds ticked past and Mike waited. He'd learned patience over the years. In the military, you learned that impatience could get you shot—and military tactics were good practice for his and Kelly's fights. So, if he had to, he could wait all night.

Kelly didn't force him to.

She threw her empty tray to the floor, made a sharp about-face turn and stomped toward the kitchen—and escape. Mike didn't let her get two steps. He caught her up and pulled her close, wrapping his arms around her tightly.

"Not a chance, babe," he said, his voice low enough that only she could hear him over the music still soaring through the room. "Neither one of us leaves until this is settled."

"Damn it, Mike, you don't want to marry me. You want to make up for last time."

Her green eyes swam with tears she refused to let fall, and his heart twisted painfully in his chest. So many years gone, he thought wildly. So much time lost. No more. Not one more second.

"Are you *nuts?*" he demanded, his voice louder now, stunned that she would think he'd offer her a pity proposal.

"Apparently," she ground out. "Since I'm still hanging around with *you.*"

"O'Shea, you're killin' me." He shook his head and smiled. Life with Kelly would never be dull, he thought. And he couldn't wait to get started on it. His voice loud enough to carry and soft enough to be the caress he couldn't afford to risk, because he was still too worried about letting her go, he said, "I *love* you. Loved you then. Love you now."

"Oh…" A soft sigh came from the woman still clutching her hands to her chest.

"But—" Kelly started.

"No 'buts,' Kel," he said and felt her relax a little, the starch going out of her spine even as the first tear slid from the corner of her eye. "Six years ago, we weren't ready. Either of us."

"Maybe," she allowed, leaning into him a little more.

"Now we are."

Her mouth twitched, and Mike felt the sweet rush of relief.

"Maybe," she said.

"And," he continued, pressing his luck, now that he'd found the chink in her defenses, "if we hurry the hell up, we could get married before I ship out."

"Before?" she asked, lifting her gaze to his, watching him with wonder shining in those incredible green eyes. "You don't want to wait until you get back?"

"Are you kidding? No way," he said tightly. "I want my ring on your finger. I want yours on mine. I want us signed, sealed and delivered. As fast as we can manage it."

"Really?" She smiled up at him and her eyes shone with the promise of forever.

"Oh, yeah," he said, sparing one hand now to cup her cheek and wipe away a stray tear. "Marry me, Kelly. Give me someone to come home to. Be my wife. Have my babies."

Someone in their audience clapped and was suddenly hushed by someone else, waiting for the conclusion.

Kelly dipped her head and said a silent prayer of thanks. She'd found the love of her life. Not once, but twice. And this time he'd fought for her. He'd come back and made her hear him. This time it would work. This time it was *right*.

When she looked up at him again, she saw everything she'd ever wanted in his steady gaze. And she knew that "the plan" had been destined to fail. He'd been in her heart since the first time she'd seen him. And now she couldn't imagine life without him.

Lifting both arms to encircle his neck, she said loudly, for the benefit of not only Mike but their audience, "I'll marry you, Connelly. I'll have *our* babies. And I swear, I'll love you forever."

The applause thundered around them, but neither of them heard. For them there were only the two of them in the world and that was just as it should be.

* * * * *

Be sure to watch for
AND THEN CAME YOU
by Maureen Child,
coming July 2004
from St. Martin's Press.

THE DARE AFFAIR

Sheri WhiteFeather

To MJ,
my amazing editor, for bringing Barbara, Maureen and me
together on this project. And to Richard Cerqueira,
my favorite cover model, whose stunning good looks,
charming personality and Portuguese heritage
inspired the hero in the story.

Chapter 1

Katrina Beaumont hadn't come to Steam to see Clayton Crawford, the owner of the posh restaurant and trendy blues club. She'd agreed to allow her girlfriends to treat her to a night on the town so she could shed the humiliation of being jilted.

She glanced in Clay's direction. He stood near the stage, with his back turned. She hadn't seen him in years, but she recognized him instantly. She could sense his presence, even from across the room.

Katrina reached for her wine, then shifted her gaze, staring at the cocktail napkin in front of her.

Clay wasn't her ex-fiancé; he wasn't the man
who'd tromped on her heart. Clay was part of her
past, and memories of their youth flickered like a
long-lost movie.

"Your mind is drifting again." Jenny Kincaid,
a brown-eyed brunette, tilted her head. Her neatly
bobbed hair hugged her chin, swaying lightly to
one side.

"We're worried about you." This from Anna-
Mae Delcott, her other concerned friend, the blond
bob.

Over a decade ago, the trio had been introduced
into society at the same cotillion. They'd even attended the same private high school and dallied at
the same college, furthering their education, in
spite of their trust funds.

Katrina sighed. She and her girlfriends occupied
a gray marble table that faced the dance floor. Couples swayed, rocking to the beat. The music coming from the band was slow and soulful, filling the
club with jailhouse tunes, songs that imprisoned the
soul. "I'm trying to enjoy myself."

"By dwelling on Andrew?" Jenny dipped a cat-
fish nugget into a bowl of Cajun tartar sauce. The
restaurant was on the second floor, but the club
served a variety of appetizers.

"I wasn't thinking about Andrew." Katrina

sipped her wine. Andrew's name left a gaping hole in her chest, the pain of being a poor-little-rich-girl, a has-been debutante, a discarded lover. "I was thinking about Clay."

Anna-Mae leaned forward. "The owner of this decadent establishment?"

"Yes." The wine slid down her throat, burning her stomach, warming it. Steam was as dark and rich as the man who owned it. Thick velvet drapes, mahogany woods, a single blood-red rose on each table. Was she the only woman aching? The only tortured heiress taking refuge in a blues club? "I haven't seen him since we were teenagers. His mother used to be my seamstress."

"Where is he?" Jenny jumped back into the conversation, fanning her mouth, waving away the spicy aftertaste of the appetizer.

"There. Near the stage." Katrina motioned. His back was still turned. "He's talking to a cocktail waitress."

Both bobbed heads strained to get a better look. And then Clay flashed his profile, moving closer to the waitress, an intimate motion that sent Katrina's pulse into a rickety shuffle.

"Swarthy," Jenny said.

"Wrong side of the tracks," Anna-Mae added.

"Or that's what I've heard. Why didn't you ever mention him before?"

Katrina faked an unaffected shrug. Clay had been her secret; the boy who used to watch her through dark, dangerous eyes. But boys like Clayton Crawford were off-limits, and delicately bred girls like Katrina knew better.

"I wonder how he afforded to build this place." Jenny's voice slipped into its gossip mode. "Do you think he's connected?"

Katrina dared another glance at him. He was no longer a boy. His features had aged, hardened into sharp angles and shadowed hues. "Connected to what?"

"Criminals."

Before Katrina could respond, Clay caught sight of her. Trapped in a timeless moment, she fought the air in her lungs, hoping she wasn't wearing her emotions on her sleeve.

"His ears must be burning."

"What?" A little dizzy, she gulped the chardonnay, unsure of who'd spoken. All she could see was Clay coming her way. Would he know that she'd been jilted? Would he sense her discomfort?

He reached their table, and she looked up at him. He wore a black suit with a narrow tie. His dark brown hair was combed away from his face. She'd always been fascinated by his eclectic ancestry, the Portuguese, Scottish and Choctaw roots that claimed him.

"Katrina."

He said her name in a voice that sizzled with summer nights, with the light rain misting the windows. She could almost feel the heat, the mugginess dampening her skin.

"Clay." She introduced him to her friends, and he offered a proprietor's smile.

"Ladies. I trust you're enjoying your evening."

Anna-Mae nodded, but Jenny studied him with a critical eye. Still wondering, it seemed, if he were a shady businessman. "This is quite a place you have," she said.

"I like it." He raised his brows at her, almost as if he'd read her mind. Then he turned to Katrina. "Where's your beau tonight?"

She took a nervous breath. He must have read about her engagement in the society column. Andrew Winston's family hailed from old money, from the kind of prestige that made the papers. Katrina's family, of course, was cut from the same gilded cloth. Clay knew that better than anyone. "He...we—"

"She's mourning him," Anna-Mae said.

Clay's brows lifted again.

"He didn't die," Anna-Mae explained. "He called off the wedding."

"I knew what you meant." The man from Katrina's past didn't offer an apology. He merely gazed into her eyes and made her knees weak.

She smoothed her French-braided hair, hoping she appeared calmer than she felt, struggling to maintain the ladylike decorum her mother had instilled in her. "It's only been a few days."

"A fresh wound," Clay noted.

"Andrew will come around," Jenny interjected. "Sometimes men just get cold feet." She sat ramrod straight, looking a bit too snooty for her own good.

Katrina supposed she looked that way, too. She wondered if Clay cared or if he took women like her, Jenny and Anna-Mae in stride. Steam was the hottest spot in Savannah. He walked on the cutting edge of society, in a world that made their privileged lives seem dull. Clay's reputation was glamorously forbidden, simply because he'd been poor. The boy from the wrong side of the tracks had come a long way.

"I'll send over a bottle of wine," he said. "On the house. For your mourning," he added with a slight tilt to his lips, a smile that seemed to mock the past.

"Thank you, but that isn't necessary," Katrina said, lacking a clever response.

"I insist." He gave her a polished nod, bade her friends goodbye and walked away, leaving her lonelier than she'd been before.

Hours later Clay stood at the bar, nursing a soda water, keeping an eye on his club. He'd built Steam on blood, sweat and determination. He'd worked hard to improve his family's station in life, busting his butt for the scholarships that had granted him a higher education. And he'd worked even harder to convince investors to trust him, to prove that he could make Steam a success.

And now?

Now he was a thirty-year-old entrepreneur, still trying to shake Katrina Beaumont from his blood. When they were teenagers, he'd wanted nothing more than to be her equal, to be good enough to date her. But Clay's wrong-side-of-the-tracks roots and minority-mixed heritage hadn't meshed with high-society women. Of course, these days, ladies like Katrina flocked to Steam, intent on being part of the flame-licking, blues-palpitating world he'd created.

As music vibrated the walls and bodies made erotic contact on the dance floor, Clay refused to suffer the way he'd done when he was a boy. He wasn't a kid anymore, and Katrina was smarting over another man.

So who the hell cared?

By the time the headlining act took the stage, Joe Morton approached Clay. The bouncer, competent as he was, looked like a no-necked jock in a dark suit, with short blond hair and a serious nature.

Joe jerked his head. "There's a little trouble at your lady friend's table. Do you want me to handle it? Or would you prefer to deal with this yourself?"

Trouble? He shifted his gaze and caught the disagreement going on. Katrina and her companions appeared to be arguing. He stalled, squinted at Joe, struggled with a decision.

"I'll take care of it," he finally said.

"That's what I figured."

Clay didn't respond. It hadn't taken Joe long to notice his attraction to Andrew Winston's former fiancé, to zero in on his frustration.

The bouncer squared his shoulders. "She's all yours."

Right. As soon as Clay took a closer look, he realized she was drunk. She'd abused the wine he'd sent to her table.

Great, he thought. Just what he needed, another

complication. He strode across the club and placed his hands on the back of her chair, snaring her attention. "What's going on?" he asked, interrupting the feminine squabble.

"They want to leave." She swayed a little, moaning to the soulful song. "But I want to stay."

"She never does this," the blonde who'd been introduced as Anna-Mae said.

"This is definitely a first," Jenny, the brunette added.

Clay wasn't surprised. Katrina Beaumont, with her properly styled auburn hair and elegant clothes, wasn't the sort of woman to lose control, to misbehave in public. But there she sat in a classy black dress and jeweled choker, three sheets to the wind.

"Short of dragging her out of here and pouring her into my car, we have no idea what to do." Jenny glanced at her glassy-eyed friend. "Katrina will be mortified later if we cause a scene. But I'm afraid there's no way to make a discreet exit."

He maintained his composure, even though he wanted to curse a blue streak. Drunken patrons were his responsibility, especially this one. "I'll take care of her."

Jenny gave him an exasperated sigh. "How?"

"I'll escort her upstairs and give her some time to pull herself together. Then I'll take her home."

Katrina's companions exchanged a concerned look. But even so, it didn't take them long to accept his offer. Apparently they trusted him enough not to cause a ruckus in his own club. And they probably didn't realize that upstairs meant Clay's fourth-floor apartment.

Katrina made a face. "You're all talking about me as if I wasn't even here."

"We know you're here." He leaned into her. Her lashes fluttered like hummingbird wings, shadowing her cheeks. "Your friends are going to let you stay. But you'll have to hang out with me for a while."

She almost smiled at him. "Jenny thinks you're a criminal."

"I do not." The brunette made an indignant sound. "I can see that Clay is an upstanding citizen."

Yeah, right, he thought. As this point, all she saw was the man who was going to take an intoxicated friend off her hands.

"Where are we going?" Katrina asked, as Clay escorted her down a private hallway.

"To my place." He knew that nothing but time would make her sober, but he intended to give

her a cup of coffee, anyway—something to keep
her busy.

"It's so secluded."

He glanced up at the security cameras that provided surveillance for his front door. Inside his
home, a sophisticated alarm system offered high-
tech protection.

"Is this it?" Katrina asked upon entrance.

"Yes." He turned off the alarm. "This is where
I live."

She gave him a fluttery smile. "It's sexy."

He glanced around his loft-style apartment. The
furniture was modern, with angular tables and can-
vas prints by his favorite artist—a Peruvian painter
who used brilliant colors and sparks of sensuality.
The glass lamps were the same style the decorator
had used in Steam, and the floors were covered in
black-and-white linoleum.

"You're sexy, too," she said.

Clay merely looked at her. "That's the wine
talking."

"I always thought you were hot. A hot-ee." She
cranked up the last syllable, putting more emphasis
on it. "Even when we were young." She slid onto
his sofa and cuddled into the cushion. "Do you
know what he insinuated to me?"

Uh-oh. Confession time. Clay sat on the edge of

the coffee table. He could see a shadowy outline
of the verandah through the partially open sheers,
and the rainy image made him lonely. "You don't
have to tell me this, Katrina."

"Kat. You can call me Kat. No one does, but
you can." One of her shoes, a ladylike pump, dan-
gled precariously from her foot. "Andrew wasn't
satisfied with our relationship. He admires my social graces, but—" the dangling shoe dropped to
the floor "—I'm just not exciting enough for him.
In bed," she added in a mock whisper, her eyes
going gullibly wide.

Clay couldn't help but smile. "Maybe he should
have gotten you drunk."

She laughed at that. "Maybe. Am I drunk, Clayton?"

"Yes, ma'am, I'm afraid you are."

"Hmm." She pondered her state of inebriation
for a moment. "I'm not sure I like it. I feel sort of
sad and happy all at once."

"I'll get you some coffee." He headed to the
kitchen, unsure of what else to do. He couldn't
imagine Katrina being staid in bed. He'd always
imagined her a little naughty, a prim-and-proper
heiress who let her guard down at night, who whispered fantasies in her lover's ear.

He turned on the faucet and wondered if she and

Andrew would reconcile, the way Jenny had indicated.

A few minutes later Clay removed his jacket and loosened his tie. Then he stared at the coffeepot. The liquid dripped like tonight's rain, painstakingly slow.

Finally he returned to Katrina with a cup of the hot brew, doctored with milk and sugar. She seemed like the milk and sugar type. Sweet, he thought. Creamy.

"Thank you." She took a sip, leaving a lipstick mark on the rim of the cup. "I can see your bed."

He squinted. "So?"

"So you don't have any walls in this place. I can see where you sleep. I can be a voyeur."

Clay thrust a hand through his hair. The wrought-iron frame was a piece that he'd ordered from an Italian designer. Strangely ornate, it fit his emotions, the entanglement of his life.

"Sexy man. Sexy bed."

He frowned at her. "Stop saying that."

"But it's true." She discovered a set of glass coasters on his end table and made use of one, placing her cup on it. Even drunk, she adhered to her Beaumont breeding.

More or less, he thought. The wine was making

her uncharacteristically chatty, even if she wasn't slurring her words.

"Can I sleep in your bed? I want to snuggle up with your blanket."

The air in his lungs whooshed out. "I'm supposed to sober you up and take you home."

"But it's lonely at my house."

He glanced at the verandah, then shifted his gaze, studying her lost expression. He had the notion to run his thumb across her cheek, to feel the softness of her skin.

She sighed. "Can I stay here, Clayton? I'm over twenty-one."

"I know how old you are."

"Twenty-nine," she said for effect. "An old maid."

Why did she have to make him smile? Why did he have to like her so damn much? "What are you going to sleep in, Katrina?"

"Kat. You can loan me something. Either that or I can climb into that big old bed of yours naked."

"What?" His heartbeat blasted his chest.

She tossed him a sly grin. "I was just kidding."

Easy for her to say. Now he was fighting an arousal, an instant hardness that made him want her the way he'd wanted her when they were young, when he couldn't control his hormones, when he used to lie awake at night and—

"So, can I?" she asked.

His mouth went dry.

She gave him a pleading look. "Please."

Well, hell, he thought. He didn't have the heart to send her home, to drop her off at her family's estate like a drunk and disorderly orphan. He knew the Beaumonts had never seen their daughter in this condition. "Maybe I should call your parents. Let them know you're all right."

She waved her hand, dismissing his suggestion. "They'll think I'm with Andrew. They'll think we got back together." She rose, teetering on one high heel. "I'll change in the bathroom. It has walls, doesn't it?"

"And a door with a lock, too. But let me give you something to wear first." He moved across the massive apartment to an antique armoire and pulled out an old button-down shirt. She followed him, losing her shoe along the way. "Here." He handed her the garment and pointed her in the direction of the bathroom.

She emerged a few minutes later, wearing his shirt and a pair of thigh-high hose that stayed up all on their own.

Damn, he thought. *Damn.*

"I couldn't get this off." She tugged at the delicate choker around her neck.

"So I see." She hadn't buttoned the shirt properly, either. It gapped in spots and the tails were uneven. "Turn around. I'll take off your necklace."

When she presented him with her back, he leaned in to inhale her perfume. She smelled exotic, like orchids blooming at dawn. There was no way sex with her could be boring. He moved her braid out of the way, wishing he could nuzzle her neck, seduce her into a slow, seductive kiss.

The clasp on the choker seemed too small for his fingers. He fumbled with it, holding his breath, curbing his urges. "Got it." The chain fell into his hand, the shimmering stones pressing his skin.

"Thank you." She spun around. Her bright blue eyes were cloudy and her lipstick was gone. But she was still pretty, her features refined.

He placed her necklace on his dresser. "Let me fix your shirt."

"It's your shirt," she reminded him.

"Then let me fix my shirt." He knew he shouldn't be doing this, but he didn't give a damn. He was using any excuse to touch to her, to make the moment more intimate.

"I'm sleepy," she said.

He undid the first three buttons. "I'll put you to bed. But not this second, first I need to…" His words drifted. He could see her bra, the small swell of cleavage. He kept going, releasing all the buttons. Her panties were black lace, just like the top of her hose.

"Can I go to bed now?"

"What? No." He snapped out of his trance and rushed to cover her, nearly missing the buttonholes the way she'd done. "Now you can. Come on." He led her to the wrought-iron bed and turned down the heavy maroon quilt.

She sank onto his pillow. "Are we still friends?"

"We were never friends."

"Yes, we were. We had a crush on each other."

"For all the good it did." Suddenly the past slammed straight into his gut, punching him like a set of brass knuckles, making him feel young and poor again. "You never went slumming. You weren't the type."

She blinked at him, confused, light-headed, mourning her ex-fiancé, the guy who'd jilted her. "That's not what I meant."

"Then prove it." Hurt, frustrated, he leaned over her. "Prove what you meant."

For a moment she didn't move. She just looked

up at him. Then she reached out to touch him, to skim her hand along his jaw, to make him more aroused. Warmth flowed through his veins, settling beneath his fly.

Cupping her face, he kissed her.

She closed her eyes, and he tasted the wine she'd drunk, the coffee she'd barely consumed, the sweet, lazy intoxication. Milk and sugar.

He deepened the kiss, taking more, sipping her flavor, filling his senses. Her lips were soft against his.

Too soft, he thought, as she pressed closer. Too vulnerable.

He pulled back, let a shiver roll down his spine. He couldn't do this. Not here. Not like this.

"Go to sleep, Kat."

Her hand fell, the hand that had been caressing his face, delving into his hair. "Don't you like me?"

Was she wounded by his rejection? Too drunk to know that he was trying to respect her? "Of course I like you." He settled onto the bed and offered her his arms, giving her a safe place to cuddle.

With a sigh, she accepted the invitation, and he sensed how much she needed a friend, someone she could trust.

The boy from the wrong side of the tracks, he thought. Picking up the pieces, protecting the broken chips of her heart. It made him hate Andrew Winston. But it made him envy the other man, too.

She shifted against him, and when she drifted into a soundless slumber, he brushed his lips across her forehead and listened to the intermittent rhythm of the rain, wondering what tomorrow would bring.

Chapter 2

Katrina squinted at the light filtering through a nearby window. She rubbed her eyes and winced. She'd never had a migraine, not like this.

She sat up and looked around, then realized where she was and why her head hurt.

She wanted to crawl under a floorboard, die a thousand deaths. She'd gotten drunk last night. And she'd slept in Clay's bed.

She fingered her shirt—Clay's shirt—vaguely recalling him buttoning her into it. Or had he been unbuttoning it? She moved her legs and wondered why they felt so tight, so restricted. Kicking at the covers, she peeked under the blanket and saw that she still wore her hose. She'd slept in a pair of thigh-highs? Like some sort of Victoria's Secret diva?

"What are you looking for?" Clay's voice shot out of nowhere, sending Katrina's heart into a tail-spin.

Mortified, she dropped the covers, wondering how he'd sneaked up on her. Then again, who could hear footsteps above the noise in her head?

He gave her serious study, and she wished she could remember exactly what had happened. Had she made love with Clay last night? Naked with nothing but her hose? Had he redressed her in her underwear? Buttoned her into his shirt afterward and tucked her into bed?

No, she thought. No way. Her memories weren't *that* jumbled. Sex wasn't something she could forget, not with a man like Clayton Crawford.

He moved closer to the bed, and she squinted at him. He looked much too refreshed, his hair damp from a recent shower, his jaw cleanly shaven. He wore faded jeans and a simple white T-shirt. Lazy elegance. Masculine beauty. She imagined she looked a fright, with mascara smears raccooning her eyes and a night-tousled French braid. Suddenly she stalled and reached for her hair. It was loose, tangled around her shoulders.

"I undid your braid," he said.

"When?"

"Last night, after you fell asleep, after it stopped raining."

"Why?"

"Because I wanted to touch your hair."

Her skin went warm, much too warm. She didn't need him creating romantic images. "I appreciate your hospitality." She smoothed the hair in question and did her darnedest to sound polite, practical. Unaffected. "But I shouldn't have stayed here."

"You wanted to." He smiled a little. "You wanted to cuddle up with my blanket."

Katrina caught her breath. How was she supposed to respond to that? She couldn't remember half the things she'd said to him last night. "I should get home." She paused, looked around for a clock. "What time is it?"

He glanced at his watch. "Eleven forty-five."

Almost noon? She tried to get out of bed, then reached for the headboard to brace the dizziness. His bed was a work of iron-forged art, scrolled and twisted into a unique design. But at the moment, it wasn't helping her cause. Her hand slipped on one of the scrolls.

"Sit still," he ordered. "I'll get you some breakfast. Something to revive your strength."

Her stomach roiled. "No food."

"Dry toast and a cup of tea." He left the bedroom and headed for the kitchen without waiting for her to reply.

She sat back and cursed herself into oblivion. A second later she cursed the vintner who'd cultivated the wine. Then she decided to curse Clay for sending the bottle to her table, for encouraging her to drown her sorrows.

Clay returned with a wicker tray and placed it in front of her. "Eat, drink and be merry."

Was that his idea of humor? She battled the dryness in her mouth and reached for the tea. She wasn't about to ask him where he'd slept. Not when she had a hazy recollection of dozing off in his arms.

Had they kissed, too? Or was that her imagination? A dream her befuddled mind had conjured?

"How's the tea?"

"Fine." She sipped cautiously. "I told you about Andrew, didn't I?"

"That he was disappointed in your love life?"

Clay sat on the edge of the bed. "Yes, you told me."

"I'm sorry. I shouldn't have put you in that position."

"It's no big deal. You didn't talk about your ex all night."

Her breath rushed out. "I didn't?"

"No." His voice was thick, as slow and Southern as his exaggerated drawl. "You kept telling me how sexy I was. Me, my apartment, my bed."

He was sexy, she thought. But that was beside the point. "I was intoxicated."

"Uh-huh. And now you're indisposed. And wearing my shirt."

She nibbled the toast, taking birdlike bites, trying to ease the burning sensation in her stomach. "I'll have it cleaned and returned to you."

"You can keep it. A memento," he added, "of your first hangover." He leaned forward and drew her attention to the pills he'd left on her tray. "Don't forget to take those."

"Are they for my headache?"

"Yes, ma'am. Kat."

She nearly dropped the medication. "Kat?"

"No one calls you that, but I can." He grinned like a bandit in a bordello. "You gave me permission."

Katrina popped the pills into her mouth, washing them down with mint-spiked tea. Kat was her alter ego, her secret childhood name for herself. She'd chosen it because it sounded casual, fun and airy, much more relaxed than her upbringing had allowed. In her family, appearances were everything. The Beaumonts didn't misbehave; they didn't garner gossip. She'd come from a long line of Savannah royalty. And in spite of her alter ego, Katrina had always been Mommy and Daddy's proper little princess.

She looked up to find Clay watching her. His grin was gone, his eyes dark and indiscernible.

"Where are my clothes?" she asked.

"I hung up your dress." He motioned behind him. "It's in the armoire. Your purse and shoes are there, too."

"Thank you." She wished he hadn't unbraided her hair. The thought of him touching her while she slept made her uncomfortable. "I guess you're an expert at this sort of thing."

"Why? Because I own a club? Or because you think I'm a drinker?"

She didn't know, not really. She wasn't privy to details about his life, not anymore. "Because you offered to take care of me." She paused, sipped the tea. "You don't have a lady friend, do you? Some-one who might misunderstand this situation?"

"If I did, I wouldn't have brought you here." He roamed his gaze over her. "Joe called you my lady friend."

"Joe?"

"A bouncer at the club."

She prayed his staff wouldn't gossip about her, start rumors about her affiliation with their boss. "I wonder what made him say that."

"I think it was the way I'd been looking at you."

The way he was looking at her now, she thought. She wanted to ask him if they'd kissed last night, but she didn't have the nerve. "I'll never do this again."

"Do what?" He raised his brows. "Get drunk? Or end up in my bed?"

Was he teasing her? Trying to embarrass her? Or was sarcasm his defense mechanism? "I already told you that I appreciated your hospitality."

He almost smiled. "Anytime."

Suddenly her limbs went weak, as mushy as oat-meal. Was holding her in his arms part of his hos-pitality? Lulling her to sleep? Touching her hair?

"Cat got your tongue, Kat?" This time he did smile, a flash of teeth against bronzed skin.

Her spine went stiff. "Stop calling me that."

He frowned at her. "You were more fun when you were drunk."

"And you were nicer when we were young."

"I'm still nice." He snared her gaze, pinning her in place. "When I feel like it."

Self-conscious, she chewed the food in her mouth. Finally, she finished the toast and took one last sip of the tea. "I need to get dressed."

He removed the tray. "Be my guest. The bathroom is all yours. Feel free to help yourself to whatever you need."

She climbed out of bed and tried to maintain a semblance of propriety, but it wasn't easy. Not while she was wearing his shirt and the lace-topped thigh-highs.

She opened the armoire and gathered her belongings. Clay's clothes weren't in any particular order, she noticed. And his footwear ranged from boots to loafers to a pair of simple white sneakers.

Katrina took a deep breath and headed for the bathroom. As she walked past Clay, she could feel him watching her, but he used to watch her when they were teenagers. So why would he stop now? Especially after she'd slept in his bed.

Once she was inside the bathroom, she gazed into the mirror and sighed. Her appearance had never looked worse. Making use of Clay's toiletries, she repaired the damage as best she could. Since he didn't have a guest toothbrush available, she made do with his mouthwash and a paper cup from the dispenser above the sink. Finally, she put everything back the way it was and berated herself for feeling intimate about washing her face with his soap and taming her hair with his brush.

Attired in the clothes she'd worn the night before, she emerged, Clay's shirt in hand. He sat on the sofa, waiting for her, it seemed.

She reached into her purse for her cell phone, flipped it open and discovered the battery was dead. "May I use your phone?" she asked. "I'd like to call a cab."

Clay studied her through those dark eyes. "What for? I can drive you home."

"It would be more appropriate for me to take a cab." To keep her family from seeing him, she thought. To keep the night she'd spent with him a secret.

He rose to his full height and came toward her. For a moment she wondered if he was going to touch her, tilt her chin, coax her into a kiss, prove that "appropriate" didn't apply. But he stopped just short of getting too close.

"You should go back to bed when you get home," he said. "Sleep this off."

"I will." She paused, adjusting his shirt over her arm. She still intended to have it laundered for him. "Thank you for your help, Clay."

He nodded and handed her a portable phone. She arranged for a taxi, and when it was time to leave, he escorted her down the elevator and out of the building, where he put her into the cab and turned away without saying goodbye.

Katrina arrived at her parents' island estate, a Greek Revival mansion with stately columns and a wraparound porch. She paused in the main foyer and looked around. She'd always considered the oak staircase the focal point, the heart of this Beaumont-built home. She'd been taught to respect its legacy, and as a child, she'd agreed to live here until she married and had a family of her own.

Fat chance of that, she thought, as she ascended the stairs. She would probably die an old maid.

"Good afternoon, Miss Katrina," a member of the household staff said.

"Good afternoon." She stopped at the top of the hallway and watched the gray-haired woman reorganize a linen closet. "Are my parents in?"

"No, miss. They left some time ago."

Where were they? she wondered as she entered her suite. Had Daddy, a sixth-generation Savannahian, escorted Mother, one of Savannah's most graceful social hostesses, into town? Or had their busy schedules taken them in separate directions?

Katrina sat on her canopied bed and fingered a lace-edged pillow. What would they do if they discovered their properly reared daughter had gotten piss-faced drunk and slept in Clayton Crawford's bed?

The phone on the nightstand rang, and she picked it up, telling herself not to worry. Mother and Daddy wouldn't find out.

"Oh, thank goodness," the familiar voice on the other end of the private line said. "I've been trying to reach you all day."

Katrina adjusted the receiver. "Anna-Mae?"

"Yes, it's me. You're not going to believe what happened. When Jenny learned that you never came home last night, she started calling everyone we know to find out if they'd seen you."

Oh, no, Katrina thought. No.

"Anyway, when Jenny discovered that Clay had an apartment above the club, she put two and two together and—"

"And what?" Her heart dove for her throat. "She told everyone that he seduced me?"

"Not everyone," Anna-Mae drawled. "She didn't tell your parents. They think you were with Andrew, and she didn't dispute their assumption." The line went quiet, then she asked, "Was Clay as wild as he looks?"

"Anna-Mae."

"You can't blame a girl for asking. Jenny doesn't care for him, but I think he's rather delicious."

She clutched the lace-edged pillow to her stomach. "I didn't make love with him."

"Oh." The other woman's voice went flat. "All of our friends think you did."

"I'm going to kill Jenny." It was only a matter of time before her parents found out, she thought. Before they heard the gossip. Mother would probably learn from the Cotillion Club and then she would sit Daddy down and relay the horrifying news.

"Jenny didn't mean to cause a scandal. She was worried about you. I'm sure she'll correct the error once you explain it to her."

Correct the error? How does one correct a scandal? Tawdry little rumors were passed around their social circle like chocolates. "You know darn well that won't work."

"Then you'll just have to roll with the punches.

Besides, if anyone deserves to have an affair, you do.''

But I didn't have an affair, Katrina thought. Her reputation was shot for nothing.

After she ended the call, she changed into a nightgown and climbed into bed, intent on sleeping her troubles away, if only for a few hours.

The phone rang again. She made a face and grabbed the receiver, certain it was her girlfriend again. "Anna-Mae, I'm too tired to—"

"It isn't Anna-Mae."

The male voice shook her to the core. "Andrew?"

"I can't believe you let this happen. Do you realize how this looks? Do you know what people are saying?"

How dare he reprimand her, treat her as if they were still engaged. "You called off the wedding. Remember?"

He made a tight sound, and she pictured him, seated at his grandfather's antique desk, wearing a pale gray suit and tasteful tie, his ash-brown hair carrying subtle highlights from the sun.

"So you're not denying that it's true?" he asked.

In spite of herself, she lied. "No, I'm not denying it. In fact..."

He waited a beat, then took the bait. "In fact what?"

"Clay said I was—" she stalled, searching for a phrase the owner of Steam might use "—the best lay he'd ever had."

Andrew turned quiet, and she could feel the tension building. Were the veins in his neck pulsing? Was he imagining her naked, her body arched in an erotic position, her legs spread across Clay's thighs?

"You were drunk," he said nastily.

"My lover didn't seem to mind." She cuddled against her pillow, feigned a morning-after air. "Now, if you'll excuse me, I'd like to get some rest."

Before he could respond, she hung up, leaving him with nothing but silence. After she unplugged the phone, she walked to the beveled mirror, intent on commending herself. But the exhausted image staring back at her was the same woman Andrew had refused to marry. The same woman who'd disappointed him in bed. Only, now she'd just fed the gossip mill, boasting that she and Clayton Crawford were lovers.

Two days later Clay knocked on Katrina's door. Or at least he assumed it was her door. He'd heard she'd been banished to the Beaumont guest house, a cottage-style dwelling flanked by white trellises, a carpet of grass and a spray of flowers. No, he thought, it wasn't the main house, the high-society mansion; but the charming little bungalow could have been a setting straight out of a Thomas Kinkade original.

Katrina answered the summons, wearing beige slacks and a silk blouse, her hair coiled into a ladylike topknot.

"This is some banishment," he said.

She merely blinked at him, her lashes making a graceful sweep. "Clayton? What are you doing here?"

He pressed a gold chain into her hand. "You left this at my place."

"My necklace." She took the choker. "Your shirt is still at the cleaners."

"I told you I didn't want it back."

"I know, but…" Her voice faded as she glanced at the necklace. "I forgot about this."

"I didn't." He'd been plagued by it for days, debating on how and when to return it. "Aren't you going to invite me in?" He slipped his hands in his pockets, tilted his head, waited.

She stepped away from the door, and he entered the cottage. "Nice digs," he said. Hardwood floors, bright bay windows, carefully selected antiques.

"I wasn't banished."

"Then what's the deal? Why are you living in the guest house?"

"I chose to stay here." She still held the choker, the faceted stones glinting in her hand. "It was my decision."

Because her parents were disappointed in her, he thought. Because she'd created a scandal.

She gestured to a settee, but he shook his head, refusing the seat. He preferred to stand. "The gossip didn't originate from my camp," he said.

"I know. It came from mine. When I didn't return that night, Jenny made a few phone calls and things escalated into what they are now."

"That's not the way I heard it."

Katrina moved to stand beside a glass shelf, where a collection of Fabergé boxes was displayed. Lifting one, she slipped her necklace inside. "What did you hear?"

He couldn't stop the smile that ghosted over his lips. "That you were the best lay I'd ever had."

Her cheeks went pale. "I don't know who started that rumor."

"Don't you?"

"No."

Ignoring her lie, he stepped forward to inspect the jewel boxes. "Andrew called me at the club."

Her voice jumped. "What? Why?"

"To give me a piece of his mind. Your ex claims that I disrespected you. First, by getting you drunk. Second, by seducing you. And third, by rating the kind of lay you were." He glanced over his shoulder, saw her fussing nervously with her impeccably tailored blouse. "Do you think he'll want to duel?" He turned away from the glass shelf, his tone laced with humor. "Isn't that the way gentlemen used to settle a score over a woman? Or were duels reserved for political squabbles?"

"That isn't funny, Clayton."

"Did I say it was?" He met her gaze, masked his smile. "I don't even own a pistol."

Katrina sank onto the settee. The daughter of the manor, hiding in the guest house. "This scandal is getting worse by the minute. What am I going to do?"

What indeed? "Why don't you meet me for dinner tonight at Steam? Around seven." He headed for the door. "We can discuss the details then."

She left her seat. "What details?"

"Have dinner with me and find out," he said, before he opened the door and exited the cottage, leaving her staring after him.

Chapter 3

Katrina entered Steam and took the stairs to the second floor. She was too nervous to embrace the elevator, to stand in a confined space with other people. Being seen in public with Clay would only stir more gossip. Yet here she was, attired in an iridescent cocktail dress, preparing to meet the man of the hour.

Maybe she shouldn't have worn something so noticeable. Maybe she should have tucked herself into a classic summer suit.

She moved closer, wishing Clay hadn't lured her into his trap. But it was too late to turn tail and run. The maître d' had already spotted her.

"Miss Beaumont." He rewarded her with a we-were-expecting-you smile. "This way, please."

He led her to a cozy table in the middle of the room. Wonderful, she thought, as he seated her. She was the star attraction at Steam tonight.

"Mr. Crawford will join you shortly." The maître d' gave her a small, customary bow. "He already chose the wine."

For a moment her expression froze. Then she summoned her wits and managed a proper thank-you, knowing darn well this was Clay's way of embellishing the scandal, of reminding her of how she'd ended up in this predicament.

As if she were likely to forget.

The wine, an all-too-familiar chardonnay, arrived. But it wasn't a waiter who delivered it. It was Clay.

He stood beside the table, tall and dark in a midnight-colored suit, looking as exotic as the atmosphere. A crystal chandelier bathed him in a soft, shimmering glow. His hair was slicked back, exposing the strong-boned angles of his face. A small smile tugged at his lips.

"Kat," he said. "Kitty Kat."

Warmth flooded her stomach.

He leaned forward and kissed her cheek, brushing his mouth against her skin. "You look beautiful," he said.

"I don't know why I'm here."

He sat across from her, an ornately painted lamp burning between them. "You're curious. You want to know what I have up my sleeve." He smiled again. "And you want to make Andrew even more jealous than he already is."

She shook her head. "That isn't true."

He poured the wine. "Isn't it?"

She touched the stem of her glass, but she refused to drink, to sip the poison he'd provided. Somewhere deep down, she wanted to keep punishing Andrew, to prove how strong and independent she was. But she hated to admit that to Clay.

"I took the liberty of ordering our meal ahead of time," he told her. "I hope you don't mind."

"It's your game."

"No, Kat. It's our game. We're in this together."

"In what?" she ventured to ask.

"This affair." He leaned into the table, the light catching his eyes. "We're going to go back to my place after dinner and make love." He sat back, tasted the wine. "On the verandah."

She couldn't find her voice. None of the private schools she'd attended, none of the blue-blooded boys she'd dated, none of the high-society events she been weaned on had prepared her for this moment. "I can't...I just couldn't do something like that," she finally said.

"You're the one who told Andrew what I supposedly said about you. You're the one who claimed to be the best I ever had." He fingered the roses on the table, tracing his hand along the side of the vase. "Don't you think you should live up to your claim? Show me how good you are?"

He was daring her, she thought, seducing her, making her head spin. This went beyond making Andrew jealous, beyond attracting more gossip.

A waiter brought lemon-garnished water to the table, followed by a gourmet meal.

Did she want to show him how good she was?

Avoiding the question that loomed in the air, Katrina sipped her water to combat the dryness in her mouth, and complimented him on the food selection.

They ate in silence, dining on pan-seared mahi-mahi, served with fried capers. The restaurant provided an elegant ambience, rich with dark woods and red velvet.

"We can have dessert at my place," he said.

Lovemaking on the verandah? she wondered.

"Broiled peaches with crème fraîche," he offered. "We can fix it ourselves."

She looked up at him, stalled, put her fork down. "I'm not very good," she admitted.

A smile tipped one corner of his mouth. "At broiling peaches?"

"At intimacy," she whispered across the table, wishing he would take her seriously for once. "Half the time I don't even—" she paused to add the telltale inflection "—*you* know."

He furrowed his brows, feigning confusion. Katrina wanted to kick him.

"You mean come?" he finally whispered back.

Her entire face flamed. "Clayton."

"Sweet, beautiful Kat." His voice turned low, gentle. "I could come just looking at you."

This can't be happening, she thought, as the room tilted. They couldn't be having this conversation, not here, not like this.

"Will you have dessert with me?" he asked.

She should have said no. She should have told him she wasn't ready to be with him, to let him draw her into his spell, but she couldn't. It was too late; he'd already paved the way. "Yes," she said.

"Now?"

She nodded. Suddenly she craved something sweet. "Broiled peaches."

"And crème fraîche," he added.

They took the gated elevator. Like caged tigers, she thought, preparing to mate. He produced a key from his pocket and inserted it in the key switch that accessed the fourth floor, giving him sole entry to his living quarters.

They walked down the secluded hallway, a path she'd traveled once before. But this time she'd agreed to make love with him, to become part of his life.

At least for tonight, she thought. Until it was over, until the passion cooled and she realized the full impact of what she'd done.

He unlocked his front door and disabled the alarm. The loft-style apartment seemed vast, with its black-and-white floor and iron-forged bed.

She wanted to ask him about his family, his mother and his sisters, but it didn't seem like the right time to catch up. For now they teetered on the edge of being strangers, a boy and a girl who'd lost touch a long time ago.

He escorted her into the kitchen and she placed her handbag on the counter. Like the rest of the loft, the kitchen boasted Clay's dramatic flair. Old copper pots hung from a chopping-block island, and a life-size painting of a half-clothed warrior dominated the only wall. Next to it were a series of smaller paintings, stunning young women with tribally decorated faces and long flowing hair.

"The artist is color-blind," he said.

She tilted her head, wondering how a painter who couldn't distinguish one shade from another could create such bold and beautiful images.

She turned to look at Clay and found him watching her. "I like your dress," he said, studying the sleek silver garment that hugged her body. "I like your hair, too."

Self-conscious, she smoothed the auburn strands that fell over her shoulders. "I wore it loose this time."

He moved a little closer. "Yes, you did."

She looked into his eyes, into the darkness that unmasked his soul.

He touched her cheek, but only for a moment. "Did you pretend when you were with Andrew, Kat?"

"Pretend?"

"When it didn't happen," he clarified. "Did you fake it?"

Her breath rushed out. "No. But maybe I should have." She glanced at the painted warrior, saw that his eyes were as dark as Clay's. "Maybe it would have made a difference."

"No. It's good that you were honest."

"We didn't talk about the times it didn't happen," she admitted. "When he broke our engagement, he said that we weren't compatible in bed. That something was missing. But he didn't blame me, not directly."

"You blamed yourself?"

"Yes, but my girlfriends keep telling me I shouldn't. That I didn't do anything wrong." She shifted her gaze to one of the painted women, wondering how many dark-haired beauties Clay had taken to his bed. "But it's obvious that Andrew was disappointed in me. That I didn't meet his expectations." She managed a shaky laugh. "I doubt Andrew was disappointed in himself. Men never are, it seems."

"Do you still love him?"

She wanted to say no, but how could she? "I don't fall out of love that easily, but he hurt me. He made me feel inadequate, even if he didn't do it purposely. I'm having trouble forgiving him."

"It won't be like that for us." Clay touched her cheek again. "This is only an affair."

"I don't want to disappoint you."

"You won't." He smiled at her. "I've wanted you for over half my life. From the first moment I saw you."

Embarrassed, she almost looked away. "We were kids."

"We were teenagers," he countered. "And teenage boys have raging hormones. I used to think about you when I went to bed at night. I used to—"

She held up her hand, stopped him from destroying the innocence of their youth. "You promised me peaches."

"Yes, ma'am, I did." He reached for a bowl of fruit. "Didn't I?"

Together they stood at the chopping-block island, cut two fresh peaches in half and pitted them. She arranged them on a pan, and Clay sprinkled sugar over the tops.

He turned on the broiler, and when the sugar was golden brown and the peaches were warm and tender, he removed them from the oven. Next he produced a glass jar from the refrigerator.

"The crème fraîche," he said, as he scooped their desserts onto clear glass plates and added the whipping-cream-and-buttermilk topping.

She tasted the simple delicacy and made a pleasured face. "Perfect."

He removed his jacket and loosened his tie, tossing both over a kitchen chair. "Let's sit on the verandah."

The verandah. Her pulse jumped, but she followed him onto the roofed structure. The June air was humid, the view from the fourth floor presenting a square of Historic Savannah.

They sat on a wooden bench, surrounded by potted plants. A small porch light provided an amber glow.

He finished his dessert and set his plate on a narrow table. She continued to eat her peach, the creamy topping melting in her mouth. When she licked her lips, he leaned toward her, nuzzling the side of her neck.

The crème fraîche slid down her throat. He coaxed her to face him, to let him take what he wanted. The kiss was slow, soft and intimate. He sipped from her, and she tasted the sugar in their mouths, the heat of the summer night.

Katrina liked the dizzying sensation, the warmth, the wetness of his tongue dancing with hers. He made a hungry sound and ran his hands down the sides of her body.

Before she could grapple with common sense, he broke the kiss and took her hand. But he didn't lead her inside. He turned off the porch light and guided her to a dark corner of the verandah, pinning her against the wall, trapping her between two tall leafy plants.

"Someone might see us out here," she whispered. See the moon-dappled shadows of a man and woman, she thought, pressed against each other.

"They won't know what we're doing. They can't get close enough to know that I've got my hand under your dress."

She blinked, nearly bumped her head on the wall. "But you don't have your—"

"I do now." As quick as lightning, he sneaked under her skirt, toying with the waistband of her panties.

She told herself to breathe, to keep air circulating in her lungs.

"You're wearing those sexy hose again," he said, his hand traveling to her thigh.

"I always wear them."

"We're going to make love with our clothes on." He spoke softly against her ear. "But you'll have to take your panties off first."

Could she do something so daring? Here? On his verandah, with strangers milling around on the street below? "I'm not that kinky, Clay."

"Yes, you are. You just don't know it yet." He pressed his mouth to her neck. "Your pulse is jumping. Your skin is hot."

And her knees had gone unbearably weak. She

slipped her arms around him, trying to steady herself. "You take them off. You do it."

"No." He nipped her neck. "I want you to give
yourself to me."

Like a woman on the verge of losing her sanity,
Katrina closed her eyes and reached for her panties.
Sliding them down her legs, she stepped out of
them, leaving them at Clay's feet.

"Good girl. Now lift the hem of your dress."

Suddenly she couldn't breathe.

"Do it, Kat. Do it for me."

She grabbed the hem and pulled it up. He
smiled, just once, before he dropped to his knees.

She held on, lifting her dress for him, wondering
if she were going mad. He didn't waste any time.
He kissed her—there, right there, between her legs.

The verandah railing shielded him from view.
No one would know that he was on the ground,
making love to her with his mouth. No one but her,
she thought.

She looked down at him, watched while he seduced her, while he made her slick and wet. She
wanted to touch him, but she couldn't. She still
held her dress, clutching the hem with shaky fingers.

He found her most sensitive spot, and Katrina

thought she might die. He tasted her with sweet, steady strokes, making her moan.

Suddenly nothing mattered but him. Clayton Crawford. Her new lover. The man who'd scandalized her, the man who was scandalizing her now.

What if the verandah railing wasn't shielding him? What if someone saw what he was doing? What if a stranger saw her, rubbing herself against his mouth?

Too aroused to care, Katrina raised her dress even more. She liked the idea of being wild and free, of feeling his tongue inside her.

He kissed her deep and slow. So deep her body trembled. Still sandwiched between two plants, she swayed on her feet. Leaves brushed her arms, heightening the sensation, the wicked pleasure, the breathy little sounds spilling from her throat.

Fire flooded her veins, melting into liquid, bending her to his will. And then she climaxed, hot and wet, right against his mouth, all over his tongue.

He sipped her like wine, and she wondered if she were drunk again. Her mind was spinning.

Clay got to his feet and rubbed against her, showing her how aroused he was. Katrina wanted to devour him, to climb all over his body.

She unbuttoned his shirt, then unzipped his trousers, sliding her hand inside. He was hard and thick, warm to the touch. When she stroked him, he brushed his lips along the column of her throat.

She heard the pounding of music, blues coming from the club. Or was it the rhythm of her heart?

He removed a condom from his pocket. He was ready for her. He'd made sure he was prepared. She liked the idea of making love with their clothes on, of groping each other in a dark corner. It made their affair seem more daring, more dangerous, more forbidden.

"Maybe I am kinky," she said.

"You are," he whispered back. "And so am I." He sheathed himself and moved even closer.

Katrina kissed him, and when he entered her, when he thrust full hilt, she lost her breath.

He made love to her like a man possessed, a man feeding an addiction, a man who couldn't live without a hot, sexual fix. He tugged on the neckline of her dress, just a little, just enough to expose the front of her bra.

A line of perspiration trailed between her breasts, but she craved the heat, the hard, pumping rhythm.

He kept his eyes on hers. Even in the dark, their gazes locked. Her dress was bunched around her waist; his shirt billowed in the air.

She ran her thumb over his mouth. Moonlight slashed across his face, then disappeared, like a mysterious shadow.

Suddenly, she wanted to push the boundaries of their affair, to slide her hand between their bodies.

"You're corrupting me," she said.

He breathed against her ear. "My Kat."

Yes, she thought. His Kat. For now, she belonged to him. Giving into temptation, she touched him, then stroked herself, making them both half-crazy.

Clay moved his mouth all over her, kissing her neck, her chest, making her nipples press achingly against her bra.

And then it happened, pinwheels exploded beneath her eyes, bursting in a prism of need. Clay lost the battle, too. Her release triggered his, and when it was over, he swept her into his arms and carried her inside.

Chapter 4

Clay carried her to his unmade bed, placing her on top of the rumpled sheets. She was still warm and damp between her legs, still wearing high heels.

Had she actually hiked her dress to her waist? Rubbed against his mouth? Made love outdoors?

Coming to her senses, Katrina discarded her shoes. Clay did the same, then climbed into bed beside her.

"Look what I've got." He removed her panties from his pocket. "And I'm keeping them, too."

Was he teasing her? Making a silly joke? Or did

he collect souvenirs from his lovers? Mortified at the thought, she lunged for the trophy. He laughed and let go, and for a moment she considered flinging them at his head.

Clayton Crawford had grown into a decidedly wicked man. And, she thought, the most incredible lover a woman could want.

She slipped on her underwear, securing the lace-trimmed cotton to her body, and he raised his brows.

"You think that's going to stop me?"

"For now." She reached for the remote control on his nightstand and turned on the TV, flipping stations, trying to keep her mind off the dampness between her thighs.

"What are we watching?" he asked.

"This." She came across a classic movie channel, settling on the middle of *Casablanca.*

He didn't argue. Instead, he propped some pillows, offering her a cozy spot beside him. She scooted a little closer, and he took her hand and held it. Suddenly, she felt young and inexperienced. Like the teenager she used to be, the girl who'd had a heart-stopping crush on Clay.

They watched the movie in silence, treating Humphrey Bogart and Ingrid Bergman like old friends, appreciating the memorable moments, the familiar lines, the emotion.

When it ended, she hit the remote and the screen went blank. She turned to look at him, and he smiled.

"Will you stay here tonight?" he asked. "I bought an extra toothbrush."

That girlish feeling came back. "You did?"

He nodded. "And you don't have to worry about what to wear to bed this time." He moved closer. "We can sleep naked."

She couldn't help but smile. "You've got this all figured out."

"I'm just trying to find a way to steal your panties." He paused, grinned. "I used to spend a lot of time fantasizing about your underwear."

Properly embarrassed, Katrina shook her head. She used to fantasize about him, too. But the images her teenage mind had conjured weren't quite so primal.

"You wouldn't believe how many times I considered walking in on you during one of your fittings," he said. "But my mom would have killed me."

"Your mother is an amazing seamstress. I don't know how we lost touch."

"You got too old for debutante dresses, I guess."

And it had become increasingly difficult to be around Clay, she thought, to want a boy who didn't fit into her social circle. "How is your mom?"

"Good. Fine. I bought her a condo." He shifted his weight, stirring the mattress. "Do you want to have dinner with us on Sunday?"

She met his gaze. "Us?"

"My mom, my sisters, their husbands. We get together every Sunday."

The invitation struck a nostalgic chord. She'd always admired Clay's family, the closeness they shared, even if they'd been working-class poor. "Yes, I'd like that very much." She paused, looked into his eyes. "I didn't know your sisters were married."

"They have kids now, too. I'm the only one who hasn't settled down."

"You've been busy with the club." Busy building a successful business, she thought. Busy seducing socialites. "How long is this going to last, Clay?"

"This? You mean us?" He shrugged. "I don't know. A few weeks. A month. Does it matter?"

"No." They both knew they still lived in different worlds, that nouveau riche and old money rarely progressed beyond sex, beyond quick, heated affairs.

"Andrew is already getting territorial," he said.

"Because I lied about you. Because he thinks you took advantage of me while I was drunk."

"Maybe so. But sooner or later he's going to try to win you back."

Her nerves tangled, twisting like confused vines. "I don't want to think about that right now." She wasn't ready to forgive Andrew, to consider reconciling with him, not while she was in Clay's bed.

"Then what do you want to think about?"

"You," she said automatically.

He smiled at that. "What about me?"

"I used to check out library books about your heritage."

"Really?" Clay found himself intrigued. He hadn't expected her to bring up something from the past. He touched a strand of her hair, flattered that he'd made a lasting impression on her, that her crush had been as deep as his. "Which part of my heritage?"

Her voice turned soft. "All of it. I read about Scotland and Portugal. About the Choctaw Indians."

Clay's mother was second-generation Portuguese and his father was half Choctaw and half

Scot, but he had no idea that had mattered to Katrina. "I have something important that belonged to my dad." A man who'd died when he was still a boy, a man Katrina had never met. "A family heirloom, I guess."

"What is it?"

"A beaded Choctaw sash. I'll show it to you sometime." When he wasn't caught up in teenage sentiment, he thought. When their affair wound down. "I have an old rosary from my mother's side."

"I'm looking forward to seeing her again."

"She's going to be happy to see you, too." But he hoped his mom didn't make too much of his relationship with Katrina. Kat, he corrected. He liked calling her Kat. When they both fell silent, he cuffed her chin, teasing her. "So, do you want something to drink? Maybe a bottle of wine?"

"Very funny. I'm never drinking again."

"Doesn't matter. You get wild even if you're not all liquored up."

She glanced in the direction of the verandah, then back at him.

Clay couldn't help but smile. His patio would never be the same. "Just for the record, that's the first time I've had sex out there."

"I'm glad. I mean…I'd hate to think you did

that all the time.'' She fidgeted with a corner of the quilt. ''Why'd you do it with me?''

''I don't know.'' Maybe it was his way of making love to her in public. His way of proving to Savannah that he was good enough for her. ''I guess it was the risk of getting caught.''

She toyed with the quilt again. ''Are you sure no one saw us?''

''It was dark. We could barely see each other.'' But he could still taste her, still feel her climax, hot and wet, against his mouth. He leaned over her. ''You really are the best lay I've ever had.''

''Clayton.'' She shook her head and swatted his shoulder.

''What?'' He grinned and tickled her.

She laughed and struggled to get away. In a mock fight, they rolled over the bed and started peeling off each other's clothes, tossing them onto the floor.

And then they kissed. Long and slow, deep and seductive.

''Proper Katrina,'' he said, as he straddled her. ''Naughty Kat.''

She skimmed his chest. ''Dangerous Clay.''

''It's just sex.'' He removed a condom from the nightstand, held the foil up to the light, watched it shine.

"I know." She rolled the protection over his body. "But it feels so good."

"To break the rules?" He knew she needed to rebel against her upbringing, to step outside her social circle. But Clay didn't care if he was her rebound lover, if they were playing a short-lived game. For now she was his.

She arched her back and he plunged into her, thrusting hard and deep. Her hair, as rich as autumn, feathered across the pillow. She closed her eyes and he rode her, taking possession, claiming her.

When she opened her eyes, they locked on to his, as blue as sapphires, as bewitching as enchanted stones. Breaking the spell, he buried his face against her neck and inhaled the scent of her skin, the orchid note of her perfume.

She wrapped her legs around him, and his heartbeat hammered his chest. He'd imagined this moment for over half his life—the hip-grinding sex, the breathy pants, the incredible pressure between his legs.

"Fantasies," he said.

She clung to him. "Mine or yours?"

"Both." They rolled over the bed again, licking each other's skin, kissing, tasting.

She thrashed beneath him, and he linked his fingers with hers, holding her arms above her head, imprisoning her, taking what he'd always wanted. She bit down on her bottom lip, almost making it bleed. He lowered his head to kiss her, to soothe the pain, to feed the hunger, to push her toward the climax burning between them.

She broke free and dragged him closer, rubbing her body all over his, clawing his back, driving him deeper.

Making everything but her disappear.

Katrina awakened at dawn. Clay slept beside her, his hair falling over his forehead, one arm slung across a pillow. The sheet draped around his hips, drawing her attention to his stomach and the line of hair below his navel.

He had a long, lean body, with rangy muscles. He wasn't bulked up from weights, so she suspected swimming was still his exercise of choice. Clay had always enjoyed water sports.

She smoothed his hair, moving an errant strand from his eye. He stirred, swatted her away like a fly, then squinted, realizing what he'd done.

"Sorry." He gave her a sheepish smile. "I'm used to waking up alone."

She moved back, keeping her distance. "That's okay." She was used to waking up alone, too. Unless she'd spent the night with Andrew, but she was familiar with his habits.

Clay scratched his head, making his hair stick up at odd angles. He looked delightfully boyish, dark and rumpled.

"What's the first thing you do when you get up?" she asked.

He stretched, dragging his arms heavenward. "It depends on what I've got going on that day."

"You don't have a routine?"

"Not really. No."

The opposite of Andrew, she thought. No matter what, her former fiancé showered at 6:00 a.m. every morning, then read the paper in the formal dining room, eating two poached eggs and lightly buttered toast.

"What do you do?" he asked.

"I usually make a pot of coffee."

"Then go ahead. But you've got to do it in the buff." When he sat up, the sheet fell below his hips. "I'll bet you never made coffee at Andrew's house without your clothes on."

"Who said anything about Andrew?" She clutched her pillow. "I wasn't thinking about him."

His mouth quirked into a wiseass grin. "You're a terrible liar, Kat."

She tossed the pillow at him, and he laughed. Why did he have to be so casual about their affair? So flippant? "Don't you care that I was thinking about another man?"

"Why should I? I'm the guy you're sleeping with. The guy who's making you—" he paused to waggle those wicked eyebrows "—you know."

Good grief. "Such ego."

"Damn straight." He lunged across the bed and made her squeal, kissing her as hard and fast as he could.

Maybe he did care, she thought, as his tongue stroked hers, maybe he was more possessive than he was willing to admit.

And maybe not, she decided, when he let her go. Maybe he preferred waking up alone.

She climbed out of bed with the sheet wrapped around her. "I'm not making coffee in the nude."

"Listen to you. Miss Priss Pot." His sheet fell farther south. "I probably have just as much money as you do now, but you don't see me behaving like a blue blood."

Her mouth went dry. He was half-aroused and too damn gorgeous for his own good. "You're not a blue blood. Besides, you wouldn't know how to conduct yourself in a cultivated setting."

"Like hell. I've been watching your kind for years."

"My kind?" He made old money heirs sound like Airedales at a Westminster Dog Show. "Fine, Mr. Smarty Pants. Since you can handle my social scene so well, you can escort me to the aquatic gala at the end of the month."

"Some boring charity event?"

"It isn't boring. And you'd do well to donate some of that nouveau riche money of yours to charity."

He flashed that grin again. "To save the mermaids?"

"To build an aquatic museum." She held fast to her sheet. She wasn't about to have this conversation in the nude, in spite of his appealing state of undress. "Do you own a tux? The male gender of my kind doesn't rent them, you know."

"I'll buy an Armani just for the occasion." He roamed his gaze over her. "Will Andrew be there?"

"Probably. We were supposed to attend the ball together. I imagine he'll escort someone else."

"Another Savannah mermaid? My, but the blue bloods like to play. Too bad my kind is so adept at stealing their womenfolk." He climbed out of bed and yanked the sheet off her body.

Her knees wobbled like jellyfish. If only she could sting him. "Don't you dare."

"Don't I dare what?" He smoothed his tousled hair. "Ravish you? Push you against the night-stand, open your legs and thrust right into you." He shifted his stance, much too casual for a naked man talking about sex. "No foreplay, no condom. No apology." He moved a little closer. "I wouldn't dream of it."

A pulse in her neck fluttered. She could feel it dancing beneath her skin. "Why? Because you're such a gentleman?"

"Because I want that coffee." Without warning, he scooped her up and tossed her over his shoulder, caveman style, her legs dangling, her arms flapping.

When he patted her bare bottom, she screeched like the damsel she was, struggling, playing his off-beat game.

He carried her to the kitchen, but all she could see was the black-and-white linoleum moving past her eyes. Finally he plunked her on her feet.

In the next instant, they looked at each other and burst out laughing. Apparently, he'd forgotten that he'd set the timer on the coffeepot the night before. Naked or not, a fresh pot awaited them.

* * *

Hours later Katrina took ladylike sips of the iced tea her parents had provided. She sat in a leather chair in her father's home office. Her mother sat in a similar chair and her father occupied his Chippendale desk. He looked like he was in charge, with his distinguished gray hair and stern posture. Even the custom-made humidor and imported cigars boasted power. But Katrina knew otherwise.

Her mother had called this family meeting. Delilah Beaumont didn't look nearly as imposing as her husband. But looks could be deceiving. The aging Southern beauty, with her soft-spoken voice and delicate manners, was far from a shrinking violet or a wilting magnolia. Delilah had always been a woman to be reckoned with, especially for Katrina.

"We hired a private detective to run a background check on Clayton Crawford," Delilah said. She lifted a file from her husband's desk and placed it on her lap.

Appalled, Katrina could only stare.

"Andrew suggested it," William Beaumont added.

Andrew. She should have known. "Why? Because Jenny told Andrew that Clay might have criminal ties? That his club could've been funded by mobsters?"

"Precisely." Her mother's genteel voice held no shame.

"And?" Katrina pressed.

"And there was no evidence of criminal activity." The older woman opened the file. "His investors are quite legitimate. But," she added, pausing to make her point. "someone had been smuggling drugs through his club. Dirty cops or some such thing."

"Was Clay involved?" Katrina asked.

"No. But Steam isn't the proper environment for a young lady of your station."

"Steam? This isn't about the club. This is about Clay. You're trying to stop me from seeing him."

"That man is using you." Her mother sighed. "He's spoiling your reputation."

"He didn't get me drunk, and he didn't take advantage of me. All of that is a lie."

Her mother arched her brows. Her golden brown hair was fashioned in an elegant twist, and a set of pearls decorated her ears. "Then you're not sleeping with him?"

"Yes, I'm sleeping with him." Katrina glanced at her father. But he remained quiet. "I like being with Clay." She thought about the coffeepot incident. "He makes me laugh. He makes me feel good about myself."

William spoke. "We don't want to see you get hurt."

"Andrew hurt me, not Clay."

"You hurt Andrew, too," Delilah interjected. "This scandal is hurting all of us."

Katrina finished her tea. In that respect, she knew her parents were right. On the other hand, she wanted to date Clay, to make her own choices. "I asked Clayton to escort me to the aquatic gala."

Her mother's face went pale.

"Maybe it's better this way." William spoke gently to his wife. "If Katrina and this young man attend a social function together, the gossip might die down. It might legitimize their relationship."

"You mean their affair." Delilah placed the file back on her husband's desk. "How does one legitimize our daughter sleeping with the owner of a blues club?"

William picked up the file. "Clayton Crawford is a wealthy young man. A self-made man. He worked hard for what he has. There's no shame in that."

Katrina's heart stirred, but she didn't dare react. Not while her mother was still upset.

Finally, the Southern belle gained her composure. She met her daughter's gaze. "If you insist on seeing Mr. Crawford, then I suggest you behave in a manner that doesn't embarrass your father and me.''

Silently Katrina nodded, wondering if that were possible. She'd lost her inhibitions around Clay. When she was with him, Kat, not Katrina, took over.

''Do you have a dress for the aquatic gala?'' her mother asked.

''Not yet.''

''Then I'll take you shopping.'' The older woman managed a cordial tone. ''If everyone is going to be ogling you and your date, then we'll make darn sure you're wearing something stunning.''

Katrina agreed to shop with her mother, hoping Clay called her later. That he would invite her to Steam tonight, to listen to music, to dance.

To make love in new and wondrous ways.

Chapter 5

Clay looked across his desk at Michael Whittaker. Michael was the owner and CEO of Whittaker and Associates, a highly successful security-consulting firm. Whittaker and Associates had provided the initial security for the club, but Michael was also Clay's most trusted friend.

They'd only known each other for a few years, but they shared the discomfort of growing up poor, as well as the determination of clawing their way to the top. Although both were Native American mixed-bloods, they rarely discussed their parentage. In spite of the financial hardship Clay's family had endured, his childhood had been blessed with love and understanding. Michael's poverty-stricken youth bore the brunt of anger and infidelity.

Tonight the men occupied Clay's office, nursing domestic beer and engaging in private conversation. Clay knew that Michael didn't like conversing in public settings, but his life was always filled with high-profile clients and top-security assignments.

"I'm working for Abraham Danforth," Michael said.

"Honest Abe II? You're involved in his campaign?" Clay sat back in his chair. He'd never met the wealthy politician, but he intended to cast his vote in Danforth's direction. The senatorial race was in full swing, and Clay thought Danforth seemed like a strong, stable candidate. "Is someone dishing some dirt on him?"

"I'm investigating a stalking."

"Damn. Any leads?"

Michael nodded. "She identified herself as Lady Savannah in the threatening e-mails she sent to Danforth's computer."

"A female stalker? Has anyone seen her? Do you have a description of her?"

The other man took a swig of his beer. "Tall,

slim, auburn hair, tinted glasses. But I'm keeping that under wraps for now.''

''I'm seeing a tall, slim woman with auburn hair.''

''Seeing? You mean sleeping with? I heard about the scandal. I know you're messing around with Katrina Beaumont.'' Michael's gaze didn't waver. ''You're doing quite a number on her reputation.''

''She doesn't seem to mind.'' Clay paused. ''She's not a suspect in the stalking, is she? You're not—''

''No, I'm not here to investigate your lover.''

Of course not. Katrina wouldn't have any reason to threaten a politician. Her family probably socialized at his fancy fund-raisers.

Tense, Clay picked up a paperweight. The small glass sculpture was a dolphin, a sea creature, a troubling reminder of the aquatic gala he'd agreed to attend. ''I hope I'm not getting in over my head.''

''How so?''

''I think she's starting to consume me.''

''Hot sex will do that to a guy.'' Michael's lips formed a quick, teasing smile.

''Yeah. But I've known her since we were teenagers. I've been attracted to her a long time.''

"So quit complaining and enjoy it."

Clay chuckled. "Figures you'd say something like that. You probably haven't been laid in months."

Michael gave him a screw-you look, and they both laughed. The security consultant worked long, hard hours, rarely taking the time off for good behavior.

"Maybe Lady Savannah will give you some action," Clay said.

"Oh, sure. That's just what I need. A stalker for a girlfriend."

They laughed again, appreciating each other's sarcastic humor.

"I invited Katrina to the club tonight," Clay said when they fell silent.

"And now you wished you hadn't?"

He shrugged, put the paperweight down, then picked it up a second time. "I don't know. I'm just not used to wanting someone this much."

"I prefer a little space in my relationships, too. But it's only an affair, right?"

"That's the idea, except I agreed to go to a charity event with her."

"A society date," Michael mused.

Clay frowned at the dolphin. "I invited her to

my mom's house for dinner, too. We've got all sorts of dates lined up.''

The other man drained his beer. ''Sex doesn't come free. You've got to pay for it one way or the other.''

''I know.'' But Clay hadn't been expecting to pay for it with his emotions, at least not to this degree. ''Her ex is still in the picture. I know damn well he's going to want her back.''

''So let her go when it's over. Stop driving yourself crazy with it.'' Michael looked up. ''Unless you don't want to let her go. Unless that's the problem.''

Clay glanced out the third-floor window and noticed it had begun to drizzle outside. The glass was misty, fogging the view. He wondered when the intermittent rains would stop. ''I just need to get her out of my system.'' He turned back to his friend. ''That's why I'm sleeping with her.''

''And that's why you asked her to come to the club tonight,'' Michael remarked.

''Exactly.'' Clay blew a tight breath. Why else would he be so damn anxious to see her?

Steam was packed, primed for a Saturday-night showcase. Tall, tanned men prowled the perimeter of the dance floor while teased-and-sprayed women posed as eye candy.

Katrina looked around for Clay but couldn't find him. Uncertain of what else to do, she turned toward the stage. Music flooded the room, as sleek and soulful as the female singer caressing the microphone.

She watched the other woman, admiring her coffee-colored skin and smoky voice. And then she felt someone move in behind her, someone tall, someone standing much too close.

He slipped his arms around her, and she leaned back, letting him hold her. When she turned her head to look back at him, he kissed her. Hot and slow. Sweet and silky.

Music to make love by, she thought. She wanted to strip Clayton Crawford, right here, right now, and put her mouth all over him.

They separated, facing each other, silent for a moment. He looked hard and masculine in the dim light, as intense as the cloud-shrouded sky.

"Would you like a drink?" he finally asked.

"I'll take a soda. Ginger ale."

"How about an appetizer?"

"Something spicy," she decided.

He roamed his gaze over her. "I like what you're wearing."

"It's a cat suit." She spun around to model the skintight outfit, a black garment she'd bought just for him. "It's all one piece."

"A Kat suit," he mimicked, gesturing to her, inserting her name into it.

"It has a zipper in the back." From her neck to her tailbone.

"I noticed." He gave a passing cocktail waitress their order, then led Katrina to a private table in the back of the club.

"What's it like to live like this every night?" she asked.

"Music? Beautiful women? A successful business?" He held her chair for her. "A guy could do worse."

She glanced around at the beautiful women, including the singer taking center stage. "They don't all belong to you."

He sat beside her. "Are you sure about that?"

"So you have a harem?" The idea boiled her blood, but she managed a noncommittal shrug. "Lucky you."

Her ginger ale arrived, along with a club soda for Clay. The appetizer, chipotle-seasoned chicken strips, showed up a few minutes later.

She tasted the chili-spiked meat. It was hot, but it fit her mood. She motioned to the singer. "Have you slept with her, Clay? Is she part of your harem?"

"Gloria?" He gave the sultry singer an appreciative glance. "She's married to her guitar player."

Katrina refused to smile. "And what about her?" She indicated the prettiest cocktail waitress in the room. A leggy blonde with a sassy walk and enviable cleavage.

He studied his flashy employee. "I don't mix business with pleasure."

She lifted her chin. "So who's in your harem?"

"You," he said. "Only you."

Suddenly she went warm, foolishly warm, right between her legs.

"Is something wrong?" he asked.

She shook her head, wondering if he'd turned her into a nymphomaniac. These days, she lived and breathed just for him.

They remained silent for a while, listening to music, nibbling the chicken. Every so often, the candle on the table flickered.

He sipped his club soda, ice crackling in his glass. "Do you want to dance?"

"Yes." Please, she thought. Anything for his touch.

He guided her to the dance floor and they found

a cozy spot in the corner. The music was slow, the beat deep and sensual. She slipped her arms around his neck; he circled her waist. They moved to the rhythm, man to woman, lover to lover. When he dropped his hands a little lower, pulling her hips against his, she bumped his fly.

Katrina didn't care if the entire world knew that Clay aroused her. She didn't care if they were misbehaving in public. Steam had been created for moments like this, for couples who wanted each other.

They danced to the rest of the set and after the band left the stage, she asked him to take her on a tour of the club.

"A tour?" he questioned.

"I haven't been everywhere."

"There isn't much left to see. Just the third floor."

"What's there?"

"Offices. Storage space."

She took his hand. "Show me."

He led her to a small staircase designed for employees. "It isn't very exciting."

"But it could be," she remarked.

He paused on one of the steps and turned to look at her. "What are you up to?"

"A seduction," she admitted, taking the rest of the stairs, letting her heels hit the wood like bullets.

He stopped at the top of the floor. "You're going to seduce me?" He made a wide gesture. "Here?"

"You did it to me on the verandah." She touched her earlobes, fussing with her jewelry. She wore diamonds at her ears and a small strand of rubies at her throat. To complement the look, she'd plaited her hair into a French braid, simply so he could undo it.

"What's in here?" she asked, as they came to a closed door.

"Cleaning supplies. Are you going to seduce me in there?"

"Maybe." She opened the door and pulled him inside. He laughed and she knew he was willing to play her game.

"Where's the light?" She searched the wall and found the switch, flipping it on. The room was cramped, stocked with items much too mundane to notice. "Does the door lock?"

"Not from the inside. We could get caught in here."

"That's part of the fun." She studied the tight quarters. "But maybe we should block the door. Just in case."

"This'll work." He moved a pallet of paper products, securing the entrance.

She glanced around for a chair and came up with a sealed box and a stack of clean white towels.

"Is that for you or me?" he asked.

"Me." Behaving like the lady she was trained to be, she covered the box with a towel and sat on the edge of it. "You're going to stand in front of me."

He stepped forward. "Why? What are you going to do?"

"What do you think?" Her face was nearly level with his fly.

Recognition dawned in his eyes, and he rubbed his thumb over her mouth, tracing the shape of her lips. "Naughty girl."

She unzipped his trousers, pushing them down, finding him aroused already. "Naughty boy."

His stomach muscles jumped, and she teased him with her tongue. By the time she took him into her mouth, he was playing with her hair, toying with the braid, loosening it.

Katrina took him deeper, and he watched her, lifting her chin, looking into her eyes.

"This isn't fair," he said.

She stopped, came up for air, smiled. "Why? Because you can't do anything to me?" She pulled his trousers down a little farther. "Poor baby."

Lowering her head, she showed him how good she could make him feel.

He groaned, and she sensed he was close. She could almost taste his orgasm, taste the saltiness spilling into her throat.

But instead of losing control, he pulled back and dragged her to her feet, attacking her zipper, peeling off her jumpsuit.

Suddenly everything changed. He had his hands all over her, his fingers pressed between her legs.

He grabbed her, kissed her, made her head spin. They bumped into the pallet against the door, stumbling over supplies.

She moaned, and he tore apart his wallet, searching for a condom. He was taking her game and using it against her, but she didn't care. She couldn't think beyond the urgency, between the desperation of wanting him the way he wanted her.

He secured the protection, spilling credit cards in his wake, scattering them onto the floor.

Finally he dropped onto the box and made her straddle him. Naked, she rode him, her head tipped back, her body arched.

Sensation slid over sensation, warm and wet and filled with friction. She dug her nails into his shirt, then ripped the front of it open, baring his chest. He leaned forward and sucked on her neck.

They were going mad, she thought, damning the consequences.

"Kiss me," he growled. "I want you to kiss me when it happens."

She covered his mouth with hers and their tongues clashed, warring like enemies, like lovers who longed to tear each other apart.

His release was swift, deep and aggressive. She felt him shudder, knowing he'd spilled his seed. Katrina climaxed, too. As warm as a waterfall, as powerful as rain, as potent as the kiss still thundering between them.

Chapter 6

Katrina sat beside Clay in his Porsche, a make and model that fit his sporty lifestyle.

They were on their way to his mother's house, and she was nervous about seeing his family, about the emotions this visit would probably stir.

"You look nice," Clay said.

"Thank you." She smiled, realizing how often he complimented her. She wore a summer dress and sandals, hoping to appear unpretentious.

He reached over and moved her hair away from her neck. "I wonder if my mom will notice the hickies."

"That's not funny." She slapped his hand away, wishing he would quit teasing her about what they'd done last night. Sneaking out of the supply room had been a feat in itself, considering her tousled hair and his torn shirt. And, of course, there were the marks on her skin, the telltale signs of lovemaking she was determined to hide.

"This is it." Ten minutes later, Clay parked in front of a modern condominium complex, trimmed in red brick and indigenous foliage.

They took the sunny path to his mother's unit, but Clay didn't knock. He opened the door and escorted Katrina inside, calling out to his family.

"Oh, my." Marie Crawford, his fifty-two-year-old mother, rushed to greet them. "Look at you." She took Katrina's hand. "As beautiful as ever. I was so excited when Clay told me he was bringing you to dinner."

"Thank you. It's good to be here." She smiled at the other woman, memories floating to the surface. She'd met Clay's mother when Marie had worked out of her home, struggling to sell her dresses to upscale boutiques.

Marie finally turned to her son, embracing him. "My handsome boy."

"My gorgeous mama." He gave her a loud,

smacking kiss, and Katrina admired their easy
manner.

The rest of the family gathered around. She
knew Clay had considered himself the man of the
house, protecting his sisters and helping Marie with
financial duties. In some ways, he'd thrived on being the only male, and in other ways he'd struggled
with the overwhelming pressure that came with
having two younger sisters and a widowed parent.

These days his sisters had charming husbands
and sweet-faced babies, toddlers stumbling along
with well-loved grins.

The Crawford brood headed to the kitchen,
where a home-cooked meal sent cozy scents into
the air. The condominium Clay had bought for Marie provided luxuries missing from his youth. He
and his sisters had grown up in a cluttered apartment, with Clay sleeping on a foam futon in his
mother's sewing room.

"I made sweet bread," Marie said to Katrina.
"I remember how much you liked it."

"Thank you. Everything smells so good." She
glanced at Clay and saw that he'd scooped up one
of the toddlers, bouncing the boy on his hip.

Katrina's family never ate in the kitchen, nor did
they hang around while meals were being prepared,
poking their noses into pots and pans. Her mother

approved the menu, but that was where the culinary intervention ended. Here everyone pitched in, including the husbands in attendance.

When someone suggested Clay set the table, he handed the toddler to Katrina. Jenna, the mother of the child, merely smiled and went about her duty: sprinkling feta cheese over a Greek-style salad.

Katrina took the youngster and nuzzled his hair. He shook the toy clutched in his stubby hand, then offered it to her.

"Why, thank you," she said, studying the plastic boat.

In turn, he grinned and bumped against her breast. His name was Danny, and he appeared to be as flirtatious as his sexy uncle.

While Clay set the table, he winked at Katrina and snatched an olive from the salad, receiving a playful slap from Jenna. Clay's other sister, a curvaceous brunette named Tiana, rolled her eyes.

By the time the meal was served, Tiana's daughter, a two-year-old with chubby cheeks and pink overalls, sat on Clay's lap, eating diced fruit from his plate.

"So what do you think?" he asked Katrina.

She knew he meant the food, the pork tenderloin, clam stew and cilantro-seasoned rice. "It's wonderful."

"Did you know Mama works at a bridal shop now?" Jenna asked.

"No, I didn't." Katrina glanced at Marie, who looked up and smiled.

"I made both of my daughters' wedding dresses." She turned to Clay. "And someday I'm going to get that son of mine down the aisle."

"Who? Me?" He shot a good-natured grin to his brothers-in-law. "No way. I'm not like these guys."

Marie snorted at that, convinced, it appeared, that her club-owner son would make a fine husband and father.

When Katrina's chest constricted, she spoke to Marie, admitting her own failure. "I was engaged. But it didn't work out."

"And now you're seeing my boy." The older woman's voice softened. "Maybe you can tame him. A proper girl like you."

Tame him? She lifted her water, took a time-stalling sip. Apparently Clay's family hadn't heard the rumors. They didn't know that he'd corrupted her.

The conversation shifted to another topic, and after dinner they drank decaffeinated coffee and ate dessert in the living room. Clay and Katrina didn't touch, no loverlike pats, no hand holding. But that didn't stop Marie from treating them like a couple, from matchmaking in her own motherly way.

When the evening ended, everyone hugged Katrina, treating her like one of the family. Marie gave her an extralong embrace and a loaf of Portuguese sweet bread to take home.

Suddenly Katrina wanted to cry.

Clay drove her to the Beaumont guest house, and she invited him inside, wishing her emotions would settle.

She put the care package in the bread box and leaned against the counter. French doors led to an informal garden, flourishing with summer blooms. But as beautiful as the setting was, the stillness made her lonely. She missed the camaraderie in Marie's condo.

"Are you okay?" he asked.

She gave him an unconvincing nod. "I'm fine."

"You don't seem fine." He came toward her. "Are you still hurting over Andrew? Is that what this is all about?"

"I don't know. Maybe." She glanced at the garden. "I guess I want what your sisters have. I think I've always wanted that."

Clay turned silent, slipping his hands in his pockets. His hair fell softly across his forehead, gentling his features. Katrina wanted to put her head on his shoulder, but she couldn't summon the courage to touch him. Not now. Not like this.

He finally spoke. "Do you want to do something with me tomorrow?"

Her heart made a girlish leap. "Do something?"

"Go to the park. Feed the birds. Just spend a lazy day together."

She couldn't recall ever doing something so simple with Andrew. "Yes, I'd like that."

"Then meet me at the big park around eleven. Near the fountain." He removed his hands from his pockets. "It was my favorite place to go when I was a kid."

"When we were teenagers?"

"Yes." He brushed her cheek with a fleeting kiss, then stepped back, putting distance between them. "I'll see you tomorrow."

"I'll be there." She walked him to the door, stood on the porch and watched him go, already anxious to see him again.

Clay arrived at Forsyth Park, sat on a vacant bench and waited for Kat. He checked his watch and realized he was early. Too damn eager to see her, he thought. Too damn attached to a woman whose heart belonged to another man.

He glanced at the famous fountain with its robed

female figure, water-spouting mermen and majestic swans. And when he turned back, he saw Kat. She was early, too.

She came toward him, the sun glinting off her hair. Their eyes met from across the walkway. Most of the benches near the fountain were occupied, but she'd spotted him right away.

He liked the way she moved, the way she carried herself. Her strides were long and graceful, her clothes swaying softly with each step. Jeans and a T-shirt had never looked so good.

She sat next to him, and he had the notion to grab her, hold her, to never let go. But he gave her a lazy smile instead.

"Kat."

She crossed her legs, returned his smile. "Clay."

He lifted the bagged bread he'd brought and handed her some. For a while they remained silent, tossing tiny pieces on the ground, watching the birds eat.

"So you used to come here when we were young," she said, starting a conversation.

"Because of the fountain," he admitted. "I like the way it makes me feel."

"And how is that?" she asked.

"Sort of mythical, I guess." He looked at the statues. "Maybe it's the mermen."

"My daddy calls them tritons." She shifted to observe the fountain. "In Greek mythology, Triton was Poseidon's son. Triton was half man and half fish. Or half dolphin. I'm not quite sure which."

Clay hadn't studied Greek mythology, but he'd heard of the well-known gods. "Poseidon was lord of the sea, right?"

She nodded. "He rides along the surface of the sea in a golden chariot pulled by dolphins."

He thought about the dolphin paperweight on his desk. "Where does Poseidon live?"

"In a golden-domed palace near Atlantis."

"Lucky him." Clay had always been at home in water. Swimming in the ocean made him feel strong and free, mythical, like the mermen. "I guess going to that charity gala with you won't be so bad. I don't mind donating money for an aquatic museum."

She tossed another handful of bread crumbs to the birds. "I'm looking forward to it. My mother already bought me a dress. It's—" She paused, laughed a little. "I doubt you want to hear about my dress."

"Why not?" He laughed, too. "I grew up around that kind of stuff. I'm used to it."

She smoothed her hair away from her eyes. She wore it loose today, still covering the marks on her neck, he suspected. The places where he'd sucked on her skin.

"I'll surprise you," she said.

"I'm sorry. What?"

"With my dress."

Suddenly the aquatic gala seemed like a prom date. "At least tell me what color it is." So he would know what type of corsage to bring her, he thought.

"White."

He tilted his head. "My mom made you a white dress for the Christmas Cotillion." The debutante ball hosted by Savannah's finest, an elegant event Clay could never have attended.

"All the debs wore white. This dress isn't like that. It isn't quite so…virginal."

He couldn't help but smile. "Good thing."

She smacked his shoulder, scattering bread crumbs onto his shirt. He dusted himself off, cupped her face and kissed her. In front of the fountain, he thought. In front of the merman protecting the water.

When she made a sweet sound, he deepened the kiss, tasting the breath mint still melting in her mouth. Then he scooped the mint onto his tongue, stealing it from her.

She gasped, but he didn't let her go. He liked shocking her, teasing her, doing things she didn't expect.

Finally they separated. "We shouldn't behave like this," she said. "Not in broad daylight."

He shrugged, even if his heart was pounding. "It was just a kiss."

"It made me dizzy." Her lashes fluttered. "You make me dizzy."

"Too dizzy to have lunch with me? I'm about ready for a burger."

"I think I can handle that."

"Good." He took her arm, and they walked along a tree-shaded path, content to be in each other's company, to be friends as well as lovers.

They dined at a nearby café, and Clay realized he'd been watching Kat eat. Everything about her fascinated him: the way she sipped her cherry cola; the way she made eating a char-grilled burger look graceful. His plate oozed with condiments that had fallen from his bun, but those messy globs didn't happen to her.

"You haven't tamed me yet," he said.

She glanced up, and he knew he'd thrown her

for a loop. Apparently she hadn't expected him to bring up his mother's deep-seated wish.

"Do you want me to?" she asked.

Yes, he thought. "No," he said. "There isn't a man alive who wants to be tamed. Chained to the bed maybe."

She blotted her mouth, leaving a lipstick mark on her napkin, a paper kiss, coral-pink and pretty. "You have a one-track mind, Clayton."

"And you're still my fantasy."

Her cheeks flushed. She took a drink to cool herself off. He recognized the signs. The lady had a libido.

She glanced at their waitress, who darted past to serve a nearby table. "We shouldn't be talking about this here."

"Just like we shouldn't have kissed at the park?" He shrugged, smiled. "Invite me to go home with you." He wanted to make love with her in her bed, in the Beaumont guest house, with sunlight spilling over her skin.

She didn't respond, not right away. So Clay waited, anxious to hear her voice. He couldn't shake her from his blood. He couldn't end the day without putting his hands all over her.

"Come home with me," she finally said, her cheeks still flushed.

They took separate cars. Clay stopped by a pharmacy to pick up some condoms, replenishing his supply and giving Kat a head start.

A short while later he traveled down the avenue that led to her parents' estate. Shadows dappled the road, sunlight zigzagging through live-oak patterns.

He turned into the driveway, passing the mansion and taking the foliage-lined route to the guest house. And then he saw a midnight-blue Mercedes parked next to Kat's luxury sedan.

When the trellised porch came into view, his heart nearly stopped. Kat stood beside a tall, well-groomed man.

Andrew Winston. Her former fiancé. Clay recognized him from pictures he'd seen in the society pages.

Time to face the music, he thought. Or kick the other man's butt if it came down to an ungentlemanly brawl. He squared his shoulders and closed his car door loudly enough for Kat and Andrew to hear. They both turned, and his breath clogged his throat.

Kat looked vulnerable, lost in a way that made him ache. Andrew's aristocratic features remained stoic, aside from a muscle ticking in his jaw.

Clay moved forward, and Kat fussed with her

hair. Was she trying to keep the marks on her neck hidden? Hoping her old lover didn't notice them?

"Andrew stopped by," she said.

"So I see." Clay met the other man's gaze, and they stared each other down. He wanted to grab Mr. Society Pages by his high-and-mighty lapels and shove him down the porch steps, but he wasn't about to let his working-class roots show. Not unless Andrew threw the first punch.

"What are you doing here?" Clay finally asked.

"I'd like to speak to Katrina."

"About what?"

"The aquatic gala, if you must know."

Kat's former fiancé turned toward her. Then he brushed her hand, a light, tender touch. A touch that twisted Clay's gut in two.

"Will you attend the gala with me?" he asked her, his voice as refined as processed sugar. "I still have our tickets."

She blinked, released an audible breath. "I'm going with Clay."

"Really?" The blue blood shifted, cocked his regal head at Clay. "I envy you, Crawford."

What the hell was this? Polite charm? A new ploy to win Kat's favor? "As you should, Winston."

Andrew's lips formed a tight smile. "Maybe Katrina will save me a dance."

A dance, a society duel. That was right up Winston's alley. "I'm sure she will," Clay responded, refusing to appear threatened.

"Then I shall see you both at the gala." Andrew smoothed his shirt, tugging at his cuffs. He didn't look the least bit wilted, even in the stifling heat. Yet Clay had begun to sweat. Now he wished he'd knocked Winston on his butt.

Kat stood like a zombie, and as Andrew gave her a slight bow and said goodbye, Clay wanted to shake her, to snap her out of the trance.

When Winston was gone, silence stretched between them, digging a deep dark hole in their sunny afternoon.

"I should go, too." He couldn't bear to be with her, not now.

"I understand." She crossed her arms, hugging herself. "I'm sorry that happened."

"It doesn't matter." He skimmed her cheek. "I knew Andrew would want you back."

She released a shaky breath. "I'm so confused."

"I know." He brushed her lips with a soul-searching kiss. He was confused, too. "Maybe we should take a break before the gala. It's only five days away. And I've got a zillion things to do at the club.''

"So I won't see you before Friday?''

"No. But I'll still be your date.''

"Don't forget to get a tux.''

"I won't.'' He'd already bought one. "Be good until I see you again.''

"Then I can be bad?'' she asked, teasing him, making him ache.

"Yes.'' He wondered how long it would take for Andrew to propose to her again. Not long, he suspected. He frowned, and when she leaned in to hug him, he held her a little too tightly, missing her already.

Chapter 7

On the night of the aquatic gala, Clay told himself that attending a charity ball was no big deal. He wasn't a blue blood, but he had plenty of money, enough to make him an equal. He wasn't as polished as Andrew Winston, but he knew how to conduct himself in social settings. He'd been studying Kat's peer group since he was a boy.

Then why was he was so damn nervous? Why did he feel as if he was going to trip all over himself? Stumble over every word? Forget the manners he'd rehearsed?

He rang the bell at Kat's guest house. She answered wearing a long, slim icy white gown. The décolleté presented an elegant display of cleavage, just enough to stir the imagination.

"Wow," he said. "That's some dress."

"I'm glad you think so." She spun around, modeling the rest of it, showing him that her entire back was bare.

He had the notion to kiss her skin, to run his mouth along every curve. She turned to face him again, and they gazed at each other. He reached for a strand of her hair. She wore it in a fancy updo, with loose tendrils falling in calculated disarray.

She smiled at him. "You look incredible, too."

"Thank you." His designer tux was hand tailored, with a peak lapel. "This is for you. For your purse." He held out an orchid corsage. "It's my favorite flower, and I figured it would look good with a white dress."

"It's beautiful." She thanked him, taking the exotic bloom from his hand. "I wear orchid perfume."

"I know," he said.

Once again they gazed at each other, caught in a timeless moment. She seemed nervous, too. But they hadn't seen each other all week. They hadn't touched; they hadn't kissed. He looked at her mouth and noticed her lipstick, a flawless shade of peach, a color that complemented her autumn-tinted hair.

"Come in." She stepped away from the door, as though suddenly aware that they stood on the porch in formal attire, staring at each other. "I need to get my bag."

He entered the guest house, wishing they were staying in for the evening. The cottage provided a warm, summer ambience, with the lingering aroma of vanilla-scented candles.

Kat attached the corsage to a white purse, where the orchid made a ladylike statement. When she turned to indicate that she was ready to leave, he decided she looked like a storybook princess come to life.

But that was her station in life, he thought. Katrina Beaumont hailed from Southern royalty. And Clay couldn't stop thinking about the dance that had been promised to Andrew.

They climbed into his Porsche and he tried to shake her former fiancé from his mind. Kat was his date tonight, his fairy tale, the woman who'd dominated his teenage dreams.

"Are your parents going to be at the ball?" he asked.

She shook her head. "No. They're out of town

this weekend, but Anna-Mae and Jenny will be there.''

He pulled onto the street. ''Is Jenny still spreading rumors about us?''

''I don't think she needs to. We've created enough gossip on our own.''

He downshifted at a stop sign. ''We certainly got Andrew's attention.''

''Yes,'' she said quietly. ''We certainly did.''

Clay drove into town, and they arrived at a historic hotel that overlooked the Savannah River. The ballroom offered a floor-to-ceiling view of the port. But even more impressive was the decor, the aquatic touches designed just for the ball. Seafoam-colored lights and streams of rippling fabric made the room look as if it were underwater.

The luxurious fund-raiser presented an artistic buffet of seafood delicacies. Although a full bar was available, uniformed servers wove their way through the guests, handing out complimentary glasses of champagne.

Clay and Kat mingled, and he could feel people watching them, wondering about their affair. He kept a possessive arm around her waist, staking his claim. He'd yet to see Andrew, but he sensed the other man would arrive in a princely fashion.

Kat refused the champagne, opting for a soda from the bar. Clay ordered scotch and water.

Anna-Mae came flouncing up to them in a beaded gown. The oceanlike lights cast a bluish glow over her pale blond hair. She gave Clay a genuine smile, and he relaxed.

"Isn't this divine?" She indicated the room. "We all look like mermaids."

"Or mermen," Clay said.

"Or tritons," Kat whispered in his ear, making him hungry for her touch.

"Oh, my. You two are simply dishy." Anna-Mae sipped her champagne. "Come sit with us. That's my date over there." She gestured to a man with the same hair color as hers. Bluish blond. "Cute, huh?"

"Dishy," Clay said, giving her a playful wink.

She laughed and led them to her escort, who proved to be an entertaining fellow, in spite of his aristocratic genes.

Ten minutes later Clay and Kat sampled the buffet, arranging salmon cakes, crab-stuffed sole and caviar canapés onto their plates. They returned to the table, eating with the rest of the guests.

Clay had always appreciated fine dining, and he liked watching Kat taste her entrées. She looked up and smiled, and he lifted a slice of Cajun toast to his mouth, the spicy flavor pumping through his blood.

"Food is so erotic," Anna-Mae said, not missing a beat. She turned to her escort. "We should have a torrid affair."

"I already thought we were," he responded in a droll voice, making everyone laugh.

Soon Clay asked Kat to dance and they joined the couples swaying to the music. He wanted to kiss her, right then and there, but he refrained. This wasn't Steam. This wasn't his club.

"Are you having a good time?" she asked.

He nodded, but when he glanced toward the door, he saw that Andrew had just arrived, with Jenny and her date trailing a few paces behind him.

The rest of the evening went to hell. Within no time Andrew claimed his dance, and Clay watched from the table, with Jenny, the gossipy brunette, pecking in his ear.

"They always made a marvelous pair," she said.

"I wouldn't know." But in truth, Katrina and Andrew did look natural together. Not Kat, he thought. But Katrina, the woman who'd wanted to marry Andrew from the start.

They moved in unison, Clay noticed, each step flowing into the next. Graceful. Fluid. A man and a woman who'd been taught to waltz as children, who'd attended charity balls all of their lives. When Katrina met Andrew's gaze, Clay downed the contents of his drink.

Andrew leaned in to her and said something. Something intimate, it appeared. She responded, her voice probably hushed.

Clay knew it was time to let her go, to end their affair. She was his fantasy, a boyhood dream he'd gotten to fulfill, but they weren't meant to last.

"Andrew knows he made a mistake," Jenny said. "He knows he shouldn't have broken their engagement."

Clay didn't react; he didn't converse with the brunette. When the song ended, Andrew kissed Katrina's hand, thanking her for the dance. Clay had never kissed her hand. He'd put his mouth all over her, but he'd never treated her with that kind of romantic care.

Now he wished he had. He wished he'd given her just one night of chivalry.

Andrew headed to the bar, and Katrina returned to the table. Clay stood to hold out her chair for her, but she refused the proffered seat.

"Do you think we could go outside? I'd like to get some air."

"Of course." He guided her to a set of glass doors leading to a nearby terrace.

They moved toward the rail and looked at the river. Moonlight shimmered on the water, then disappeared like a lost treasure.

Katrina fidgeted with the flower on her purse. "Andrew wants to start dating again."

Clay masked his emotions. "And how do you feel about that?"

"I don't know." She looked up. "I honestly don't know."

He breathed in the shore air. "You're still confused?"

"Yes."

She reached out to touch his face, but he stepped back, leaving her hand empty. He couldn't bear to vie for her affection, to know he would lose. Nor could he be her balm, the man who kept soothing her ache. "I think you should give Andrew a chance."

"You're telling me to reconcile with him? To stop being with you?"

"We had a good time, Kat." He slipped his hands in his pockets, the free-spirited club owner. "But it was just sex."

"Just sex?" She sounded hurt, much too vulnerable. "I thought we were friends, too."

"We were. We are." Something in his chest twisted. Was it his heart? His lungs? The air he couldn't seem to breathe? ''But Andrew was your fiancé. You had an affair with me to make him jealous. This was always about him.''

''That's not true.'' She paused, traced the orchid petals, softly this time. ''Not entirely. I slept with you because I'm attracted to you. Because you make me feel—''

''Erotic?'' he supplied. ''Wild?'' He studied the river, searching for moonlight, wishing it would return. ''We both knew it was a game. We both knew it would end.''

''So, that's it?'' Her words quavered. ''It's over?''

He turned to face her. ''Yes. It's over.'' But he would never forget the time he'd spent with her, the desperation, the dare that had made her his lover.

On Tuesday evening Katrina worked her hair into a French braid, her fingers tense with each movement. She glanced back at her mother, who sat on the edge of the bed, watching her.

''You're dining with Andrew tonight?'' Delilah asked.

''Yes.'' Katrina turned back to the mirror and noticed the circles under her eyes. She hadn't slept well since the night of the gala. She couldn't stop thinking about Clay; she couldn't stop wondering where he was and what he was doing.

"How long are you going to remain here?" Delilah gestured, indicating the guest house.

"I don't know. It doesn't matter."

The older woman rose, then stood behind Katrina. "Here. Let me do that." She took over, fixing the braid. "You should be with Daddy and me. It doesn't make sense for you to live here."

Katrina shrugged. "I feel so empty."

"Andrew will help you overcome that scandal."

"I miss Clay, Mother. I know I shouldn't. But I do." Her affair with him wasn't meant to last, but his rejection was more than she could bear.

"You'll be all right once you spend time with Andrew."

"Will I?" She met her mother's gaze in the mirror. In spite of her age, Delilah's skin glowed, her makeup carefully applied, her head tilted at a graceful angle. She reminded Katrina of the wisteria that bloomed in the spring. Beautiful yet vigorous, she thought. A plant that climbed its way to the top, flowering along the way. "Did you love Daddy when you married him?"

"Of course I did. I would never marry a man I didn't love." Delilah smoothed the braid, then rested her hands on Katrina's shoulders. Her manicure shone in the glass, the tips of her nails a pristine shade of white. "Are you doubting your feelings for Andrew?"

"Clay told me I should give Andrew a chance."

"And that's what you're doing." Delilah paused. "I want you to be happy, Katrina. Maybe Clay wants you to be happy, too."

By the time Andrew arrived, Katrina was dressed in a mauve dress, low heels and a strand of pearls. Picture perfect, she thought. A mild-tempered heiress.

Andrew looked just as sedate, with his dark blue tie and neatly trimmed hair. He was a handsome man, tall and refined. She'd dated him for years, but now he seemed like a stranger, someone she couldn't relate to.

He escorted her to his car, then climbed behind the wheel. Rather than start the engine, he turned to study her. They sat in awkward silence. They weren't used to each other anymore. Their lives had changed.

Andrew cleared his throat. "I want you back, Katrina. I want to work out our problems."

"Why?" she asked. "Why now?"

"Because you seemed different when you were with him. And I want you to be that way for me."

She glanced out the window. Suddenly the guest

house looked like a lost cottage, a twisted story-book setting, a place where aging debutantes disappeared. "Do I seem like that now?"

He frowned a little. "No."

"Maybe I can only be that way around him. I think he put a spell on me." She turned away from the window. "You were right to break off our engagement. And you were right about us not having any chemistry."

He touched her cheek, a tentative caress. "We can try to change that."

"Can we?" She gazed into Andrew's eyes and saw their past, the uncertainty of their future. "What if it doesn't work? What if we can't make it happen?"

His ego bristled. "Was he better in bed than me?"

She fidgeted with the hem on her dress, refusing to compare, to pit one man against the other. "It isn't a case of who's better." She sat back, took a deep breath. "Clay gave me what I'd been missing. I think somewhere deep down I've always needed him. That he was always there, buried inside me."

Andrew's expression remained tight, but he didn't lose his temper. He simply looked at her, as if he were trying to see beyond the wall that separated them, to understand it. "Are you falling in love with him? Is he in love with you?"

Katrina froze, her heart slamming her rib cage. Love? She hadn't let the word enter her mind. She hadn't let herself think that far. "I don't know. I—"

"You what?" he interrupted.

"I wish I could be with him. Just one more time."

"Then go," he told her. "Finish your affair."

She gazed at her former fiancé, stunned by his suggestion, by the honesty in his voice. "And then what am I supposed to do? Come back to you? Try to make it work?"

Andrew didn't respond, but she knew the decision wasn't his to make. The choice was hers.

Chapter 8

Clay paced his apartment, unable to focus, to think beyond the tension in his gut. He had a feeling that something was about to happen, something emotional, something that would make his life more complicated than it already was.

He walked into the kitchen and frowned at the dishes he hadn't washed. He didn't like that he couldn't get Kat off his mind, that she'd been invading his thoughts since he'd let her go.

His cell phone rang, and he sensed this was the trouble he'd been waiting for. ~~But not answering~~ didn't seem like an option.

He flipped open the phone and said hello.

"Clay, it's Joe."

"Yeah?" He waited for the bouncer to continue. The club was about to close, but Clay hadn't made an appearance tonight.

"Katrina Beaumont is here and she wants to see you."

Clay cursed. He wanted to send her away, but knowing she was in the building made him lonely for her. "Will you escort her to my apartment?"

"Yes, sir. We're on our way."

He waited by the front door, wondering what had possessed her to come to him. To torture him, he thought.

Finally he heard footsteps in the hallway. And then he saw Joe and Kat. The bouncer was the only employee who had a key to Clay's floor. The men exchanged a silent glance before Joe nodded and left Kat in Clay's care.

She fussed with a strand of pearls around her neck, looking much too proper. Her hair was fashioned in a ladylike braid and her dress was soft and subtle.

"I was supposed to go out to dinner with Andrew," she said.

He raised his brows at her. "But you came here instead?"

"I wanted to see you. Andrew agreed that I should." She glanced over her shoulder, and he suspected she was uncomfortable standing in the hallway with the security cameras aimed in her direction.

"Do you want to come in?" he asked.

"Yes. Thank you."

She followed him into the apartment, and he wondered if he should offer her a cold drink. She seemed a little wilted from the weather. He knew the night air was humid. He'd left the door to his verandah open, but there was no escape from the heat.

"I'll get you a soda." He entered the kitchen and filled a glass with ice. While he poured the cola, she came in and stood beside the counter.

She took the drink and sipped gratefully, leaving her signature lipstick mark on the glass. Clay wanted to put his mouth where hers has been, but he grabbed a soda for himself and drank from the can instead.

"What are you doing here, Kat?"

"I told you. I wanted to see you."

"Why?"

"Because I miss you."

He missed her, too. He literally ached for her,

an ache he'd been fighting. "Why did Andrew agree that you should come by?"

She took another sip. "I told him that I wanted one more night with you."

Clay's chest constricted. "One more night?"

Her breath rushed out. "Andrew asked me if I was in love with you. If you were in love with me. But that's…"

"Impossible," he finished for her.

"Yes. Impossible." She set her drink on the counter, but her voice was shaky. "One night will be enough."

"Of course it will. For both of us." He held out his arms. An automatic reflex, he thought. A need he couldn't seem to control. She put her head on his shoulder, and he felt her tremble. He brought her closer, inhaling her fragrance. "Sometimes I smell your perfume when you're not here."

She looked up. "I'm here now."

He touched her braid, thinking how beautiful she was. "You wore your hair like this on that first night."

"The night I drank too much wine. That seems like a lifetime ago."

"You wore it this way another time. The time you put your mouth on me."

"When I seduced you in the supply room?"

He nodded, praying one more night would be enough. "You never fail to surprise me." He led her to his bed, and they undressed, opening zippers, peeling away fabrics.

He caressed her skin, roaming her body, rubbing his thumbs over her nipples, making them hard.

In turn, she skimmed his stomach, then lowered her head to kiss his navel. When she took him in her mouth, he wished their lovemaking could last forever.

Wanting more, he adjusted their positions so he could taste her, too, so they could pleasure each other at the same time.

Beautiful madness, he thought. Warm, wet foreplay. He and Kat seemed like painters, memorizing this moment in their minds, creating slow, sensual strokes.

He licked her until she peaked, until she shuddered against him. But he didn't let her bring him to fruition. He wasn't ready for it to end.

He rose above her, and she smiled at him, still dazed from her climax.

"I'm so glad you're here," he said. To say goodbye, to be together one last time.

"Me, too." She kissed him, making him long for her even more.

Finally he straddled her, anxious to make love,

to claim her. He reached for a condom and frowned at the foil packet. He wanted to come inside her, flesh to flesh, but he knew it was wrong. He had no right to risk conception.

He used the protection, then entered her, as hard and deep as he could. She gasped and arched, as sleek as a cat, as soft as a kitten.

"Kat." He said her name, and her heart pounded against his.

They made love in a rush of emotions, in tangled limbs and sweet whispers. She slid her hand between their bodies, touching him where they were joined. He buried his face against her neck, absorbing her scent.

The sheers on the window billowed, just a little, just enough to haunt the bed, to send a gust of warm air over his skin.

The moon glinted in the sky. He could feel it bathing the building, shimmering over Steam like a jewel.

She moved with him, stroke for stroke, as fluid as a dance. The music was in their hearts, in their heads, in the blood flowing through their veins.

He thrust deeper, needing more, needing all of her. She climaxed beneath him, making sweet little sounds, taking everything he gave her.

And when he looked into her eyes, his seed spilling from his body, he knew he was falling in love. That it wasn't impossible after all.

Katrina awakened in Clay's arms. She nuzzled against him. His body was strong and warm, smooth and muscular. She ran her hand across his chest, and he stirred in his sleep.

She lingered for a while, appreciating him, fighting the urge to stay, to keep a man who didn't belong to her. Finally she climbed out of bed, and as she gathered her clothes, she turned to look at him. Suddenly he opened his eyes, and they stared at each other.

"Where are you going?" he asked.

"To take a shower. Then I'll go home," she added, wishing daylight hadn't come so soon.

"I'll shower with you." He sat up but he didn't smile. He seemed disturbed, as though his mind were cluttered.

They walked to the bathroom and closed the door. She dropped her clothes on the floor. There was no point trying to salvage them; they were wrinkled already. He turned on the spigot, and the moment they stepped into the tub, he grabbed her and kissed her. Hard, she thought. Desperate.

She kissed him back, and the water rained over their naked bodies, pounding against their skin. He didn't take the time to caress her, to play nice. He was already aroused, already pushing her against the tiled wall, wanting her.

She wanted him, too. With a vengeance. She said his name and dug her nails into his shoulders. He lifted her hips and thrust into her.

They made frenzied love, panting and kissing and biting. No protection, no gentle words. The shower was hot and steamy, and her world was spinning out of control.

He rubbed his hands all over her. Rough hands, aggressive fingers. In turn, she clawed him even deeper, drawing blood. He didn't seem to care, to feel the pain. All he wanted was the hard, driving rhythm, the power of unbridled sex. She could see it in his eyes.

Would this be her last memory of him? The image that haunted her every night? The idea terrified her, knowing she would miss him for the rest of her life.

He pinned her arms against the wall. Maybe he'd started to feel the pain. She'd scratched him like a cat, like a tigress damaging its mate.

He kept thrusting into her, pushing toward a release. Their gazes locked. Water streamed unmercifully down their faces.

And then it happened. They climaxed at the

same time, at the same insane moment. She felt a jolt of electricity shock her system, leaving her weak.

His entire body shuddered, and he spilled into her, as hard and fast as the shower pummeling their flesh.

Breathless, he released her arms. She nearly lost her balance, stumbling against him.

"If you get pregnant, I'll marry you," he said.

Stunned, Katrina blinked. That was the last thing she'd expected him to say. She glanced at the marks she'd left on his shoulders, unable to respond.

They stepped out of the tub, and he wrapped her in a towel. "Did you hear me?" he asked.

"Yes." A lump formed in her throat. "Did you mean it?"

He stepped back. "Of course I did."

"Thank you." She wondered how she could feel so romantic yet so sad. "I appreciate your..." She couldn't think of the right word to say, so she let her sentence fade into the air, into the stillness that surrounded them.

"Are you going back to Andrew, Kat?"

"Not if I get pregnant by you."

"And if you don't?"

She couldn't imagine being with Andrew. Not

now. Not after being with Clay. "I'm never going back to him. I don't love him anymore. Maybe I never really did." Because she loved Clay, she realized. Because somewhere deep down, she'd always loved him. "I guess Andrew figured that out before I did."

Clay didn't react, and they both fell silent. If Andrew wasn't an issue between them, then they were free to be together, with or without a baby. But she didn't have the courage to say that out loud. And apparently, neither did he.

Clay picked up his toothbrush and added a glob of toothpaste to it. Katrina reached for her toothbrush, as well. The one he kept in his bathroom for her.

They brushed their teeth, taking turns at the sink. It was strangely domestic, she thought. The sort of things married couples did.

"I'm sorry I scratched you." She slipped on her panties and bra. "I'm sorry I made you bleed."

He was still naked. "It's okay. It doesn't matter."

She lifted her dress off the floor, wishing she'd brought a change of clothes, wishing this wasn't so awkward. "I guess I should go."

She searched for her purse and found it in the kitchen. Clay went into his room, or the unwalled area that served as his room, and put on a pair of jeans. She could see him from her vantage point, dragging the denim over simple white boxers. His hair was in damp disarray, falling around his face.

She watched him, the thought of leaving him tearing her apart. Should she hope for a baby? Or was it wrong to force a man to marry her? To trap him into a union based on a child?

He entered the kitchen. "Ready?"

No, she thought. No. "Are you going to walk me out?"

"I have to. The club is closed."

When they stepped into the elevator, he didn't press the button. He just looked at her, and her eyes started to water.

"Don't cry, Kat."

"I'm not." She sniffed, and he moved closer. Then he took her in his arms. She clung to him, realizing how often he held her, how often he offered her the comfort of his embrace.

"Stay with me," he said.

She looked up. "For how long?"

"As long as you want."

She chewed her lip. Shy, nervous, trapped in emotion. "What if I want forever?"

He touched a strand of her hair; it was as

damp and tousled as his. "Does that mean you love me?"

She nodded, her heart going weak.

"Oh, God, Kat. Me, too. But it scares me."

Her knees nearly buckled. He looked so serious, so lost. So incredibly beautiful for a man who'd just bared his soul. "Why?"

"Because of Andrew. Because of him being the type of guy your family wants you to marry."

"My family wants me to be happy." She leaned forward. "I've been in love with you since we were teenagers."

"That's how it was for me, but I didn't understand my feelings until now."

"We were too young."

"I tried to get you out of my system, but this affair wasn't about sex. I thought it was, but I was wrong." He paused. "Do you want to live here with me? Help me run the club?" He paused again, his gaze searching hers. "Maybe marry me?"

"Maybe?" Her heart pounded a glorious rhythm. She took a deep breath, cherishing this moment, letting it flow through every cell in her body. Clayton Crawford loved her; he wanted to make her his wife. "There's no maybe about it." She couldn't imagine living another day without him, surviving without his touch, his voice, the shelter of his arms. "I'd marry you in an instant."

"You came here to say goodbye, and now we're getting married." He grinned at her, his lips tilting in masculine wonder. "I think we're losing our minds."

"Yes," she agreed, returning his smile, equally awed by the beauty of being together, of planning a future. They were crazy. Beautifully, madly insane. The perfect ingredient for being in love.

"We have less than two months!" Delilah Beaumont flipped through her Rolodex. "Less than two months to plan a wedding!"

"They're anxious," Marie said about the bride and groom. "They don't want to wait."

Clay glanced at his mom, and she smiled. The Beaumonts and the Crawfords were gathered in the Beaumont sitting room, sipping iced tea and eating finger foods.

"We'll need a coordinator. Ah, here." Delilah produced the number she'd been searching for. "We'll make it the grandest wedding Savannah has ever seen. Even if we have to work day and night to make it happen."

Clay didn't say a word. He just leaned back and watched Kat's mother fawn and fuss over his upcoming nuptials. He didn't care what sort of ceremony they had, as long as he was marrying the woman he loved.

Kat sat beside Marie, a stack of bridal magazines on her lap. They'd been working on ideas for the dress, a gown Clay's mother was designing.

"We could have the wedding here." Delilah gestured to French doors leading to a formal garden. "At dusk, with tea lights floating in a lily pond. Wouldn't that be elegant?"

"And romantic," Marie chimed in.

Kat looked up from a magazine. "We don't have a lily pond, Mother."

"So we'll build one. And we'll build a park temple or a limestone pergola. Something far more appealing than a gazebo. We'll redesign the whole garden if we have to." She clasped her hands together. "What about Greek statues?"

"As long as there's one of Triton," Kat responded.

"That's a marvelous idea." Delilah reached for a cucumber sandwich. "Poseidon's son." She paused to taste her food. "Maybe we should order a statue of Poseidon, as well. What do you think, Clayton?"

"That sounds perfect." He looked at Kat and

felt his heartbeat quicken. More perfect than he could imagine.

"It all sounds good to me," Kat's father said, although no one asked his opinion. He was a quiet man, with a good heart and a respectful nature. Clay liked him immensely, and he sensed the Beaumont patriarch liked him, too.

"I'll call the landscaper." Delilah all but beamed. She was in her glory, planning her daughter's wedding. Just as Clay's mother was in her glory, eager to send her son down the aisle.

"Why don't you two take a walk," Delilah suggested, sending Clay and Kat into the garden. "You've been cooped up all day."

Clay took his lady's hand and they strolled through the grass, surrounded by acres of flowers and a view of the sea. It was a stunning location for a wedding.

"My mother hasn't even started in about the reception yet. The dinner menu, the cake, the—"

"It doesn't matter." He cupped Kat's face and kissed her. "All that matters is us being together."

She looped her arms around his neck. "I love you, Clayton Crawford."

"I love you, too." An array of scents mingled in the air, creating paradise on earth. "You're everything I need."

They kissed again, then separated to gaze at the sea, at the blue-green water shimmering in the distance. "I'm not the only one who fell in love at the club," he said.

"You're not?"

"Sophia and Nick are together and so are Kelly and Mike."

Kat turned to look at him. "I have no idea who you're talking about."

"Sophia was my assistant, and Nick was the DEA agent who swept her off her feet. They're renovating a steamboat, turning it into a casino."

"So he's not a cop anymore?"

"No. And she's not my assistant anymore, either." He smiled, thinking how amazing Kat looked, with her bright blue eyes and sun-glowing skin. "I guess you'll have to be my new right hand woman now."

"With pleasure." She leaned against his shoulder. "Who are Kelly and Mike?"

"Kelly's a cocktail waitress at Steam and Mike's a Navy SEAL. They call him Mad Dog."

"Does he go mad?"

Clay laughed. "He's mad about Kelly. I'll invite them to the wedding. And Sophia and Nick, too. I want you to meet them, to get to know my friends." He touched a strand of her hair. "It's going to be a beautiful wedding. The best day of our lives.''

''Every day is going to be the best day of our lives.'' She picked a carnation and tucked it into his shirt pocket.

He looked up and noticed an archway blooming with roses above their heads. ''I'm in heaven.''

''So am I.'' She reached for his hand and led him farther into the garden, into a moment made just for them. For lovers, he thought. For a couple who was ready to spend eternity in Savannah, a place to enjoy warm afternoons and blues-filled nights, a place where their babies would be born. A steamy Southern town, he thought, that would always be home.

* * * * *

Be sure to catch up on all the scandals in the Silhouette Desire series,
DYNASTIES: THE DANFORTHS,
*all year long. And watch for
Michael Whittaker's story,*
STEAMY SAVANNAH NIGHTS,
*by Sheri WhiteFeather,
— coming in August
from Silhouette Desire.*

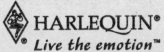

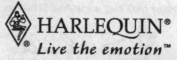

If you enjoyed what you just read,
then we've got an offer you can't resist!

Take 2 bestselling love stories FREE!
Plus get a FREE surprise gift!

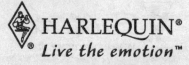